# Celtic Blood

James John Loftus

I dedicate this book to my wife Janice without her unfailing help this book would never have been written.   I would also like to acknowledge the fine editorial efforts of Michelle Sandelier and Tim Scurr.  Ross Wilson, thanks for the friendship and writing mentorship.  And last, but not least, the noble Mackay clan for inspiring this Celtic Blood.

# CONTENTS

# CELTIC BLOOD

I felt the wind and heard the rain, I felt an ancient hand.  The spirit of my ancestor drove the pen which touched the page and enabled me to visualize that which had occurred.  He called out to me from the past with the voice of long ago.

# SOLE SURVIVOR

WITH AN UNQUENCHABLE thirst the ship drank in the ocean. White tops came crashing over the sides forcing every man to go down on all fours to avoid being cast overboard. Woven trimmings trembled under avalanches of water. The wind was bludgeoning. Most of the men huddled together for warmth and protection under the covered stern of the ship. Seward, thirteen, although none would call him so young by his look, held a rail with an iron grip. Tasting the sea-blown water on his lips, Seward felt exhilarated by the turbulence of nature, and was afraid.

On the railhead, droplets of moisture were held captive by the wind. Watching the drops of water bend out of shape and realign, Seward felt amazed at how these tiny drops could endure, telling himself if they could, so could he. The ocean surged and the ship heaved. Looking beyond the bulging water spheres to the pattern of the woodwork lost in the fine wood-grain was Seward. Abrupt movement. The deck, once beneath his feet became a cliff, behind and above him ... nothing was beneath his feet, and he was falling into space. He hit the water. Above his head the ship. A moment ago he had been on the deck. In another ship not far from him, men were bailing out water. That ship came close and almost touched him. It swept past in a blur, curled up in a wave. Then whipped upward again he slid across the wooden hull looking for a place to hold. Then, with another sudden jolt, the deck broke and screaming men tumbled to water. Seward was certain this was the last journey he would make, bar the one unto God should fate be so kind.

Carried by confused ocean currents out away from both ships. A lead weight of water poured on him, like a blow. A mass of liquid crashed into his side. Like his legs were meant to touch the ocean floor, a hundred feet below, he was sucked down. He thought he had died for he saw and heard nothing, and felt, nothing. Seeing his hands through the water Seward realized that life was still his, though the rain still fell, and the dark sea still held him captive. A wave rearing up and up and up came crashing down, sending him into depths cold enough to take his life. He held his breath deep underwater. Suddenly he saw white as he surfaced to the sinister sound of hissing surf. A piece of the mast came rushing past him. Grabbing at it, his outstretched fingers met water and nothing else. Friends and comfort were lost to him now he thought. Without the ship, what could he do, drown? No! Fight on, he told himself as his limbs fastened to the uppermost level of the sea and he swam.

Gulping air while rising high, so very high, and seeing far in each direction, he saw coast and rocks and what he realized could be life if he made it to the shore. A dark mass arose, tossed him forward. Much closer to the shore, a wave rolled him along. Stumbling onto a beach Seward, from his new perspective, heard nothing but a strange internal ear sound. These strange silent waves. When some water escaped his ear, the waves were alive, pounding, booming. The very next instant, it seemed, an owl hooted on the branch of a small tree. The moon was high much time had passed. He had fallen asleep, he realised. He sat alone gazing at the ocean pondering what to do for a considerable time.

A hill overlooking the coast would be the best place to find survivors. He set off. Finding a fresh water rivulet, he cupped his hands and drank, ascending the hill thereafter. When his physical powers deserted him all he could do was lodge himself behind some bushes out of the wind resting trying to regain some strength listening to the sound of sea and surf. He almost slept until something caught his eye. Mounted armed men, and screaming men, below. Horsemen rode out onto the dunes with swords drawn. Two men, survivors from the shipwreck, his friends, were running. Soon horses meshed with the men afoot. The bodies of the Danes were then cut down in pools of red as flashing blades struck right and left.

He could not stand by and let his friends perish without his aid. Seward made a nervous quick grab. He held a sword from a rider's sheath. He ran down toward the fight. A horseman came in pursuit. Seward turned in time to see, but not to avoid a blow to his head. The sword dislodged from his grasp it lay at the hooves of this horseman, too far to reach. Seward realized he could not regain the sword; any attempt to do so, would fail. He stayed where he was. From the ground, Seward looked at a solid, sunburned fellow, good-looking, if watery eyed - a man uneasy within his skin. Seward was waiting for the death stab from the man who towered above him. The horseman threw himself off his horse and took the sword which he passed to his comrade. He mounted. The man pointed at him and laughed, spun his horse and with the speed and coordination of a life long rider and warrior stretched out his hand and lifted Seward up behind him. Kenneth's horse now had two riders, Kenneth and Seward.

In a strange way Kenneth, Earl of Ross, felt more pity for the boy than his companions did. With weighty concerns he was apt to pity another. The land he called his own was beset by enemies. These very murdering men on the beach amongst them. Kenneth and his party departing, Seward turned in the saddle and attempted to see if any of his shipmates survived. The unforgiving sea was all that he saw.

A long ride amongst bare hills, was followed by travelling through dense woods. They came out into an open valley of scattered pine and oak scrub. A flat-topped hill with a wooden fort stood in the distance. They rode toward it. Entering its courtyard, surrounded by a crowd, he fell from his horse. If they would kill him, so be it, he thought. "I am not going to sit back and let these folk laugh at me."

He stood and addressed them in his own tongue, "I am a seafarer, not a knight. I wonder what skills you have." He looked at blank faces. "I am far from home in an unkind land." Their amused faces perplexed him.

"Not a brain to rub together amongst all of you." He looked away. He should strike someone. He learned long ago the weakest dog gets kicked the most and he was not a weak dog.

Someone noticed Seward's combative attitude with distinct interest. An instinctive fighter who would fight his way out of any corner, handy for trouble to come. Kenneth realized it. "The boy needs feeding and clothing supposed Christian people." Kenneth said, searching and finding the quality he was looking for. She seemed kindly disposed. "You there," he said to her.

"Aye, my Lord."

"Help him."

Her compassionate arms assisted Seward to his feet. He cautioned himself to be brave, not to shame himself. Growing up with stories of heroes he would put up as good a showing as any of them, he told himself. By not succumbing to despair, Seward caused immense interest but provoked no sympathy. The crowd moved closer and immediately commenced chattering.

This foreign singsong language was unknown to him. He stared at them and they stared at him, studying him closely. A mere boy yet, but the curve of his biceps showed that potentially he would be brutally strong. Yet somehow, his smoothness of face was angelic. His eyes of palest blue had the light of intelligence behind them. His hair as pale as angel's wings, hair to win the heart of the most fair of maids.

"What a sight he is, poor, young man. He's bonny though," the woman hastened to add as if he had heard and understood their tongue. Foreigners weren't always ignorant, so she'd heard, and didn't want the shame of an uncivil reception to fall upon them.

"This boy the men have caught is solid," was observed and spoken by another.

Many comments passed around, "He has good looks."

"Aye, and a hard look."

"We will clean him and feed him and make him our poppet to spoil on treats."

Aye, I'd spoil him," harped a cold-eyed crone.

"Aye, I know what sort of spoiling you'd give him," replied her friend while others laughed, though Kenneth was not much amused and the woman felt abashed at his stern look.

Then someone said. "You'll be alright son - don't be alarmed. We'll feed you and see to your health." Seward looked closer into blue eyes that shone in a ruddy face, eyes that were warm and wise.

A little girl determined to have her say pushed through. "You poor, miserable boy." Her tone hard was uncaring. She stared at him unflinchingly. The cruel words hung in the air. He knew they were cruel by the looks returned from those around him. Give him a big long stick and he'd show the cruelty. The thought made him smile.

Seward felt a finger prod him. It was the girl. "What happened lost boy?" The language was foreign and meant nothing to him, yet the intent he knew. To her he poked his tongue out. A look of surprise flickered across the girl's face and she laughed.

He felt a hand on his shoulder. Then taken indoors by a kindly man and placed next to a warm fire. Someone put a rich broth before him. Looking into the fire, the ordinariness of it allowed the memory of sea and blood to fade. As they still spoke to him, as their voices began to take shape, he was excited.

These people spoke Scandinavian, outlandishly accented, but it was understandable. Was the place so far north that Norse was spoken? He asked someone

"It is a trading language." The one who had taken him indoors told him.

"Where am I?"

"In Scotland."

"I never thought to come here."

"But but you're her-here n-now." A bearded man got out despite his impediment. The stammerer's looks and personality matched his speech. Jigging about, clapping his hands, as the Scots laughed at him. Indeed he was a sight.

These were sturdy folk for the most part dark haired, however, the firelight caught various contrasting shades of red hair and the odd dull blond, none with his striking white hair. To the Scots he looked strange for such blondness in one his age was unknown. He was fascinating. He looked at a slight black-eyed man who spoke, and answered the question:

"Where are you from?"

"Denmark."

"Where is that?"

"Across the sea ... it is a part of Scandinavia, the place of the Vikings. Over the sea to the east."

The man nodded. "Are you a raider?"

"No, just a fisherman."

"There is no such thing as just a fisherman." Replied another fellow, at which laughter ensued.

"He is a great one for fishing. A serious fisherman. Eat, boy, eat." The man who took him indoors said.

"Thank you."

After the second helping more questions eschewed, "Tell us what happened? How did you come here?"

"By ship."

"We know that, but what was your design?"

Then a series of questions, too fast to reply to, until. "Obviously you have suffered troubles." At that, everyone looked expectant awaiting his answer. He wanted to explain, but needed a moment's pause to collect his thoughts.

"Let him eat, there is plenty of time for all that," said the wise fisherman on his behalf.

Seward smiled. Sitting, surrounded by kindly expressions; whispers circulated the room. He guessed on what, on the Norse and what they knew of them, how they looked. As his own people would, if the situation was reversed. They would have commented on the Celts facial features. The pixyish upturned noses and ruddy cheeks would have drawn comment.

The young girl he had poked his tongue out to, was smiling. She appeared playful now, not spiteful. Fair haired, dark-eyed, good-looking, terribly appealing, in a little girl kind of way. She would make a good companion to play a child's game with. On closer inspection, seemingly in need of a protector, she seemed the runt of the pack. It was not what she wanted him to think. She had bumps under her gown that he'd notice soon enough if she slipped it off, she thought. Watching him, she knew what he thought of her, she was a perceptive girl and he wasn't hard to read. Reaching out to him with her eyes, pleading with him to notice her as a man would a grown woman, and to smile at her with more than friendly favour, to notice those bumps she was so proud of. She did gain his attention but not in the way she wanted, he gave her a look a brother might pass to his sister. That wouldn't do. She was a posey. A pretty girl, as pretty as any here. He looked back at her, noticing there was nothing childlike like about her eyes. He turned away.

A number of the smaller children, who began to touch him, withdrew their hands with squeals of delight. Seward felt a link of good fellowship with these strangers. He knew their hearts were kind. At the very least, his body didn't lie on the beach, face down, or condemned to the tides where it would be torn apart by the fish and sea. For a moment he imagined his eyes on the ocean floor, meat for a crab. There was a sense of unreality about this. He was tempted to touch someone to verify their existence. He had drunk the mead they pushed on him and shouldn't have for it lessened his mental balance.

Deciding, he must brighten up and be good company, satisfy their curiosity, and not disappoint them in his exoticism. He entertained them, and now sought to do so even more. On impulse, he caught the children's eyes and smiled in an insane disquieting way and jumped out of his chair and pulled a contorted face that would scare the devil himself.

The children disappeared out the door, terrified. He felt ashamed for real fear he had seen in them when he had expected laugher. His unusual behaviour was attributed to his foreignness, or a bump on the head. The Scots, seeking to avoid a repetition, explained that women and children seldom ventured far. Never had they met a true Viking. Scandinavians lived in parts of northern Scotland. Settled farmer folk however who had been in Scotland for hundreds of years, far removed from the fierce raiders who descended on the coasts. As a son of Denmark some of the children were genuinely scared of him. Hereafter, he must be much more gentle in his actions.

Youngsters peered around the corner at Seward who motioned them up to him. They edged forward warily. This was a truce but not peace as yet, he realised upon seeing their temper. Intent upon rectifying this, he began to tell of the storm and the shipwreck. A natural storyteller, Seward thrilled his audience. The wind, the rain, the cold, booming surf filled the room. The previously uncertain children crept closer and he caught smiles passing between them. Bold young fellows demanded what Seward knew of the serpents that were known to inhabit deeper oceans. Thus he began a tale regarding them, and of his ship being menaced.

"When we were attacked we took to the beasts, riding on their backs and inflicting grievous wounds upon them. Some of us died when the serpents dived below the water. We fought long and hard. I never thought we'd get past them. I don't know how we did."

The tale, moved his audience. Seward paused, dramatically, "I must wet my lips before I end this story."

"No Seward, no," protested some youngsters. "Tell us more. You must tell us what happened. Please Seward." One pleaded, "Don't delay in the telling."

He relented. "It ended thus, when one of the creatures gulped us down and swam off, the better for having eaten us."

Laughter. Seward noticed him then. The boy had sad lonely eyes. What a bedraggled figure the child was, disappointed as were all but at least they laughed, he thought. An unhappy child, this Morgund MacAedh, Kenneth's son. Seward felt he must get to know him, as this was the son of the man who had saved his life.

A man approached Seward and bent over and whispered confidentially as if saying something important which didn't include the others, a simple straight forward wit, he'd elaborate later to make himself important to his listeners. Secret information worked well in enhancing his status. "Seward, you are called to attend upon the Lord Kenneth."

Once, in changed clothing, Seward was hurriedly conveyed to a central hall where Kenneth was seated on a raised dais. Seward examined Kenneth. He was dark haired, blue eyed, broad-shouldered, with a stern leader's manner. Yet, it was not convincing. Kenneth was nervous. The kind of man who expected someone to sneak up and stab him in the back and end his days.

Kenneth forced a smile and said, "I am conversant with your tongue, Norseman." Kenneth then smiled at Seward, "I am part Norse myself or at least my kinsmen are, so I am not averse towards you," he said.

"Thank you for your kindness," Seward replied.

Kenneth continued. "I am the self-styled Lord of Ross. Why I am self-styled can wait for another occasion. It is a long tale full of woe. Too long to tell here. So Seward, tell me how you came to be shipwrecked on the coast of Scotland?"

The crowd remained very still as Seward took his mind back. "Our ship was lashed by savage storms. We lost control as we were taken close to your coast. We were wrecked. Many of us drowned. For the others, you know what happened to them on the beach."

"Thank you, Seward. I am sorry for your shipmates. I will explain. Until recently Norway dominated northern Scotland. Many Scots including my forebears took the side of the Norseman. Now William, the Lion, the king, has improved his control of northern parts. Unfortunately your complement of fishermen came ashore at Buelly. There is a strong royal castle there. The castellan is a brutal man with no love for Scandinavians. He probably deemed it good sport to hunt them. Seward, I am aggrieved for you."

Seward considered these words. As he did Kenneth stood and addressed the assembled Scots. "You have all heard him. I say we help this lad by accepting him as one of our own. Malcolm The Black we know you have a fine house. Have you room for Seward?"

"Yes." Malcolm responded. "We will take him in. I have heard the boy has the gift for story telling. What a great thing that will be on cold winter's nights. Often we sit around our fire with nothing to say." Malcolm, to reassure Seward, winked at him.

Kenneth warm in reply, "I can always depend on you Malcolm." He then looked at the others, the inference being that with them it might be otherwise. Kenneth spoke to Seward. "You will be content amongst us then. Never fear, lad. Some happiness you will have, I will see to it."

Kenneth was a good but overly trusting man who failed to understand what motivated men. Some close to him meant him ill, and stood near waiting for their moment. Seward himself sensed ill intent and that all was not right here. He turned his eyes from the predators. Kenneth stepped forward and squeezed Seward's shoulder. "You have courage. It is a great base upon which to build. Good luck, Seward."

Seward having heard tales of knightly conduct, knelt and immediately bowed low. "Thank you my, Lord," he said.

"Seward, one day I will seek to return you to your homeland. But it may take time."

"Aye, my Lord."

"Good, Seward.  You will be well cared for here."

"I will make myself useful to you and I will never forget the great kindness you have done me, my Lord."

The crowd murmured.  Seward had acted nobly.  Some thought back to another Seward, he of Northumberland, who came from Birnam Wood to Dunsinane with Malcolm Canmore a hundred and fifty years before.  MacBeth was slain and thereby Canmore, was made King.  It was a good and lucky name for Scotland, many thought.

Later in the night, a man with wild and curly, fair, unkempt hair, attacking a plate with abandon.  Sitting beside him, his companion, who was much younger, sixteen, no more.  They sat in a corner lit only by a flickering fire, whose light coloured the fair man's hair yellow and boy's dark hair, gold-red, black.  It painted their faces with long sinister shadows.  The blond man burped loudly in Seward's ear and said, "Greetings."

"Greetings," Seward replied.

The blond man said, "Your friend Kenneth is dead already and he doesn't know it."

Seward replied, "He looks well enough to me."

"Too good for some of us ..."

"Some people are never loyal." His mother's words came to mind. They would have earned her wrath if she came striding in, and they would have stayed their tongues then. He turned to more agreeable company. Almost immediately a scuffle erupted between the man and his young companion and they were evicted. "They could pass for Norseman," he said to someone who laughed.

He thought of their reference to Kenneth and what it implied. This place was dangerous and Kenneth, the man responsible for saving his life was the centre of it. Kenneth was surrounded by evil, Seward could almost see the noose tightening around Kenneth's neck. He needed a distraction and looking for it outside, walked to where young lads were wrestling. Upon asking to join in they told him, "You know us not. We understand one another. With us there is no chance of ill intent. Wait till you know us better."

He returned to the four walls with a hollow feeling of despair. When faced with great danger the act of surviving provides initial relief, however the mind eventually becomes negative gnawed away from inside. That was learned. Realising it would take a considerable time to cast aside his uneasy feelings, he sought distraction by concentrating on those about him. Whilst speaking to them he enjoyed the conversations yet continued to grow ever more weary.

Noticing this, the girl, the tongue poker, Suana watched him admiringly. She wanted to find him a pillow and direct him to a place to rest. She would have talked to him but was lost for words. What could she say? Across the hall, another girl watched him just as intently as she did, Gormlaith. Suana made sure Gormlaith didn't notice her watching Seward - it would cause a fuss.

Gormlaith was a spiteful girl who would not accept any competition. As Suana watched Seward, his head sank forward on a bench. His hosts noticed this and presently a girl of eleven or twelve appeared. Seward had noticed her watching him for some time. She curtsied, and took hold of his hand. "I am Malcolm's daughter, my name is Gormlaith. We are going home now Seward. Bid farewell to your friends." Gormlaith hummed like a bee. "You will like us. Mother sings and father is kind." There was a moment's pause. "Did I tell you we have a hound?" Wistfully, "Our dear hound. Father likes you, he has heard of your stories." Her voice came from far away and it barely penetrated the haze of his exhaustion.

Inside a dwelling he was directed to some bedding, and falling headlong into it, a moment later, he slept. Much later he awakened. Recalling the day's events and the disturbing unreality of it all. His head throbbed. The sway of the ship he felt beneath his feet, tasted salt water. The wind hit his face. He attempted to regain his bearings. Looking around the sparse room he saw a fire blazing in one corner. A sequence of recent events flashed through his mind; Kenneth, his kindness, a woman who had helped him in the courtyard, and a disturbing vision of the massacre.

A glistening of sweat appeared on his brow, "Kenneth is dead already." What did that mean? A dog stared into the flames, such a comforting domestic scene that it calmed him. His breathing steadied. He eased himself down and closed his eyes once more. With morning a fair woman. Perhaps in her forties, old seeming to Seward. That she had been a beauty was plain, but something had aged her, some sorrow. Bending over him and adjusting his bedding, they studied each other, he looked at her through squinted eyes. Blue, kind eyes he thought she had.

Gormlaith was at the door and the woman spoke to her. "We will not disturb him, Gormlaith. Bring in a pail of water so he can wash. Look at him curled up like a hedgehog in the burrow."

"Sleep peacefully, young hedgehog," Gormlaith said, giggling as she closed the door.

Sleep did not return. After wetting his face, he left the room. His steps took him to the others. Malcolm sat in a chair near the fire. The same hound was by his side, the one that had kept him company the night before, still mesmerised by the flames. Mother and daughter prepared food at a long table.

"Good morning Seward," chorused mother and daughter together.

"Good morning," replied Seward.

He saw he was in a fine house with a high ceiling, well built and well kept. A second table to which Malcolm motioned Seward to be seated. In the middle of it was a large cooked fish that smelt delicious.

"A treat boy, to welcome you," Malcolm said.

Seward, looking at smiling faces, felt a sense of belonging. He thought this was strange, but it did not make him feel uneasy. A curl of his lips grew into a small grin, which he tried to fight, not wanting to appear too overjoyed, in case they thought him overly emotional. But his teeth wouldn't be contained, they sprouted like mushrooms after a storm. Gormlaith and her mother Sienna, smiled back as broadly, a warm glow shining in both their eyes. "What a handsome boy he is," they thought.

Sometime later Seward asked Malcolm about the danger to Kenneth. Malcolm told him it was a complex situation and better to be well practised with sword and not let it be known he was all for Kenneth. Lest the day come when he could pay a high price for that. A day would come when loyal friends would be needed. Such was the case that those who cherished him must bide their time and let those who would harm him place the words in their mouths that would condemn them.

# THE MOURNING

THE PASSAGE OF time had turned Seward into a powerful youth. At seventeen, Seward had thrived on climbing the steep highlands and wading through freezing semi-arctic, waters. The highlands was the perfect environment to toughen body and mind. A society, directed towards producing warriors, rewarding valour and prowess at arms, therefore, holding Seward in high esteem. Bent down, drinking from a stream whirling between rocks, hereabouts, trees, large and stately, right down to the waters edge. After standing Seward looked like he had things of great importance to decide. Which, in fact, he did. With his fate for good or ill, linked to Scotland, he would travel to Denmark to let his parents know he was alive and well, but not until he turned eighteen. Then, at least, he would be able to protect himself, according to Sienna, Malcolm's wife, who had become like a mother to him. After reassuring his family, he would return to Scotland to serve Kenneth. Kenneth needed stout retainers. His ancestors paid dearly for pressing a rival claim to the throne. Now, Kenneth held his Earldom by default. The king's power did not extend to the MacAedh northern homeland. A temporary state of affairs that the King of Scots, King William, would soon rectify. Only by giving loyal service to the current dynasty could Kenneth's line be made secure. The MacAedh must submit to the king.

In Scotland there was a new power to be reckoned with a power that could thrust itself into the highlands. The Norman conquerors of England had revolutionized weaponry and tactics in the medieval world. Heavily armored, mounted on giant horses, superbly trained and disciplined. Since their appearance in the Brittish Isles they had vanquished all opponents including the Scots. King David the First of Scotland grew to manhood amongst them as a hostage in England in the 1120's. The Normans impressed King David. Returning to Scotland, several Normans came with him. That was many generations ago. In the reign of Scotland's current king, any who opposed royal authority had the Normans to face, not a prospect to be taken lightly, and Kenneth's kinsman Donald Ban talked loudly against the king, their patron, making things even more dangerous for the MacAedhs. All the highlanders knew the Normans were superb knights and acquisitive. War was coming. Most dreaded it, some like Seward looked forward to it, knowing, destiny would be written, furthermore, that God did not give great physical gifts without reason.

After receiving training in the art of war it was apparent that Seward possessed a gift for weaponry. The originality of his mind was suited to solving problems associated with the use of arms. He came up with theories, by implementing some, whilst discarding others, he improved all aspects of his swordsmanship. Seward was the tallest man in the village and still growing, a statement expressed often and with awe by a people not noted for their height. He thrived on practicing his martial skills till every sinew burned. Other noted swordsmen held him in high regard, none held any degree of certainty that they could beat him.

That is, all but Dolfin, famed for his skill, who Kenneth held in high esteem. Dolfin thought any talk of Seward's supremacy premature. Seward, a hulking giant, and slow, who was inexperienced in actual combat. Although he showed promise, it would be a few years yet until he was a threat to the very best, such as Dolfin knew himself to be.

Seward stood tall and strong awaiting tidings from a messenger who had ridden all night with an urgent royal missive for Kenneth. A council was to be held in Edinburgh and as the Earl Of Ross, Kenneth was invited. He had never contested William's rule. He thought perhaps the MacAedh past was forgiven. It seemed logical. Should this bring him close to the crown, his Earldom could be made valid. His cousin, the king, to whom he had made no warlike gesture towards, must need him to stabilise the north. To make this council he must depart as soon as possible and with a light escort. Must, risk crossing the lands of a warlike neighbour. He instantly made his decision and chose twenty of his best men to ride with him.

As they were preparing to depart Kenneth's wife ran forward, and clung to his robes. Mary thought she would never see Kenneth again. Clasping him as if to never let him go. She thought her heart would rip in two. He looked calm. She thought he looked too calm, like a man who did not respect the dangers, not like a man with his life at stake. "Don't go, Lord. At least wait until a strong force can be assembled to protect you."

Staring at her, Kenneth thought her worried face would darken his journey and weigh heavily on his mind. He looked away. Dolfin, a friend, came near, comforting her. Kenneth addressed him, "My lady, gentle though she is, is headstrong." He gave her a warning glance to say no more.

She ignored him. "What of time?   Surely your safety can be worth an hour."

"Time enough, there is not, Mary.  I will fare well.  See to thyself and our son for I must away."

*"I fear thou will be dead by tomorrow."*  But words could not be given to such thoughts.  "God willing, we will triumph, and be saved hereon," she said.

"I will return anon.  God willing," he replied.

"God willing."  Thereafter she relapsed into moody silence. A single tear set course down her cheek.  Seeing it, Kenneth turned away.   It was an omen almost too dire to ignore. Perhaps, he was going into the jaws of death.

Never before had Mary felt tragedy to be so close, that she could feel it, close and palpable.  Looking out at Kenneth as he turned to wave, she thought he looked happier than he had a right to.  Looking, as if he was on a great adventure, and not with his life at stake, and not with the odds stacked heavily against him.  Then he was out through the gate into the night.

Further on he rode, harness jingling, silhouetted against a bright moonlit sky.   The route was little known.   Kenneth believed they should meet no others, yet having voiced his plans to a number of his closest supporters, Kenneth felt that perhaps one too many knew his intention.  It was bleak, the deep feeling of uneasiness and foreboding.  His wife's words still dark in his mind. He tried to clear his cloud of fear and dread. He felt he had forgotten something important and must remember it.

He recalled the words of one his trusted supporters. "Stay in the highlands where the Normans cannot fight. The conditions do not suit them here." Thurloc had said.

Dolfin, vehement in denial. "They will come here as everywhere else before. You must go and make things right with the king."

Thurloc was equally passionate, "No, I say treachery is afoot, Kenneth, and doubt not, is close at hand."

With that, Dolfin's eyes had lingered on Kenneth. Kenneth saw those eyes again, upon reflection felt sick to the pit of his stomach at what those eyes told him. He remembered that when he said, "I am going regardless of any doubts." Dolfin had smiled. Attempting to analyse that smile. No reassurance was gained therein.

He recalled Thurloc warning him. "Kenneth, he is more than glad to see you go, yet absents himself, suffering an illness too extreme to sit a horse ... he looks well enough to me."

Kenneth put these thoughts away for they gravely affected his confidence. Returning to the present, urging his horse up a steep slope. Atop this slope, whispers floated in the night air. He heard, "A traitor does dwell in your midst, a sore carbuncle that festers in your breast, a traitor."

Kenneth suffered a sense of bereavement at his own death. His wife's response to his leaving was too vivid. His lifetime was nearly finished he felt. He could not escape the vision of Mary crying at his departure. Kenneth wore the pallor of all his misgivings and his face was a death mask.

Looking over his shoulder to get warning of an action toward him, the more he looked behind the greater it did vanquish comfortable spirits in him. Kenneth was sweating. His horse, good beast, obedient to his urging and took him higher up in the mountains. With a rainy mist descending, the pace slowed. The riders closing up into tighter formation. Ahead, a bridge spanning two sheer cliffs. This route made for a fast journey, but it was also an ideal place for an ambush. Kenneth warned his men.

For an attack to succeed here it would take careful planning. If such did occur, it could mean only one thing, the king was involved in a conspiracy. For Kenneth's presence here, where he was most vulnerable, was directed by the king's writ. It all seemed too contrived, a more careful methodical mind worked here than the king's for the king was not known for his subtlety. It was not too late to turn back. Continue or turn back, Kenneth could not decide, whilst all the time closing on the bridge. The best way to negotiate an obstacle is quickly. Kenneth recalled the military maxim. Nearly upon the bridge, Kenneth called his men together. "We will ride at the gallop tight packed across the span."

Before Kenneth finished issuing his instructions, mounted riders descended from above. There was only time for men to exchange worried glances before the attackers were amongst them. It was hopeless. No time to organise a defence. Seeing a prospect of escape, a few retreated up a rocky slope, on foot. The rocks hindering the enemy horses from overtaking them and for a time, it seemed some might escape.

In deathly silence, hidden by the thick mist, the survivors made their way. Suddenly the enemy burst through the gloom. A man wore an axe in his face and another had crimson across his belly. Sword points flashed. William MacRuari, a young member of Kenneth's escort, caught a blur of movement out of the corner of his eye. He turned quickly, and ducked just low enough. Horsemen galloped past. He saw a break in their ranks and ran towards the bridge. The clear space that drew him suddenly disappeared. Now surrounded by jostling riders forcing him closer to the cliffs edge, William ducked to avoid an axe, stumbled, felt nothing beneath his feet, he was over the edge, and plunging downward.

Below, the water of a stream rapidly heading up to meet him. Colliding with something. A small tree which grew from the cliff wall and that saved his life. He used it, lifting himself onto a narrow shelf. Checking himself for any injuries, he found none. There were sounds from above, horns were blowing and men shouting to one another, the sounds of battle won, a battle, over. Another realisation, he was trapped half way up a mountain.

Along the ledge William noticed a small opening in the cliff wall. He cautiously edged towards it, spread-eagled, gripping the cliff. Gaining entry, it was cave as he had imagined, but much larger than expected. Water dripping down from the moss covered surroundings. The rain swept in upon him as he crouched lower creeping further into the hollow. The gap opened up larger and led downward, he realized. The place would bear investigation in daylight.

Protected from the weather he sat and watched the now fierce descent of moisture from above. The wind often changed course. Howling gusts punctuated by lightning, illuminating William's face as he stared into the night sky. William, wondering if he would see his friends and family again? Furthermore, if he attempted the climb and didn't make it, his body might never be found. The cave could have an exit. He would look for it in the morning.

Thinking back to the battle, he remembered Kenneth's last words. "I curse those who've betrayed me. Alas my poor house."

William brows knitted together as he remembered Kenneth's attacker. The man had said, "Feel my blades length."

The attacker then plunged his dagger in, killing Kenneth. William shed a tear for his master and his friend.

"Rest in peace Good Lord Kenneth," he said, as much to himself as the ghosts of the night air.

---

MARY'S SHUTTERS SWUNG open, and rain and hail rode in on the wind. Down below, the courtyard was a sea of mud. Hailstones then steady rain. It was an hour when none stirred. She dreamt of Kenneth and what was happening with him - not easy speed. A white face piercing the dark. She gasped! Mary went to look outside, hands shaking.

The weathers course took the wetness aslant and away. Earlier fears, she felt were groundless. As is often the case, when untouched by a storm it is then you decide that the world is a better place. It rained heavier, wetting Mary. She closed the shutters. Her last thought before sleep was that Kenneth should be far by now, or dead.

A fly, in a web, above her bed attempting to free itself became more entangled. A spider meanwhile crept closer but was slowing. The cold from the wind sapped its energy and it stopped, was dead, and so was the fly. Mary dreamt of Kenneth, of his face on the mountainside. He was tilted up to the wet and his eyes were open and staring and dead. His look said he realised what a fool he was to have trusted the men he had and perhaps he was.

Rain fell on the roof, heavier, then lighter, dripping, gone. Although it was an hour when few stirred, Seward was awake. Normally he slept soundly. But this night, whilst staring at the ceiling he felt a craving for an activity, and not just any activity, an overwhelming urge to ride to a particular location, the bridge in the mountains. Dressing and went to Malcolm who surprisingly agreed to go with him.

Together they rode out. Beyond the gates into the unknown. Their horses hooves pounding driving them on. Engulfed by forest, the moon casting its glow sending the forest branches like claws down to grab them. Leaving the forest they started climbing. Before long, they detected an eerie presence which seemed to be following them. Seward and Malcolm exchanged glances and looked back. The horses were skittish and shying, like there was something here that the men could not see. Seward shouted to be heard over the sound of galloping.

"Malcolm do you feel like we are being followed?"

"Yes, I can feel it and I don't like it."

Further into the mountains this presence became stronger and stronger until it felt like they could reach out and touch it, so powerful, the air seemed to crackle with unnatural energy. Ahead was the bridge between cliffs where Kenneth met his misfortune. Swirls of mist twisted and turned to form fantastic shapes. Moon glow filtered through. The wind blew a gap in the shroud revealing parts of the landscape, Seward pointed, his face deathly white, "Over there!"

Figures were strewn across the field, the remains of Kenneth and his men. Their imagination spilt forth, giving life to the dead, and Seward and Malcolm heard screaming men, horses galloping in terror and the clash of arms. They rode closer as wispy condensation created the perception of movement. The moving mist seemed filled with horsemen. A sense of panic grew on both Seward and Malcolm. They turned their horses and rode off believing themselves pursued by the souls of the slain. Seward and Malcolm re-entered the gates just before dawn. They were sworn to secrecy. A party was sent to ascertain the truth of the matter. As luck would have it, Mary still slept. If, Kenneth was alive would remain a matter of uncertainty for hours.

---

IN THE GREY light of early dawn William slid between a rocky crevice and into the cave proper. The cave a short way on led to an opening, a large roomy vault with connecting chambers, burdening him with a decision.

Sounds of water came from one.  As he pressed on into it, the light faded.   Then, closer to the underground stream visibility increased again.  Somewhere above was an opening admitting light.    Reaching the stream, he drank long and delightedly.    Such  a  splendid place!   William wondered whether it was known?    If these caves were known to men surely the wonder of them would be spoken of widely.   The clan would certainly be aware of them.

A  narrow  beam  of  sunlight  granting  Wiliam  a  view encompassing more of the chamber.  Head up, he turned to the opening in the overhanging rock.  Deciding he could be lowered down through it.  Blurred shapes, caught the light and his eye.  Approaching them, he saw they were large leather chests.    A  closer  inspection  revealing  they  contained  vast amounts of gold coins.   "What wonder.  What amazing good fortune,"  he said to himself, dumbfounded.

Clansmen like William seldom saw such wealth.  Wealth was  alien  to  the  highlanders,  as  foxes  to  hounds,  bar  the nobility, the exception.    William savoured the coins, digging deep enjoying the caress of the coins as they trickled through his fingers.    He had no way of knowing that the likeness stamped  on  the  coins  represented  the  Roman  Emperor Caligula.   Once long ago, a Governor of one of Caligula's northern provinces who fell into Caligula's disfavour was ordered to Rome.  The call to Rome was dreaded by any who received it.    Even Caligula's friends were in danger and the Governor was no friend of the Emperor.  He decided to sail away from Roman boundaries and on taking his vast hoard of wealth with him.  His plan did not go unnoticed.  Barely did he escape harbour.  Although his vessel was quick one pursuer had him in sight long after all the others disappeared over the horizon.

As the winds freshened the distance separating the two crafts gradually narrowed. The ex-governor decided to land. Pulling into shore the chests were off-loaded and taken inland. Someone stumbled into the cave, where the gold was laid. The governor's men melted further into the hills to avoid pursuit. All of them were caught by tribesmen and killed.

The indigenents judged them as invaders. Romans venturing into foreign lands were seen as such. William staring at the coins, had no way of knowing this, he concentrated on the task at hand, how to get off this mountain. He decided against exploring further, for away from the light he might become lost. Determined to take some of the gold along with him, he undressed thereafter tied as many coins as would fit into a bundle made from his clothing. William retraced his steps to the entrance. He thought of shouting out so that a member of his clan might hear. It was tempting, but would expose knowledge of his cave should the enemy still be close. An unworthy risk.

Nothing for it, but to climb. Up until lately he had faith his escape was a sign from God that he would survive, now he was not so sure. Before he commenced, he dropped the bundle of coins away down over the side. Watching the slow steady descent this height was alarming. The bundle landed heavily on a bank next to the stream. It had taken so very long to land. For a moment he stared down at the waters of the mountain stream that crested boulders and surged downwards.

"Straight up or ahead," he cautioned himself, "Don't look down." Bile rose to his throat at the magnitude of how far up he was.

Dark clouds gripped the mountain, he prayed they wouldn't open. Time for action, he thought, for nothing would get done by thought alone. He took his belt off. Tying his dirk to his belt, throwing it forward, when it held, he dragged himself higher. Not accustomed to using his muscles in this way, he discovered he was tiring quickly.

Higher now, and the weather remained thankfully calm. Clumps of growth provided footholds as he scrambled from one to the other, aware that down an expanse of grass and rock, and to his back, nothing, only open sky. It was as if he was climbing a stairway to heaven. A single slip meant an end. Indeed this climb could lead to heaven if such an favoured outcome was destined. A step away from heaven, here, so far up. Such a beautiful moment to be embraced by death. Contemplating a longing to release his fingers, which came and went. The death, of close comrades, the terror, he had seen befall them all, had that dispelled natural calm? A tremor went all the way up his arm, for he had nearly let go. Perhaps a flaw in his make-up made him think of letting go. All sorts of dangerous thoughts had to be contended with, to live, he realised.

After ascending for some time William believed he felt the peak's life-force. The mountain accepted him. Favoured in that one sense a deep pleasant feeling came. A complete reversal to his previous mindset. Earlier, believing that this terrain was painful and dominating. Now the mountains were Gods commanding the air, Lords of all they surveyed, dominating the landscape full of power. The elation, uplifted his spirit, invigorated him, as again, he concentrated on where to put his feet.

When they were firmly placed, he moved.   A mild tempered swallow tarried near him causing him to protest the injustice that wings were affixed to it.  "Swallow lend me thy wings," he said.   But the swallow had urgent business and had trifled long enough.  It wondered why the man was there.  This was no place for a man.  Even the swallow knew that.

Continuing on, ever more carefully yet still making steady progress, until suddenly he realised that he had blundered, missing a ledge with his foot, having moved when not sufficiently on.  Spraying out his feet on the slippery surface, he felt for a ripple to hold onto, only one foot secure, the other clawing at a smoothly vertical wall.   Slightly along, a hole the size of a bucket.  Pushing off from his one secure foothold he gained purchase in the bucket sized hole and safety.

A sudden intense fear greater than anything he had ever felt.  Seeing himself falling, imagining, himself torn to pieces on the rocks below.  He didn't think of how different these thoughts were to what had gone before.  Once, he'd felt communion with this towering feature and felt embraced by it, now he thought of falling to his death and how horrific it would be.  He managed to decrease his panic, by closing his eyes and slowing his breathing, numbing his mind to the immensity of his predicament.

---

WHEN WILLIAM EDGED his legs to another foothold, thereafter, he moved his hands higher, and then when a grip above held his weight, again, moved his foot position higher, repeating the process, thereby, ascending. A short time later, he stopped, forced to, what stopped him was a geological design, an inconsistency where a tongue of rock protruded from the cliff face. Surveying further to his left a reasonably shallow incline consisting of odd stones having fallen from higher to form a shallower slope. These stones were the link to higher parts, a deep chasm between him and there, but he could jump over, and did.

Continuing past the bridge of stones, to a narrow shelf threading up. Finding purchase in clefts between rocks, grabbing a bush above. Larger boughs, reaching up grabbing the branches and climbing still more. Above these large branches he cut himself a sharp stake, using it to push himself and for balance. Almost at the summit, the mountain confounded him, as high as he could go, for the last part of the mountainside protruded at an impossible angle.

William sat pondering his options. Climbing down may prove much more dangerous than ascending. Consoled by the thought that this position offered good shelter he decided to wait for someone to come, then call for help. The sun came out. Laying back enjoying the sun on his body when a small bird alighted on a tree opposite him. It stilled. He wished the bird would not fly away. But it did. Cheeps and tweeks filled the air, and William's eyes followed the feathered movements, as they hopped onto the branches of a large tree on the opposite bank.

He longed for that other bank. Though steep, the opposite side was much more gradual in its gradient but between him and there, the ground descended in a shadowy waste. If he could cross the chasm, he could scale the rest of the mountainside easily, but the bird had wings and he did not. The bird hopped and fluttered from branch to branch in the bough of that nearby tree whose limbs reached out tauntingly close to William. If birds could fly why couldn't he? Well, he would find out if the birds alone could rule the sky.

Running as fast as he could, until ... at the cliff's edge jumping with arms and legs flailing, attempting to gain distance. Falling down, wondering if the branches on the other side would hold him. They gave, and held. He kicked his way through the smaller boughs. One last limb gave way and he fell onto ground which he had never felt happier to touch. William solving his problem in an instant and in doing so conquered his fears and pleased at that. Legs trembling, he sank down on his haunches, but an experienced fighting man he did not feel concerned, he just waited for the trembling to subside, and when it did, kept going. The jump had offered some exhilarating moments, he even wished there was some valid reason for doing it again. This was foolish, he realised, and that like everything else once the trauma was over only the good was remembered. He had experienced similar thoughts after a battle won.

Walking to the bridge he saw dead horses with equipment scattered about and the spoiling flesh of his comrades, each one of whom was headless. He stayed distant not wishing to stray near them, their entrails made him feel their moment of torment. Walking a little further he saw a line of horsemen approaching him. They were members of his clan. While waiting for them he grabbed a patch of clothing and covered his lower parts.

They warily approached him and did not initially recognise him.  Upon reaching him, William learned that the clan was in uproar.  They had heard of the battle these men had been sent to look for survivors.  Seward Gunn and Malcolm the Black had ridden upon the site in the early hours of the morning.

William thought this was strange.  It was surprising on two counts, firstly, that there were no other survivors and that anyone should ride here so soon.  No explanation was forthcoming.  William who was hurriedly given a horse was told that the clan needed him.  A gathering was to be held to decide on a future course of action.  William could provide useful information regarding the identity of the murderers.

"And what of Morgund?"  he asked.

"He is now in danger and cannot stay in Ross for someone who had Kenneth's trust has betrayed him.  Any time now Morgund may receive a dagger."

# MARY'S WOE

MARY SAT BEFORE her mirror a blankly expressionless face staring back at her. Though a multitude of thoughts captivated her she was unable to seize and identify a single one. Crowded thoughts that didn't sit right on her, of her son, of Kenneth. He was good man in so many ways and foolish. He should never have gone. The thought of Kenneth's tragic death caused lines of worry. A worm was inside her head eating the apple that was her brain. The terrible premonition she felt before Kenneth had departed was simply a woman's fancy she told herself. Or indeed something may have happened. She could not decide. The terrible sense of impending doom at, and before Kenneth's departure was too real. Her brow and cheeks white contrasting with her eye sockets, grey. She felt worse when she looked upon her son Morgund who was slight and not martial. His father despaired of him becoming a man worthy in warrior skills and had seen him as perhaps a priest in the making. To be a MacAedh was to be in danger. No priest could he be.

He was far too young to fend for himself with Kenneth gone. Kenneth's death had been in her dreams. She knew he was dead yet she didn't know how, but she knew, or thought she did, for one moment of decision was reversed the next. She wished she had an answer for what to do, or knew whom to trust for a sour atmosphere of distrust was shadowing her. To be a woman was to be in a prison for she was limited in how well she could protect her son, men didn't give weight to her decisions nor did she have the strength to fight the enemies that surrounded them. They used cold steel something she could not.

A man with a sinister eye looked at her, a truer servant she thought did not exist until now. Waving him away, she couldn't fathom if it was him or whether inside her head was the true source of her discontent. She felt unwell, but real enemies existed, as she only too well, knew.

Eionghall entered. "Don't be afraid ma'am I am sure Kenneth's journey will be a safe one."

Mary glared at Eionghall as if she were mad, her words of comfort were insincere. The woman's eyes were as wide as puddings. Eionghall had never seen Mary like this. It was deeply disturbing. Mary stared at her with distrust. Eionghall looked into the eyes of a stranger.

"Madam lay yourself down. I will wipe your brow with a warmed cloth."

Mary took a step away. Mary's view of everything was black. She felt a treacherous deed had been done. It quickened her heart, logic fled.

"I see something ..."

"What is it you see Mary?"

"A field. Upon it dead men, and there too is Kenneth."

Eionghall, forgetting the correct term of address, gasped, "Mary God no." Eionghall dropped the basin spilling the water.

The look she saw on Mary's face stilled Eionghall's breath. The air was evil. She wanted to run, expected to hear footsteps of approaching assassins. Death was near. It danced alone but looked for a partner. Someone was dead, or soon would be. Not herself, she prayed, nor her kind mistress, nor Kenneth, nor Morgund.

Why did men indulge in blood letting. The act availed nothing, save that it wrought sadness and the undoing of a mothers work. Women bore children and that was where their relevance ended. It would be a different world if they ruled it, a woman could not be so cruel. Hardihood not compassion was the precondition for success. Feminine skill, was not valued.

"I feel I am sick," Mary said.

"I can see that."

"Leave me, for I can best deal with this alone."

"Better alone madam?"

"Yes."

"As you wish." Eionghall departed leaving Mary to her darkness. A wise woman might set things right and Eionghall went to arrange such.

Thinking of Kenneth brought a sadness Mary couldn't abide. Her fingers nails dug into flesh which pained her but she couldn't loosen. She bit her lip hard then relaxed with considerable effort. Aware as she did, that she could sever her lip easily, if she lost control.

A draught of wine calmed her enough that some sleep came. An inner escape to horrors only, for the knots of despair did not loosen in her sleep.

"I am sick, I am sick." She said, clenching her fingers tight as the pain inside her head worsened.

"Mary Mary, wake child. Mary!" She looked up into a face that banished bewilderment. It was Margaret, a woman whose smile was warm, who was loving and strong, intelligent. Margaret was respected in the village, she was canny in many ways, and used her skills for good and never ill.

"Why must I wake?" Mary asked.

"You've slept overlong. The village is in turmoil. Terrible news I have to impart. You must prepare yourself to hear it."

Mary got up intending to go, go where? She knew not where. "I must get out and be away."

"Be still and listen, for it is not fact until it is told."

"Oh, no, do not tell, for I know already. My Kenneth is fallen."

By art of her eyes Margaret made Mary relax. With those same eyes, imparting the knowledge that it was Mary's duty to uphold herself and that she could. Margaret put her arms around Mary, let her cry for a time, then set about gaining her something to eat and arranged that others surround her, having told them to keep all talk to easy subjects.

She went about the grim task of informing Morgund. After ascertaining that his state would not distress his mother, she brought him to Mary. Later they went into a smaller room and spoke of what must be done. When actions were concentrated on, grief was less, it was manageable and not destructive.

"Kenneth was a good man." Margaret said.

Mary nodded and didn't prolong the conversation. Margaret knew she wasn't needed for these two together could sustain each other.

———————

WILLIAM NEARLY KILLED the horse and himself getting to the village and, thereafter, breathless and exhausted, he reported to the counsellors.

The king's Normans were exerting heavy pressure to acquire Celtic land, therefore, some of the Celtic Earls could be expected to protect the rights of a traditional Celtic landholder beset by an aspiring contestant. All were decided, such motivation was behind Kenneth's death. It was decided that Morgund must leave Ross, forthwith, south, seek the protection of the Celtic Earls. Going to Ireland would allow the king to ignore him, his familial lands would be lost forever, if he took such a course.

Regarding the identity of the Kenneth's slayer most deemed MacCainstacairt to be the culprit. MacCainstacairt was Kenneth's worrisome neighbour, canny, treacherous, ruthless and restless, only time would tell if this assumption was correct. MacCainstairt the hereditary Abbot of Applecross, was much at court, was warlike, and would like nothing better than the fall of the MacAedhs.

Morgund would seek sanctuary with the king. The council considered the king had no part in Kenneth's death. Morgund's means of travel was discussed. The council decided a number of swordsmen would escort Morgund. Dolfin, the leader, would select and lead them. A small number would be best, five other men accompanying Dolfin. The first four picked were proven fighters. The fifth remained undecided for some time. Certain names were mentioned, Seward hearing his own, registered surprise. Dolfin considered him too young, but by virtue of his being an accomplished swordsman, and skilled in field craft, most thought, he was a natural choice, and Dolfin was persuaded to include him. Seward took his place with the other men.

As they were departing Seward leaned over to Morgund, silent, pale, and sad. "Morgund, your father was a fine man. He was a great friend to me and I shall be yours." He smiled at Morgund trying to convey warmth and support. Morgund remained expressionless. Uncertainty over his future held terrors for him. With a heaviness of heart, Seward said, "I will be your shield, sacrifice my life to save you." Morgund stared at him for a moment then turned his eyes away.

Dolfin was shouting instructions. "We must be off before the killers of Kenneth descend upon us."

A horseman galloping past bearing an urgent warning to Donald Ban MacAedh. The MacAedhs, already depleted by many years of warfare were rapidly becoming extinct. As they rode out past friends and families, Malcolm and his wife and Gormlaith, out in front.

"We're proud of you, boy, protect Morgund," Malcolm shouted to Seward.

Gormlaith ran beside Seward's horse full of good advice. "Keep eyes and sword sharp." Tears stained her features. "Would she ever see Seward again?" She hoped so. "I wish I could go with you. To protect you." Shouting. "I'll pray for your safe return Seward ... Seward ... don't forget me."

She screamed until he was beyond hearing, continuing her run long after he faded to a small figure. Before he disappeared he stopped to give her a last wave then rode to catch up.

Another girl was crushed. One day Suanna had hoped to wed Seward, that shiny haired boy she poked her tongue out to when first they met, and whom she had loved since that day. Twinkling diamonds suddenly released from her eyes spilling down her cheeks. She ran, hiding her devastation from those around her, holding a medal of Saint Andrew whilst she prayed, "Please Lord, allow Seward to come home." She was so afraid that he would not.

----

THE ROUTE THEY were taking was one of Dolfin's own making. Dolfin alone knowing the way ahead. He cared not to repeat Kenneth's error, he informed them, he would not risk it. "I trust we shall fare better than Kenneth," he said light-heartedly.

Dolfin looked too cheerful on mentioning Kenneth. Seward didn't like it. His instinct warned him of danger. It was not manly art to make mirth of dead friends! "A grave loss," Seward said. "Kenneth."

Seward may as well have spoken to the air, none took notice, perhaps it went unheard, he thought, he was surprised he had the nerve to speak thus. They rode eastward then angled off to the south, into land only Dolfin knew. Dolfin talked too much as they rode, Seward only half-listening, felt that trouble stalked, the noose of discontent tightening. Dolfin began to engage Seward in gentle conversation which Seward had scant regard for, it could be said to be light, harmlessly charming, but there was an edge to it. Something was amiss.

"Seward ... tell us a tale." Looking at Seward's reddened face, he said, "Pray tell, what troubles you?"

"It isn't a time for tales, Dolfin."

"Why not?"

"Shouldn't we be vigilant in case of attack?"

"Certainly. Good thinking Seward." Dolfin threw his head back and laughed. "Seward you worry too much. I've got everything under control, trust me, things will work out well."

Dolfin produced a wry smile and nodded to the others in mockery of Seward. Seward noticed how many joined in, and those that did, he liked not. But after some further distance he had a change of heart. He told himself that Dolfin's wisdom went beyond his own. Feeling embarrassed by the ridicule he was content to ignore his fears and see what transpired. Shortly thereafter Dolfin complained of stomach pains and they slowed.

Meanwhile William resolved to make south. Being the sole survivor of the massacre it could be supposed that William might identify Kenneth's killers. Dangerous. So therefore leaving Ross forthwith with the aim to find Morgund, and help him. After following for some distance it became obvious to William that Dolfin was making no effort to hide their track. Slow travel over rocky or high ground would make trailing them difficult, was Dolfin was attempting to put speed ahead of concealment? It seemed so but then a thought occurred to him, this could be another betrayal. Dolfin could be in league with MacCainstacairt? Good sense dictated that precautions be taken. Why leave a clear trail and travel slow? There was something decidedly odd about this, especially when it appeared that the pace had become even slower. William was alert, not wishing to be caught unawares by MacCainstacairt.

Several miles to the south, Seward, was equally confused. Dolfin had been one of Kenneth's most able lieutenants. Not disguising their trail worried him. That the route was known to Dolfin alone was another cause for concern. What if trouble struck and something happened to him? As if in answer to his thoughts suddenly Dolfin fell ill and the pace dropped dramatically. Seward then demanded Dolfin tell them all what his plans were, this slowness could be their death.

Dolfin told them he knew a gap in the mountains through the thick forest.  Once up in the pines they could see any pursuers who would be travelling over open country.  Torching the forest behind them would blind their enemies and eradicate any sign of their passage.  It might have seemed a sensible course of action when Dolfin had devised it but now that Dolfin had fallen ill an alternative plan was needed for they might not reach the forest.

Nothing was said but eye contact was revealing that others were having doubts.   The pace soon dropped even more.  Seward thought that perhaps they should leave Dolfin behind and take their chances.   Seward remained silent until a mile further.  In another hour it would be dark, reassuring himself with it.  Travelling all night would make them vastly more difficult for an enemy to detect them, it might bring them to safety.

Any doubts Seward held that perhaps he had been too hasty with fear affecting his judgement were soon dispelled. Then it happened, Dolfin wanted to stop for the night.  Seward realised that under the cover of darkness was a safer time to travel.  The country was getting higher they had to push on. Seward dismounted to drink from a stream.   After remounting he drew his horse close to Dolfin who was talking to two other members of the party.

"Why are we stopping here when we may reach the forest by morning?"

"Seward, your intentions I don't doubt, but leave the decision making to me, for I am more experienced.  You are just a boy."

"But this is folly, Dolfin. I say we must press on and at least camp in brush where we can hear an enemies approach. Here we might be overrun. An enemy could descend upon us in our sleep, thus slaying us."

"I say that will not happen. The night will be very dark and our trail has not been followed. In the morning with rested horses we will leave them far behind."

"How do you know that our trail has not been followed?"

"Because I know, that is all, and I am not accustomed to be being taught by a young pup."

A long silence ensued. Seward could see two members of the party were unconvinced. He decided that too much was at stake to not voice his doubts. He pulled close to Dolfin. "Dolfin I cannot understand your reasoning. I sense a trap. Someone close to Kenneth is a traitor, and passed his plans on to MacCainstacairt. Now Morgund has been led to a place ideal for a night killing. My suspicions could be wrong but a sensible man guards against all possibilities. I say we go on."

"Go on?" Dolfin looked mystified. "So I am a traitor."

Confronting Dolfin so directly could lose Seward the support of other men. It was a concern but when Dolfin glanced at two confederates he learned the truth. They looked at Morgund with a purpose, he couldn't pull away for he knew his suspicions had been correct, half the party was in league with MacCainstacairt and intended to kill Morgund.

"Is it that you plan him harm?" Seward asked, calmly, despite his pounding heartbeat, desperate to purchase more time to formulate plan.

"Choose your words with care Seward."

"I seek truth Dolfin."

Dolfin reached for his sword. "Do you wish this upon you?"

"Nay," emitted from Seward's lips, looking tense whilst trying to assess where lay his best option.

"Do you think to offend me and live to tell of it Seward?"

Seward realised this was all gaming for the benefit of Morgund and for the men loyal to Morgund's cause. Dolfin's two confederates rode close to them. Seward warned the men he deemed independent. "Draw swords, they are traitors."

"We are ready for them," said one, as he drew.

Battle lines drawn, the sides were evenly matched and Morgund was the prize. But now having lost the element of surprise Dolfin changed tactics.

"Seward, you are a smart young fellow, as are your friends. Don't die on Morgund's account. The MacAedhs are finished. King William is dead. It is a lost cause. A plan of action was devised by MacCainstacairt with the aid of the new king Alexander. On King William's death MacCainstacairt would move against Kenneth. And thus, it was done. Seward, MacCainstacairt will be Earl of Ross. You support a dead cause."

"It is not dead. He lives."

"No doubt, but soon will be dead."

With a measure of detached coldness Seward had drawn his sword. Dolfin was mentally taken aback by this calmness, also, by how highly Seward regarded Morgund's life. The boy had few friends and was totally inept. No less, surprised at Seward having the nerve to confront him, confidently. Observing Seward's confidence and fearlessness Dolfin decided to proceed cautiously. Dispassionately a part of him admired Seward, he acknowledged his great presence of mind in adversity. Seward deemed it irrelevant if his two companions succumbed. Irrelevant, how could it be? To challenge death, with little hope of survival, was calmness, rare.

Some few feet away stood Morgund. Morgund who felt a great distance between himself and these men deciding his fate. They were capable men, it was within them this power and willingness to fight, how unlike him they were. He sought for a way to obstruct these larger fellows, but it was an impossibility. If he had a bow and arrow, then at least he could fly an arrow at them. What a hopeless mess he was in.

Unable to undertake his defence caused an emotional tightening up, a wetness to gather at the corner of his eyes, internally a feeling alike to suffocating. His fear was a solid thing, on all sides closing in on him. He wanted to flee but fear prevented it, for he knew if he ran, he would be caught and die. He could do nothing but wait. Not a dusty cloud in sight, uncommon, as if the skies were watching the unfolding storm occurring between men. Such a listless pathetic thoughts, when about to die written large on his face.

Dolfin's voice broke the spell. "Why you would risk your life to protect this feeble youth whose prospects in life are slim when compared to the wily and experienced MacCainstacairt? Seward, by sacrificing your life you merely delay the inevitable."

Dolfin was a compelling speaker, swaying men by his oratory in the past Seward wondered if he might persuade these two stalwarts to turn against Morgund. He looked to them, it would not happen this time. He hardened his resolve. He thought of what he had told Morgund, that he would sacrifice his life for him, how soon it could affected. Nothing could stop him from noble purpose. "I will not surrender him to you Dolfin and if I knew Morgund not, but knew what his fate would be at your hands I would act as now. You are a betrayer Dolfin. A skulking coward."

"Enough! Nothing will serve but that I must teach you by sword point Seward."

At that, a smile spread over Seward's face, it was not what Dolfin was hoping to see. He should have taken more notice of him in the village, stories of his ability sprang to mind.

Seward, riding some distance away from the others, addressed Morgund. "Ride Morgund." When at first Morgund didn't move, he raised his voice, "Ride to safety, I will hold these for a little." When Morgund still didn't start, he said, "Go, or die upon this field."

He saw Morgund spur his horse towards snow-capped peaks. Dolfin sent a rider after him. Thereafter the of sound of several long blasts on a hunting horn. Seward knew that MacCainstacairt was near. The horn confirmed it. Seward called to one of Morgund's supporters. "Go after him!" The man looking startled. Seward shouted again, "Go! I trust you, alone he is dead. Go!"

Seward had to risk that this man he sent after Morgund was loyal. Morgund could not out ride nor outfight the traitor who pursued him. Watching the clansman galloping away, Seward knew he had to send a man after him. He had done the only thing he could. The time for misgivings was past, he needed all his senses as Dolfin pointed his sword at Seward and charged. Thereafter, contact, wherein intense concentration and will and flashing swords. The shifting melee of combat ablaze.

Upon hearing the sounds of the other pair engaged in battle, Seward gave himself almost totally to the contest with Dolfin. A small section of his brain detached and alert for a lull in the other fight which might spell danger. Blow after blow rang out. If either man was too slow or weak he would be slashed or stabbed. Alternately changing between attack and defence amidst the panicked shuffling of horses caused a strain on the less-experienced swordsman, Seward. Dolfin abetting it, hoping to put him at a deadly disadvantage.

Planning to make Seward react a split second late Dolfin needed just part of a second to slay Seward. Seward brought his sword to Dolfin's throat, who pushed it away. Thereafter Dolfin aimed a blow which Seward ducked. Then Seward struck thin air. Dolfin missed with his strike. With Dolfin, left open, Seward likewise misjudged. With horses rearing and turning, it was awkward. Anguished, Seward pulled on his reins, his mount rose, turned, blocking Dolfin's attack. When Seward's head was strikable again, Dolfin struck the air, then his sword was parried, then, again, and again. Whirling steel came upon whirling steel. Dolfin swayed to add leverage to his attack. Seward turned, spoiling the attack.

Dolfin's next blow was met with steel and steel again. Carbon crystals densely joined, strikes were jarringly unthinkingly absorbed. Seward pushed onto Dolfin's edge, lowered it, struck, but Dolfin slipped by. Slashing, crashing, with all their vigour drenched them in salty sweat and yet another smell permeated the air, fear.

The fighting entered a new phase Dolfin almost unseated Seward with forceful blows. He thought Seward was beaten, any moment he expected to end it. Just then Dolfin's mount stumbled, allowing Seward to break contact, but rivers of sweat fell down his brow, his strength was almost gone. At this point Seward was more concerned with remaining in the saddle. No amount of practice could have accustomed him to the reality of this, this was overpowering. Seward saw his death in Dolfin's eyes, allowing Dolfin to dictate the course of the fight he couldn't see how he could change Dolfin's ascendancy. Needing all his senses just to survive he felt outmatched. The effect on him, was grievous, it made a sluggard of him. But he managed to maintain the pace long enough for change.

To Seward's relief his slowness was now match by Dolfin's own. For the first time since the fight began Seward saw himself surviving. Feeling old and tired Dolfin was surprised he had not downed Seward earlier. Beginning to feel exhausted, nagging doubts crept on Dolfin. "If I don't strike the killing blow soon Seward will kill me."

Feeling Dolfin waning Seward found renewed strength. When Dolfin swung, over committed in the process he almost toppled out of his saddle. Seward latched onto him, with one hand. Held by the shoulder, immobilised was Dolfin, his back was facing Seward. Seward plunged his dagger into Dolfin's ribs. Blood flowed onto the grass, glistening along with the dew of the late afternoon. From the ground, dead eyes looked up at Seward, or seemingly. Seward wasn't sure if Dolfin was dead, or not. Life persisted in Dolfin. Breathing causing shudders. The brain struggling to solve how things had come to this Dolfin thought he should have tested his persuasive powers, which after all, had resulted in Kenneth's death.

When younger his prowess at arms and his pride in display had prevented debating. As he aged he took more pleasure in the power of his mind than he had, his middle years were his best, he had power of mind and body then. Lately weary bones brought a distemper to his disposition, lack of patience was his downfall. Engaging Seward in another ten minute of speech would have enabled MacCainstacairt's men to arrive. Dolfin expected to be obeyed instantly and lost patience when he wasn't. With that, his brain closed down and he stopped thinking ...

Exulting in his victory, Seward was eager to test himself further, who better than on Dolfin's surviving supporter, who, on foot, dealt a last fatal stab to his downed opponent, a man loyal for Morgund. At least Seward could kill the killer of his confederate, Seward thought galloping forward.

Dolfin's swordsman turned. Attempting to remount, realising his mistake in dismounting, his face opposite to Seward's, his eyes resigned. The greatest fear was upon him death, and over, blinding pain entered, torment of a kind a man should not live to tell, was felt. That if known, soldiering would not seem so worthy a profession. Regret on his face, regret at the many things he'd meant to say to his beloved and hadn't.

He entered a state where pain did not exist. A flight of geese slowly making their way across the sky. "Such a peaceful flight they are." Enjoying these last moments of life until finally his head slumped and his eyes closed, by then, Seward had gone, following paths in the grass left by Morgund and his pursuer.

---

PRESSURE POUNDING INSIDE Morgund's head, swamping his senses into disorientation. Panic tearing at his insides Morgund played out his worst worries. Not strong enough to control a large powerful horse, not going as fast as they, the pursuit would not be long in catching up. Dismounting at a stream. A place to hide? There wasn't one. He scanned the surrounds. Heather growing on a ridge nearby. They wouldn't find him there. Morgund, by picking his way towards it left no twigs broken. Come dark he would get as far away as possible. After a time Morgund got up on his haunches. Peering through the undergrowth, he couldn't see anyone. Running quickly splashing across a stream chastening himself, "Why didn't I scare my horse off further?" Too late he had realised that having his mount close by would draw them. Fighting his way through heather and bracken bushes soon blood was streaming down his legs. "I must get further away." Barrelling his way forward, glancing over his shoulder. His face ashen, looking ahead, stumbling, landing in a bed of reeds, breathing deeply attempting to gain clarity.

If someone picked up his trail no matter how fast he ran they would catch up. Wade out into the stream and walk out on stones downstream, leave no trace, this might save him, it seemed logical. Entering the water Morgund felt the shock of the cold water, deeper and more biting than he had imagined. He swam, then, waded. Leaving the stream, walking through shadows of the forest. Then came again to the stream. Splashing downstream, until water became deeper again, up to his neck.

Morgund's assailant killed the clansman sent by Seward to protect Morgund and suffered a cut to his shoulder in the doing. The shoulder ached yet there was excited at the prospect that he would take Morgund's head to MacCainstacairt, it went some way to alleviating his pain. Earning a reward. No doubt, gaining much respect. A dark smile lingering. Trailing Morgund's horse to near to where he had first hidden, from where at a trot Dolfin's man easily followed Morgund to the stream. Galloping on a high bank looking down at Morgund walking slowly, soon he would be a lot slower, he would be dead, this thought parted his lips in an expression of evil.

Morgund came to the end of the stream, a waterfall falling twenty feet over a sheer cliff - impossible to climb down. Morgund set off again, one foot in front of another. Not thinking clearly, tiredness having sapped him, he thought he should have attempted to make a descent beside the falls. Unbeknownst to him, his pursuer gaining on him rapidly. Dolfin's supporter took in Morgund in stumbling gait. On foot there was less chance of Morgund seeing him, he could not risk that, the sun had set, light was fading fast, escape was possible. With his horse tied to a bush, MacCainstacairt's supporter sprinted to Morgund.

Out of the corner of his eye he saw a horseman galloping down, someone attempting to steal his reward, no doubt. He was angry, the fool could scare Morgund off. Thankfully Morgund did see either of them and he would get to Morgund first. Then Morgund saw his assailant. Sinking down, exhausted, burying his head in his arms, he cried, "Sir make my death quick,"

The pursuer smiled as he said, "What have we here? A pretty lass indeed with such a pretty neck indeed." He then placed his sword to Morgund's throat. Stepping back he laughed. "A sorry spectacle you are MacAedh. Laughing more until recovering himself to say, "Your head will be an ornament hanging off MacCainstacairt's wall. Morgund sadly waited, remembering all his bad luck and ruing it. Waiting for the deathblow.

Laying waste to the boy's emotions, was a pleasant a thing as the attacker had ever done. The clean lean face so ready to depart  this life, so utterly defenceless. Closer, so as to strike the killing blow, but nevertheless, delaying, letting his rival approach. Stealing Morgund's head at the last moment would thwart his opponent, there was another motivation, these frightened eyes he loved watching. The reason, the one, for delaying Morgund's death, the most pressing one, wanting the fear to last, not wanting to extinguish the flame just yet. He turned to gloat at the latecomer, the one whose reward he was about to take .... it wasn't a MacCainstacairt clansmen ... it was Seward wielding his sword. Morgund's assailant commenced an upward parry, which came too late. With a whirl of steel, his head went toppling. The day had been long, at last it had ended, Morgund thought of his own death. Almost he had died, he himself, had almost died moments ago.

Seward who felt he had grown ten years during the course of this day, said,  "It's over Morgund." Seward meaning the day as much as anything else, placed a reassuring hand to Morgund's shoulder and Morgund looked up at him through a face shattered by tears. "Are you injured?" from Seward.

"Thank you Seward, I am unhurt." Morgund sobbed anew. His emotions he couldn't contain.

"Get up quickly Morgund, MacCainstacairt is nearby. The fallen man's horse is close. We must put as much distance between them and us as we can."

With Morgund not responding, Seward half-pushed-half carried Morgund as far as he could, then lay Morgund down. Morgund somewhat recovered, Seward led the way, looking about anxiously lest observed by the enemy, sword at the ready. They set off, to the meadow, then back the way they came, risking meeting MacCainstacairt's men in the dark, they had no choice, for by morning the whole area would be crawling with MacCainstacairt supporters.

As all this was ongoing MacRuari entered the meadow from the other side, his horse's ready ears pinned back, listening, as did its owner. Horses galloping, men shouting. MacCainstacairt's ambush, William thought. MacRuarie turning his horse to reclaim his wealth, to go south to live a life of ease, thought an era gone no MacAedh's for the north. Pondering whether to risk spending any time in the village seeking help to recover the gold. He decided not to. For now the gold could wait. With luck thus far, he'd just take what he had thrown near the stream, in the future return for the remainder. The next day William would place his coins in his saddlebag starting for Edinburgh. Travelling mostly at night and keeping to trails not used by the main populace, he would pass south without hindrance.

As William left the meadow Seward was pulling Morgund's horse along beside his, leaving the meadow going in the opposite direction, to William. By morning, both were exhausted. Seward made a camp amongst large pines, the horses picketed nearby, well hidden.

When Seward awoke darkness had already fallen. It was time to be going. With a full moon to guide their way yet darkness to disguise them, night was the best time to travel. Saddling his horse whereafter rousing his companion. Too sore to travel fast they meandered.

It was important to keep moving but equally important that Morgund be restored for he might need speed and strength to escape danger again. A certainty, more like. These dangerous times required constant vigilance and Morgund was of unlucky folk, danger plagued, as was being made only too apparent. Seward had chosen a great companion, he reflected. In this kind of environment he would become a great swordsman, or die. Night begat day. Travelling across a series of mountains as it rained steadily, getting colder the higher up they were. At the end of long afternoon, a grassy well-watered meadow, met them.

"We will camp for a couple of days and rest and eat whilst there is still good forage for the horses. It is better to stop now, further up it will be barer and we do not want the horses to lose too much condition."

# ACROSS THE MOUNTAINS

SEWARD WAS CONFIDENT they were travelling correctly. Many times he had listened to tales of travel and read maps. He chose a route which avoided the great loch, which they could not cross without assistance and where parties of men could be out searching for them.   Seward, returning to the present, concentrating on the most pressing task at hand, had Morgund assist him in building a shelter.  It was safe to so and they built a large fire.  Deeming it good to be near flame again, sitting round it devouring it, sharing it's embrace.  During the past two days they had gone without it.   The warmth was reassuring.

The day next Seward scouted ahead.   With an explorer's heart, this was much to his taste.   Walking across high mountain meadows  he enjoyed the views and stillness.  To be so far from the world of men was peaceful.   The highlands were remote and scarcely populated and here he found no sign of humans or domesticated animals.   Upon his return, Seward proceeded to tell Morgund  that this area seemed to be uninhabited, further to that, reported that in all his travels and he did see for many miles, the way ahead was high and he hoped traversable but he had some doubt on it.

The base of these mountains grew dense vegetation. Together with unfavourable weather it could make it hard to find their way.   The prospect of starving in the mountains was entirely real.   The good news, that they seemed to have left any pursuit, far behind, or lost it entirely.   Seward had gathered herbs and now set to make a drink which tasted pleasant, containing an ingredient that Seward knew would help them both relax.

At calm repose in this isolated place was Seward. "Why hurry back to the world of men with intrigue and violence." Seward remarked giving voice to what was on his mind.

Staring into the fire they spoke little of their bloody encounter or of Kenneth's death they spoke things of little consequence, for they had endured too much in the recent past to seek topics of such gravity.

"It's good to be alive Seward," Morgund finally said after being engulfed in the fire's calmness.

"I have not been dead so I am not qualified to judge whether life or death is the better state," Seward replied wittily, attempting to make Morgund laugh.

Morgund ignored the statement and made one of his own. "Seward, teach me to be a swordsman as good as you."

"Like me?" Seward replied, attempting to look questioning, attempting to solicit praise.

"Yes." Both smiled, Seward's fishing for compliment so obvious, it was humorous. Morgund's eyes turned serious. "I don't want to be that weak coward that I was when that man stood above me about to strike me dead. Next time I will fight and if need be die honourably defending myself."

"I'll do my best to make you formidable Morgund."

"Therefore, again, I thank you. I am lucky to have your friendship Seward. You'll stay with me always." Morgund looked like a hunted animal. "I admit I am weak I have never been as strong as others. I despise my weakness. I will give everything I have to become strong. If I give my all, can I become strong?"

"You can," Seward answered solemnly.

"I can." Morgund said to himself, earnestly, surprised. "Perhaps I can. Seward, you must teach me and also help me to be brave. I don't want to be a coward again."

"You will need skills to stay alive, and with hard work you will attain them."

"Is fighting about courage more than anything else?"

"It is." Tossing it about in his mind then confirming it, "Putting your life on the line bravely is its essence. We all know how to fight but some must look harder inside themselves to find the spark." Morgund looked baffled, prompting Seward to say, "It's a tortuous path alike to assembling a puzzle."

"Tell me what I have to do."

Seward who did not allow him to explore further, said, "It is better always to keep things simple. Don't go into specifics, it is too early. I'll tell you when you're ready. Don't worry Morgund, I will train you well. As well as I can ..." Seward laughed. "I will have to, I might need you to save me one day. That would be one of the strangest things? Your father God bless his soul, saved me, I saved you and one day you may save me. Surely it would be one for the balladeers if it occurred."

"Yes, I suppose so Seward but truthfully train me well and I may assist for there will be many dangers ahead."

"Yes," Seward replied, feeling angered at the prospect. He had picked  very dangerous companion. He had no choice Kenneth had saved his life.

Morgund kept on not having noticed Seward's discomfort. "There are great numbers of men out to kill us."

"Enough, enough!  One day the pattern will change Morgund and we shall become the hunters."

"Do you think so Seward?  With so many dangerous enemies."

"Not really."  Seward was forced to admit.  "Can we not talk about our limited prospects of survival."

They remained silent.  A little later Morgund broke the spirit of contemplation by saying,  "You know what I feel like?"

"What?"

"Cooked lamb."

"Why?"

"I don't know, I just feel like it.  This is my longest without eating meat.  One or two hands full of oats."

That left Seward speechless.  The noise of creatures of the night lulled them to sleep.

The next morning well rested and well nourished they continued. It became a pleasant ride. Whilst browsing along, they noticed forest trees were becoming scarce and stunted the higher they climbed into the majestic mountain heights, cloaked in purple and white heather, sights appreciated more when the clouds parted and sun shone, which was mostly. In the afternoon, showers, forced them to shelter, whereupon they made camp for the night.

The next day travelling on the roof of the world the sun was bright and pleasant and now much higher there was little of woodland to speak of, the majority of the trees they had left far behind. Suddenly, it was colder. The pattern of the country changed. As they rode, the mountains closed in around them. Abruptly, edging into a valley the explosive of sound of a waterfall. Looking up through the crags to get a view of waters hurling over and downward. When the wind become gusty a trillion tiny petals swept down upon them, these, the waterfall's cast-offs, searching for places to cling to, and Seward and Morgund they found.

Morgund held up his hands, "Come on let us find shelter away from this."

Gazing enthralled upon the swirling galaxies that were descending. A drop hit Seward squarely in the eye, after which, one of Seward's eyebrow went up and then a few teeth showed through. "Aye," he said, "Lead away Morgund."

Riding across a burn, the horse's hooves were crunching on small round pebbles. Slightly further on, an overhang abutting waterfall. Winds howled hauntingly, sounding faintly like voices, but no matter how hard they listened, it was impossible to hear them clearly.

The words contained most sacred knowledge, of what they couldn't say, they remained hidden, but feel them, they did. Above the muffled roar of the water, in that dank hole, dark with moisture, a host of breathless souls whispered soothing messages. Dwarf trees poked out of crevices in the rock. They almost expected to see a gnome duck below a stone, or jump up and run away from a place of concealment, such an enchanting place it was.

Movement, onwards, wherein they left the waterfall behind them. Ascending higher thereon they concentrated on staying on track amongst tumbled rocks. That night they slept long and well. The waterfall lived in their dreams.

In the morning feeling refreshed and eager to be away to see what lay beyond the next ascent, beckoning. Morgund with likeable ways and by deferring to Seward, which Seward liked, bonded well with him. All Morgund wanted was to Seward's friend, and likewise that was all Seward sought from Morgund.

Mid morning they stopped. Seward put Morgund through a series of exercises designed to accustom his muscles to fighting. These exercises strengthened his body and helped developed lightness on his feet and co-ordination. The same drills were to be repeated every day, as Seward told Morgund.

Seward was attentive to detail. "Nothing is difficult in these movements. They are simple Morgund. Make the body strong in the moving and correct in relaxed movement and extension of the arm when that is suitable and when moving, using the full hip and foot pivot, learn the steps in the dance, that is what you are trying to do." Morgund took in all such advice and his body responded, quickly.

One day from Morgund, "What is your land like Seward?"

"Largely flat and heavily wooded. It abuts the sea closely thus our people take to the sea, as it is at our door."

Journeying further Morgund seemed to have thought about it. "Scandinavians love adventuring?"

"Journeying prevents staying at home and listening to nagging wives, which most do not admit as the cause of the rush to be off." Seward laughed. "Of such things are warrior made, fit to conquer all, except she who rules them."

"But to cross oceans." Morgund's eyebrows betrayed his doubt. "The bold Norseman, I don't believe it, they desired conquest."

"If the Viking women went out, then you Scots would realise how terrified we are of our womenfolk. If we come home empty handed, we would suffer, we don't wish to suffer." It caused amusement in Morgund, Seward enjoyed making Morgund laugh.

"It is a famous name you've made Seward."

"Yes, we have sacked Constantinople, conquered England, pillaged Paris. Our fame is immense, but at the end of the day what good is it?"

Morgund returned to his earlier subject, "A strong desire must have caused men to leave."

"Yes and no. A love of the sea, of a fight. You Scots aren't seamen but you delved into England often enough to rape and pillage. Imagine with ships, you'd be elsewhere to discover what the world holds and fight to possess it, which is what we Vikings do."

Looking disappointed Seward said, "Because Christianity has made such deeds dishonourable the fire has diminished. Only an odd flicker resides of the days of raiding. They are gone, almost."

"Can you see yourself pillaging, burning, or raping, Seward?" A sarcastic Morgund.

Seward ignored the tone. "Why I think we all can under the right circumstances."

"Perhaps," Morgund replied and then immediately added a new thought, "The Scot's prefer their homes, I think." He said this to nettle Seward which it did.

"Oh I'm sure you're more compassionate." Bowing his head in annoyance but not before giving Morgund a look which told him what he thought of his foolish statement.

A moment later Seward decided to take him to task over it. "In times past human sacrifices were made to bring bounteous crops. That was common in Scotland, I'm told." After letting Morgund digest this, he said, "The Vikings seem dastardly only because they conduct their depredations so successfully."

Silence again.  Morgund relented in his devilment.  The
niggling was soon forgotten.  Bad weather did not impede as
they gained distance across the spine of the mountains.  From
there on, it was steadily down.  Halting to drink at a stream  on
a spur in a wholesome belt they saw deer sign.  Whilst
Morgund guarded the horses Seward tracked and shot two
deer.  Tying the horses, they skinned and gutted them.  The
pair made use of a stream with a high overhanging bank
throwing up some beams then covering them with pine
boughs.  The fire lit, they sat before it.

"We must eat as much of this deer as we can."  Seward
said.

"And enjoy every mouthful," Morgund replied, biting at the
air in parody of hunger.

A tongue appeared at Seward's mouth, accentuating his
own need theatrically and they laughed.  After hanging the
carcass, Seward demonstrated two new sword techniques,
most effective if mastered.  Morgund was a keen student and
was improving.  In a few months Seward would have the
makings of a swordsman, he realised.  The following morning,
was sharply chill.  Above, the sky was steel grey.

Seward brought this to Morgund's attention,  "Morgund,
snow will fall soon.

Many hours later, snow had yet to fall,  and Seward was
looking into the fire, pondering.  They must stay for a while
and rest, he thought.  Morgund was tired he needed rest.

The winds outside got louder, sufficiently so to dispel his thoughts and to redirect his eyes. As he watched, light rain turned to sleet. Transforming, into feathery wisps buffeted by winds, slowly drifting to earth. Water dripping from the bank, stilled. A small tree, stood near, its leaves bobbing and weaving and when a strong gust came it looked like a child's toy being fought over by two children, going one way and then the other, with force. Seward covered himself further. He didn't hear the leaves now, the wind was too shrill, he spent the hours listening to it and feeling chilly vapours. On the far side of the stream, the dense forest and falling snow merged into one.

At snows sudden increase his eye went upward towards the source, to the dull the sky, moonbeams piercing through it, and lower to the ground a fast moving mist like a breath exhaled on a hand before dawn, on a cold day, driven fast, by a man's breath. The moon in a circular phase made silver, of all.

Combating the cold, Seward packed more wood on the fire and sat watching the dancing orange-bluish flames shoot up. The flame calmed his mind and allowed him to travel back in time, to investigate his predicament, to decide why he was here. To protect Morgund, that's why he was here.

The night of Kenneth's ambush, there was a feeling that magic swirled, he had felt it then, he felt it now, which made him wonder if he had the gift of second sight, as some said in the village. He could find lost things. He had never given it much thought. He could often tell if a pregnant mother would have a boy or a girl, lucky guesses he thought.

Although hearing tales of people with such abilities never before had he seen any evidence that they existed, now he realized something of the like was probable. If he had this gift, he must develop it, use it to his advantage. Recalling his brush with the supernatural, thinking of them, these forces that dwelt in air, swirling with a pattern their's alone, it seemed to bring their onset, perhaps in this way he had found access to this other world, these ideas filled his head until he slumbered.

In the morning after a breakfast they packed the rest of the cooked deer meat. Across the frozen landscape they rode. Steep mountainside gave way to gentle aspects with cattle tracks and makeshift fencing. In summer this area would be populated. It felt good to have some semblance of civilization. Such signs as had favoured them lessened, the land flattened out. It was scrubby now, and not much good for grazing, which explained the lack of people. At a line of mountains ahead, they realized, they had not seen the last of climbing, however these mountains were not as great as those behind. Common stuff, offering little to the eye, surrounding them, not much, excitement lay in expectancy.

Climbing steadily, they had to reroute several times to avoid sheer vertical cliffs. Backtracking again and again, selecting a winding path between trees and brush. Avoiding large boulders. Traversing through dense pines, climbing steeply. Reaching the summit, they looked down at a valley and although not in their direct line of travel the place had a seductive allure, a place that once seen, lived forever within the memory.

When they had nearly left the proximity of it Seward halted and asked Morgund to accompany him, to explore for pleasure alone.  Seward told Morgund, it would fill their hearts with joy.  And Morgund agreed.  They tethered their horses long enough to allow them to forage on grassy slopes.  Setting off with a positive feeling and imbued with a sense of freedom, Seward experienced greater pleasure as he was older, and therefore more aware of the impending dangers.  He would make the most of this opportunity to enjoy himself.

Quickening strides brought him past lush meadows.  To, flowing brooks, mountain flowers.  Each step, almost, opened up new splendours.  At a clump of tiny flowers of vibrant colours, Seward stopped to look more closely at these delicate mountain buds.  The air was fresh alive with the scent of clean pure freshness.

Coming to the lip of the valley, thereafter, they made their way down to undulating hills interspersed with flowing streams.  Somewhat lower they were quieter and some of them had a good quantity of quality wood.  Looking at a well-fed stream ahead Seward could not pass up its drawing power.

He smiled and looked at Morgund  "We will investigate it, touch its substance.  Some secret may be passed on to us, for this is a sacred grove and stream."  Seward  made this statement feeling the energy of the earth, so openly displayed was it.

Scattered entities assuming elongated shape plunged to earth.  Moments later, with tiny bumps they hit the ground discharging their bounty of moisture.  Seward and Morgund sought shelter under a great bough until the rain slowed.

The valley floor levelled out and they lost sight of their destination, which was a landmark beyond the stream and above it, a chimney like piece of black-spiralled rock. It was now hidden by dense, lush forest. Breaking clear of the woods they came out to numerous grassy channels through the timber, islands of pines bordering. Small lakes with mirror like surfaces. Individual conifers gazed down a them with limbs quivering on the wind. Cuckoos sang from shadowy hides. Onwards. At the top of a slight height Morgund observed the landmark in the distance the elongated heap of dark rock, Morgund looked at Seward, who nodded and they walked faster. At times thick scrub blocked their view but when they came out in the open again they saw it, it was behind them. They tried to keep it directly ahead.

Shrubs gave way to a variation between pine and faded foliage. These last golden leaves were fated to fall when the cold did fall harsh upon them. The two joked but mostly kept silent hoping to glimpse something, a badger or deer, which by remaining silent they might see. In around forest flares, a bright leaf moved with the wind, large amber circumference held the eye for long.

"Here God had created splendidly, so serene and captivating. At times the Almighty must have lost himself completely in making it. So complex is it," Seward ventured.

Seward nodded, words he realized couldn't do justice to this. If they knew how soon nature would turn hostile they'd not be so preoccupied with sights, for if they could see from whence they came, a threatening black they'd see. A little opening between branches gave sight of basalt that shot up cylindrically, but it was still far.

Lichens grew densely. Toadstools red and white appeared. Black mushrooms poked out of the forest floor some with pale coloured hats. As their steps carried them further, all at once, they heard water.

Again not hindered by branches and standing slightly higher they saw the object of their quest, the shadowy, angled rock, which was part broken, but elsewhere so sharp and square as if man-made. Water swung around the rocky outcrop, reflecting solid black. Their heads went up at electricity. It began to rain heavily. Concentrating on the sudden grey, the water rising as they tarried, Seward looked away from the water and back towards the summit. It had started snowing high up. It would be colder up on yonder hillside, so they must return quickly. They eluded the snow, it broke in an arc to the west. Only at the top of the rise where they had originally started from did it begin to fall.

On the way back they collected wood, more than was necessary, enough should decent fuel be scarce in the areas ahead. Making themselves comfortable, they sat in front of a fire. Its various qualities, warmth, ashy smell, myriad collage of coloured lights, always changing, hard to look away from. Occasionally with a crack a spent log folded in on itself and then the fire gained greater intensity as heat and oxygen penetrated further within it. Using a stick to stir disorder had the same effect, and they did it often. Wispy papery wood igniting, floated up, crackled loudly consuming fuel, going on to give them warmth. Both young men relaxed in the fire's presence.

It created a new dimension to their friendship.   Perhaps the fire burned deeply enough to touch upon a memory of earlier days when men had been stalked whilst poorly armed, who when the fire burned low could expect jaws to clench at him from behind, or worse still from front on.   All people exposed to a naked burning when in dangerous places can account for it, this feeling of safety.

Looking at the stars blinking down at them, Morgund said, "Perhaps they look at us and debate over the strangeness of us."

"Unlikely it is they care for us. "   Though Seward chided Morgund softly, he knew how he felt.

Field craft was a necessity to the traveller and was for them the difference between life and death.  If they knew what hardship lay ahead of them, they would have chosen to stay. Seward looked over to Morgund who had fallen asleep. Seward listened to the rain pattering on their deer hide shelter.

Soon Seward dreamt of maidens he desired, with huge breasts, knowing eyes, who ministered to him skilfully, then of Asgarth, who had besotted him in Denmark.  He called her name whilst trying to convince himself that he'd see her again. Morgund dreamt of his father and mother, of when they had all been together and happy, of a time when his father's calm presence had watched over him.

The next afternoon, riding across a clearing towards a ruin three parts surrounded by woods.  They blessed their good fortune in finding part of the roof intact meaning warmth and shelter.  Standing in the shadows a solitary figure waited for their approach, observing them with a keen eye.  He stood tall dignified.

As yet the figure escaped their notice. Their eyes were immediately drawn to skies rumbling. Suddenly a downpour so wet, the insides of their eyes felt touched by it. Dismounting, as the man walked out from the ruin. Wearing a dark robe, bald of pate, a long grey beard but the man's eyes were his dominant feature, unusually potent, they squinted narrowly looking at Seward, measuringly.

"Who are you?" Morgund asked suspiciously, when first they met. Morgund who was caught by surprise by Duibne's presence was tempted to ride off and have Seward follow him and leave this stranger to himself.

"Never mind who I am who are you, and what are you doing here? You're as surprised to see me, as I am you to see you." Seemingly, seeing strangers in a distant place not noted for them, he was explaining it to himself. Then with an open welcoming expression, he said, "Do you want to eat?"

"Aye," replied Morgund as thoughts of a flashing fire and warm food flickered through his mind.

"Let us stop and repast, these mountains are tough." The man with the eyes said. "Have you any food?" The man asked, with his mouth slobbering in a pretence of one suffering from great hunger.

"When you asked us if we were hungry, I thought it was yourself who would provide the victuals," Morgund replied.

"My provisions are scant."

"Oh," Morgund said, disappointed. "What we have is not much."

Seward introduced himself, "My name is Seward Gunn."

"And you, young man what is your name?" he said turning to Morgund.

"Morgund," He quietly answered, not sure what to think, there was something disturbing about his eyes. He had never met anyone remotely like him.

Before long had they had entered the ruin and seated themselves comfortably around a fire, upon which was a broth about to boil. The stranger added some turnips to the pot. "See I do have something. And where would you boys be going or more correctly, what are you running away from?"

"Why running?" Seward asked, and gave Morgund a warning look. He didn't trust people asking questions. "The better question is how we get home. We got lost in the mountains, exploring. We are trying to find our way home."

"You don't look the type to get lost to me Seward. Keep your secret I'll not do you a false turn."

Thereafter they engaged in some inconsequential banter that Duibne was far better at than themselves. They reclined comfortably on rolls made of sheepskin.

"It's beautiful here?" Morgund said.

"Is your friend alright? Duibne asked.

"He has hit his head." Seward laughed and looked at Morgund smiling. "No, he has suffered much, and can see the worth of things."

"We have come across the mountains," Morgund said.

"You've been on a desperate journey."

"Not so desperate," Seward replied.

"It is a trek of great difficulty that you have been on, to come that way is a worthy achievement. I'm sure it was filled with moments of danger and you saw some grand country."

"Do you know it?" Morgund asked.

"Young men will hunt those mountains and stories come back describing certain parts of them. It is small knowledge I have personally." He held his beard and changed tack. "Where do you go now?"

"To see the king," Seward replied.

"What do you know of the king?" Morgund asked. This conversation he would recall many times hereafter.

"I've not seen the king but I hear he is redheaded, as well as being a lad reckoned on being worthy to rule. He is yet sixteen."

Morgund interrupted. "He's fair minded and apt to give myself a fair hearing."

"His father was placid, and honest enough. So I suppose, he would be too."

"But you have heard otherwise?" For Seward could tell by Duibne's demeanour that there was something else.

Morgund stared intently at Duibne awaiting his response, finally prompting him. "It is said he is untrustworthy? Go on, is it?"

"Aye it is said of him." Seeing grave concern on Morgund's face, Duibne tried to reassure him. "Rumours are often unfounded, perhaps it dealt with some childish indiscretion."

"Where did you hear it?"

"Fairground gossip, it is not to be taken seriously."

"I hope so, Morgund said. "What exactly is it that you have heard about him?" Morgund couldn't subdue his fear.

"Nothing more than that. The king's father, William, was a sovereign true and honest, I guess his son will most likely take after him. It takes time for maturity to make the man."

"But you have heard he is untrustworthy?" Morgund pressed.

"Aye."

Morgund wished to dispel his concern. "He will be good enough."

"I hope that is so," Duibne replied. "In any case be not worried he may be gone from Edinburgh when you arrive as he is setting off into England."

"Why?" Seward asked.

"I do not know ... something regarding a certain charter or treaty."

"It is important that I see him," Morgund said.

"Then I hope you catch him before he leaves and that you find his favour," Duibne replied.

An hour had gone and it was darker and colder. Duibne's eyes swept around suspiciously. "I feel a presence."

"Yes," Morgund replied, "Obviously," mustering some confidence, adding sarcastically, "Ourselves."

"Not you two, another, a spiritual entity. One not of the flesh."

"Who?" Morgund asked.

"Him," he said, pointing with his two fingers beside his head, "The devil."

Duibne's eyes looked warily around the walls as he spoke. "This ruin is a former pagan temple. The Romans worshipped Cybele here in secret. It keeps its secrets but I will have them to be my own." Duibne raised his voice addressing the building itself, but seemingly speaking to Seward and Morgund also. "It keeps its power. Yet, whatever I seek to enslave, so it is, enslaved. The standing stone atop the mountains. I am their keeper. The priests of the Christ-God choose not to venture here. I pray to the older, darker Gods."

He shouted again looking to the walls. "Three wayfarers who only seek shelter." He smiled then, "Sleep, you be tired I see it clearly."

Morgund whispered. "Seward he frightens me, he is strange. He could gain our confidence, and whilst we are asleep he could kill us. We should go."

Seward looked out upon the scrubby landscape of tortured heather with red-sided seams of sandstone, he acknowledged that to be away here would be harsh. They were in an amphitheatre like place. Out in the open the wind would beat down on them. It was not a landscape to favour the traveller. Seward nodded to Morgund, "A word with you, outside."

"I can think now," Seward said. Seward gazed away at the hills. Should they stay or go. Could they listen to what the mage had to say? What harm was in that, none that he could see. Morgund was timid, overly so, because of the trauma of having come so close to death. It was natural, he reasoned. To leave would deny him an answer to why the man had waited and how he knew him. Seward felt there was more then mere coincidence to this. This man had some prior knowledge of them, Seward was sure of it. Strong winds roared, another reason to remain sheltered. He brought his hand down onto Morgund's. "We'll rest inside to warm ourselves a bit."

"The devil with you," Morgund responded, "Stay here to get my throat cut not likely!"

"I suppose you're right." Seward realised his young friend had been through so much, that his fear of Duibne would make him leave and Seward was not prepared to see him go unattended. "Morgund, at your suggestion, we will depart forthwith."

"What is this Seward?" Seeing that he could influence Seward made Morgund's eyebrows arch. "Seward, are you prepared to heed of me?"

"I cannot afford to be at odds with the young Earl of Ross Morgund. The MacAedh, himself."

"I am not that," Morgund replied.

"Your father held the lands thereof. He gave himself the style of it. It is yours by right of inheritance. If the king sees fit to grant you the title it will be yours again truly."

"I am not a nobleman Seward."

"Nobility is not easily extinguished, Morgund. You are descended of kings."

Morgund was brightened by this talk, which was Seward's intention. "Gather our gear so we will away Morgund," Seward said.

Duibne was distressed when he saw Morgund picking up their gear," What do you do? No harm is here."

"Ignore him Morgund," Seward held a steady gaze upon Duibne. Morgund remained aloof to as they walked out.

"What are you doing?" Duibne asked, as they were mounting. "Do you leave?"

"Your hospitality was not to our taste," Seward remarked without turning to face him, said more to the night than the distant fellow for within moments Duibne was lost to the distance and encroaching darkness.

Duibne spoke, thus: Although well out of hearing range, he cast his words after them. "You commit a great wrong."

The snowflakes soft and feathery became large and icy, inflicting pain with each stab dealt. The landscape was difficult to navigate by, featureless. Upon a plateau that offered no geological discernments, they rapidly found themselves engulfed in a blizzard with visibility decreasing by the second.

This ethereal bombardment demanded they find shelter speedily. It was frighteningly and dangerously cold. What they could see was of no help, only a short distance. Always there was danger that they might pass over a cliff or travel in an endless circle until they succumbed to the cold. Then they saw Duibne running out of the snow. How had he caught them? The two travellers saw the figure moving in the snow pacing forward relentlessly, despite the crippling cold. Did he exist? Was he real? Had their minds became unhinged by the conditions, or he was some mirage caused by the glare.

They both knew the surreal nature of this had affected their thinking, they didn't see how it could not. He was closer to them now. It was Duibne. Seward was reassured and his heart beat a touch slower. He hadn't been sure it was not a figment of their disturbed minds racing towards them. What would he of done, if it was, he didn't know.

Their collective mentality gone, no future existed here where they needed their wits to survive. That there was no, insanity, emboldened Seward. "Hold stranger, you have come far enough. Tell us your intent." Seward said.

Although they now regretted their decision in leaving the shelter offered by Duibne they were still wary of him. Just staring, Duibne did not speak. After long moments in which crystal vapours wafted about and of noisy breathing, he spoke with great clarity given the conditions, he made of Seward a hero who would perform great deeds.

Then to Morgund. "Boy, I knew your father, he was a good man, as shall you be, perhaps." He approached closer to Seward whilst addressing Morgund. "Keep mind and sword sharp though, Morgund. For to do less, is your death." His eyes were on Seward. They were not eyes, Seward thought. They are glowing coals, they are evil, possessed eyes, a madman's eyes.

Duibne spoke to Morgund, "If you survive Morgund you shall found a great family."

"Go away, strange one." Seward pointed towards the depths of the night. The storm lessened immediately on Duibne's appearance.

The sun almost peaked through the swirling clouds. It was as if Duibne somehow had control of the elements. Seward put this thought from him, deeming that luck was with them and the worse part of the storm, they had already seen. They could see higher ground not so far away now. "Strange men are better left in the company of others, like themselves. To your own kind, I say."

Seward looked to Morgund for support, a slight movement of brow and tightening of his lips registering some indignation at Morgund's fear. "Was he forever afraid, afraid of everything," Seward thought. Although in terms of physical ability Morgund showed promise as a swordsman he must develop character, poise, and courage. Controlling his fear if he was ever to be worthy.

The weather swarmed, chilly skies releasing their icy white shavings. Duibne remained unmoved, staring into Morgund's eyes enjoying the impact he made, the fear Morgund had of him. The snow fell heavy upon them but none moved. Seward worried for Morgund. Morgund looked like a maiden on her wedding night, desperate eyed, a maid best suited to stay a maid. Gentleness Morgund had but only by ruthlessness could he ensure his life.

The village knew he was placid, amongst some in the village he'd been the subject of laughter, they thought him a weakling, and if he had the time Seward would have made a change in Morgund and Morgund would have gained their respect.

"Remain calm Morgund," Seward ordered.

"Seward do you know what to do?" Morgund replied.

"Aye I do."

Then the snow enclosed them in its world, taking Morgund's thoughts away to where Duibne could not reach, to his father, that kind loving man. Morgund remembered no crease of unease in that face, happiness, hardihood, only.

No wonder his father had been angry with him for his ineptness at arms. He had no choice but to become a warrior now. His father had seen that. How important it was then, when he hadn't realized it. Try, he would. He wished his father could be there to be proud if he succeeded. It caused him sadness knowing his father wouldn't be. Snow flicked his eyes.

Through the hazy darkness, two dark shapes moved, Duibne and Morgund. Duibne moved closer, stood next to Morgund. Morgund looked at Duibne. Duibne returned the look with interest. In that moment Morgund knew he would not lose control of himself again and Duibne knew it and respected him for it. The unlikely fate he foretold for Morgund now seemed not so unlikely. For the first time Duibne could see a trace of his father in him. Morgund could see his father's face. The outline of it appeared out of the snow. Morgund could not bring himself to speak for memories of his father would disappear if he did.

Duibne extended his hand, "Young men, share a fire with me, what food I have is yours. On the morning I will take you on to a lodging made for kings. Trust me."

Duibne's words were wasted on Seward. "I don't see the need to listen to your ramblings, let us depart Morgund."

Duibne continued to follow them. "You misread me. I meant no harm."

"Be off with you, or feel the flat of my sword, move." Duibne was warned by Seward. If he didn't heed the warning he would make him senseless in the snow. The pair rode off.

Then a booming voice, echoed behind them. "Seward Gunnerson we will meet again and icy coldness will clutch at you. You have insulted Duibne to your peril."

Thick snow, they could barely see because of it. Straining to penetrate the murk, Seward made out the vague outline of hills. Saw them again, between the snowflakes. Riding forth the trees grew darker. Luckily they found a cave amongst the timber growth. They made a fire, surviving the storm, listening to it blasting.

In the morning, Seward noticed a leather thong fastened around his neck, a gold medallion was on it, which bore the image of a horned nymph playing a flute. Seward touched it and it felt good, like it belonged there, he hid it from Morgund tucking it in his tunic. Seward thought Morgund would tell him the coin was better gone as anything associated with Duibne had to be a bad thing. Duibne must have placed it there when he brushed beside him.

Morgund drew his attention to the mouth of the cave, "Look, the sun is out, the storm is gone Seward."

They did not waste time and departed quickly and that day they met the first people they had seen since coming into the mountains and Seward inquiring about Duibne was told, "Yes, he comes here. But a more silent brooding man I've not met, he doesn't waste his words on the likes of us."

At another place they were informed, "He is a nuisance, always begging ale. Some say he is learned, having been a priest, holding that he can see into the future."

A man interjected. "An invented tale, to win the coin of superstitious wives."

Yet another thought differently. "Do not underestimate him, he is what he says he is." This speaker was not keen to elaborate, for when questioned, he had remained silent. It was a strange night.

In the hut this man shared with this young family it was like Duibne's magic had followed them and that he, in invisible spirit, had seen fit to spend the night with them watching them, his energy seemed to inhabit the dwelling with them. They talked of Duibne and the events in the mountains. Seward couldn't get his mind off the mage, he was deeply intrigued at the man's origin. Morgund was just happy to be away from him and the scene of such.

"I can tell from the cut and design of your clothing that you come from the north." Their host said. Neither answered.
"Are you Rossman?"

"Aye, you are correct." Seward ventured feeling this man could be trusted. "We are of Ross."

"And come from the far side of the mountains, a route that designates you are desperate men."

"Desperate enough ," Seward said and from then on their host was silent and made them feel they were better gone. It was late, so they rested and kept their weapons close.

The day following, topping the summit of these mountains and looking downward.  At the foot of these mountains, isolated farmer's huts and fields.  They looked back to the wilderness, from whence they came.  Far distant, weathered rock folded in and out, dark-reddish where the light caught, occasional dwarf trees clung tenaciously to the rock.  Lower down, to their front, creamy limbs seemed to cast looks between themselves, swaying branches in communication which was almost perceptible to man.  Taller, spindly trees grew in numbers, in the lower fields.  And further down again, a narrow stream flowed over a drop, then going on to the lower pine covered slopes where openings in woodland gave sight of the sparkling water.

The mountainside was a riot of varied shade and hue. The deep emerald pine boughs lightened to a greenish yellow at the tips, with new growth starting.  The wild-berry bushes were populated with white and pink flowers.  Scottish pines shimmering.  All about the ground pale patches of snow reflected the light of the sun.  Far into the distance the cliff face, from whence they had come, weathered and old,  stared at them.  Seemingly from a what appeared to be an old man's mouth, the image formed by the play of light upon the rock and the rock structure itself,  the suns rays cast upon its craggy surface so one might easily recognise the essential features of a stern man.  A stream fell from the mouth, whereas other contours held an uncanny likeness to the brow and nose.  The rock-man studied them intently, vast mouth agape as if uttering an  eternal, silent scream.  A narrow funnel of water found its way over and to the valley floor in a long ribbon of white phospheresant.   The old rock-man looked as if he knew Seward and Morgund's fate, that it would be unkind, it was trick of the light, but not a pleasant one.

# NORTH TO SOUTH

BACK AT THE village Gormlaith discerned the cause of the depression that engulfed her. It was her rival, she was annoyed at the presumption. Suana had no business challenging her for Seward's affection. Gormlaith hurt this much because she imagined herself missing out on winning Seward's love and thus becoming the object of ridicule. Gormlaith decided to end Suana's quest. Convincing herself she was doing it for Seward, and that he would thank her for it. Regarding the success of her mission, she deemed it assured. Wounding Suana, would be a just reward for the girl. One so low, should know her place. Gormlaith had a cruel aspect to her personality. She wept when Seward rode out but thereafter when she learned that Seward was enamoured of another, and that it was Suana who held his interest, it made her want to hurt the girl. Gormlaith made the leap into adulthood by being ruthless. Gormlaith came across the other dark haired girl, who was something of a wood sprite, alone in the forest.

"Are you seeking the friendship of creatures because no one wants your company?"

Suana didn't reply. Some acted cruelly towards her. Her father was dead, her mother and herself had to be provided for by the other villagers, both contributed to the common good, however some chose to ignore this. Gormlaith was one. Gormlaith's father was an important man, she liked to look down on Suana, this was not the first cruel word Gormlaith had given her. Moments of pause were overtaken by Gormlaith's mounting anger.

But as Gormlaith said it, she trusted, that it was necessary to be rid of Suana's aspirations, to relieve Seward of her, and it was for the girls own good, for Suana was making a fool of herself. She'd find herself a pregnant girl, abandoned.

"Suana ... Seward is not kindly disposed toward you."

"That isn't true?" Suana replied with a wounded look.

"He told me when he left that he didn't like you because you are a sneak who is always watching him from the shadows like a goblin. Yes, that is what you are, a goblin ... we laughed at your disfigurement."

The attacker knew it was a lie, no disfigurement existed, but she knew that Suana would think it true. This would surely spare Seward the admiration of Suana. How could she even consider herself Gormlaith's match. None were as good and clever as Gormlaith. She came of good family, was pretty, and was a good cook. And how dare Seward put Suana before her. Gormlaith's detractors had sound judgement, for although she had the abilities she attributed to herself, they were aligned to a proud, rude, and arrogant nature. Suana buried her face in her arms and ran away.

Words followed that would haunt her. "Run you disgusting goblin, go into the woods and live with your kind, Seward doesn't want you... nor do I, nor anyone else in the village." Gormlaith gave no thought then to how badly she had hurt Suana, only caring that she was successful in turning her against Seward which she must accomplish ahead of all other considerations.

Gormlaith's actions did foster a change of feeling that was difficult to put aside. This encounter led to endless days of torture for her. She did not want to blame him for thinking that which was only true, she shouldn't hate him, she thought, on reflection, but as much as she tried not to, she always felt a dull thud of pain, when thinking of him.

Gormlaith came to regret her words when she had had time to think about them. She was not so harsh that she didn't attempt justifying them by speculating on what enjoyment and improvement in status a commitment from Seward would bring her and the humiliation she would have felt if she had been overlooked. It would have reflected badly her family who had been so good to Seward. She convinced herself she had no choice. Gormlaith wavered in her feelings towards Seward. He had hurt her deeply by giving her friendship and by not seeking more, she despised him, she told herself, but as with Suana, such an effort was half hearted.

As Gormlaith had her pressing concerns so did king Alexander in Edinburgh. Edinburgh, a large town overlooked by a massive stone castle, currently a hive of activity. The new king Alexander was mustering an army to travel into England. If it was an army, for what occurred here largely lacked warlike purpose, the mood pageant-like. Since the time of David, the first, kings of Scotland had paid fealty for two English baronies, Huntington and Northampton, which brought much needed gold into Scotland but was also a source of discontent. The Celtic Earls often felt, that as Scotland was an ancient kingdom, far older than England, it was belittling to their king, that he bow low before England's king.

However on this occasion they were in good spirits. The English had recently fought a civil war, king John had lost. At Runnymead a bill of rights would be presented to king John, which he must abide by or risk losing his kingdom. Alexander and most Normans had a vested interest in this for most held lands in England. It would also provide a good opportunity to gather intelligence. No less important, it offered the possibility of aligning with disaffected English. Naturally Alexander and his counsellors realised that by threatening invasion, gold and other concessions could be gained, a weak England always presented rich pickings.

After gaining entry to the stronghold, Seward and Morgund were granted an audience with Richard De Soulis, the governor of Edinburgh castle. They were seated with at a table with the old man who looked like a wise and trustworthy fellow. To Morgund he looked like someone's doting grandfather, which he was.

De Soulis said, "Why do you want to see the king MacAedh? Your family and his, are enemies.

"To find the kings protection, and to be his friend." Suddenly a tear arose in Morgund's eye. "To have MacCainstacairt punished for his attacks."

I say no good can come of it, I regret your father's death, but MacCainstacairt is close to Alexander. He will not suffer."

Morgund pounded the table and stood aggressively, surprising them all. "What a poor king he is then to support a murderous monster like MacCainstacairt!"

"You're a fool boy," De Soulis replied. "You will suffer as fools always do. Go back to Ross, go anywhere but leave this place for only ill awaits you here."

"I'll not retire gracefully and have my lands usurped by Fearcher MacCainstacairt."

"Have it as you will. Sit, I will contact the king and have his direction your regard."

De Soulis felt saddened that Morgund would not relent, for he knew what sort of concession Alexander would afford him; a quick death, as opposed to a lingering one, was all. He left seeking the king. Two families at the crossroads; the MacAedhs, once claimants for the throne had lost ground, whilst the De Soulis's prominent in Scottish affairs would go on to become Stewards of the royal household and later become kings of Scotland. Morgund represented the Celtic decline and the De Soulis the Norman ascendancy.

Seward and Morgund waited patiently. After a time the door opened and a large man entered with a remarkable serpent-like face, accompanied by several men at arms. The interloper was William Comyn, the Earl of Buchan. His venomous eyes turned on Seward first. Seward almost expected him to flick out his tongue and bite. "Who are you?"

"Seward. Called Gunn, as surname."

"It is unfortunate, Gunn, that you chose such a companion."

He stared long and hard at Seward. His eyes were without humanity and Seward felt relieved when he was finally released from the burden of his stare, for that stare was elsewhere now, on Morgund.

"Does anyone know you are here?" Buchan asked Morgund.

"No."

"Then you'll follow your dear departed father to hell, Morgund MacAedh."

Seward and Morgund found themselves held by their arms, and on Buchan's orders disarmed. It seemed their end was imminent until another melee ensued at the door. A new presence entered the room. It was Alan Durward, the Earl of Athol, the champion of the Celtic cause in Scotland and a brave and valiant man.

Buchan turned to him, "I am master here."

Athol smiled and his look said, "I acknowledge no master and certainly not you Buchan. I heard you boys, had guests," he said to Seward and Morgund.

Comyn replied through gritted teeth, "What does the good Earl of Athol wish?"

"As the premier Celtic Earl of Scotland I hold Celtic interests dear so I am making it my business to see no harm comes to this boy who is of noble Celtic stock."

"So, you are supporting a rebel family?  Jackals who would tear out our young king's heart if they could?"

"A jackal."  Athol paused to let the ridiculousness of the statement sink in.  After all Morgund was a slight boy, unthreatening in looks.  "This boy has committed no crime, nor had his father before him, a man of good standing," Athol said.

Buchan: "Good standing amongst Celtic curs only."

Athol:  "Say that and you proclaim loudly your ignorance. A cur, is what you are!"

Buchan:  "Once Athol, I'd have killed you for that."

Athol:  "Killed me?"

Buchan:  "Yes."

Athol:  "Shhh. I believe you, now go back and have sup with the king."

Buchan:  "He is the son of a traitor!"

Athol:  "Kenneth MacAedh was my friend, and is dead, so speak no ill of him.  A sad passing."

"Sadly distressed I am at the death of one who ever sought ill to our lawful king," Buchan said.

"That is not so," Athol corrected Buchan, "Any treason by a MacAedh was long ago."

"Leave this in my hands, Athol, " Buchan's voice was threatening and accommodating, somewhat conspiratorial. "I will ensure his safety."

Then his face took on a new shape, and Morgund was amazed that this serpent like face could become so servile. Athol, looking at the boys, whispered, "At least snakes made no pretence of harmlessness."

"I am the declared kings agent and by that license I may not be disagreed with, Athol."

"Infamy remains infamy, no matter at whose hand."

"Do not correct me like child. The king shall hear forthwith."

"Aye, tell the king, and I hope you remember the king is not yourself, and remember that the king must act by lawful right."

Buchan insisted. "I must have my way." He shook his fist, his face cherry red. "If you do this I will have my revenge." Finally he looked into Athol's eyes and said. "A great mistake you make Athol. I see your fall, for nothing is surer, when you cause offence to me thus."

Athol mocked Buchan. "Explain why he was accosted in this way." Whilst he said this, his teeth were on display, twisting the knife. "Was murder intended?"

"I do not owe an explanation, and how dare you ask me for one. I'm not to be gamed with. Do you know who I am?" Buchan addressed his men. "Ready yourself men, we may yet have to use force."

"Children aren't wise enough to curb cruel ways. Are you Buchan?" Athol smiled charmingly.

Buchan exploded. "Forget your display of insolence. Be good Athol, and yet show some sense. I am the right-hand of the king."

"No, the boy is mine ... Go now," Athol said.

"Do you dare challenge me Athol?"

"Your men at least have sense." Buchan's men had shuffled towards the door, overpowered by Athol's personality. He was a renowned swordsman, and he had friends who would avenge him. Many of them wouldn't risk their lives on Buchan's account.

"You are out of your depth, Buchan." Athol, tired of waiting, tired of the pregnant stillness said, "Still here? Buchan? Go!

"A command, from you? Who besides the King commands?"

Athol raised eyebrows. "Start moving or I'll cut your head off."

Buchan knew it was no empty threat. "So be it, he is in your care."

These two had history and this was but the latest in the series. Buchan silently gazed at Athol as he retired. Athol held his glare, overpowering Buchan with his own. The swords of Seward and Morgund were tossed to the floor.

Buchan was furious at having his actions blocked. "Doubt not," he said from outside the door, "I will end this dangerous collusion. I go to see the king, Athol. The king. His Grace." Turning to his men he said, "The fool does not know what he does this Celtic Earl. It will not be pleasant when I tell His Grace how he has acted towards me."

Athol laughed and shouted. "Do what you will Buchan, but take your ill wind, with you and quickly. The stench of you is not to be born." Buchan who had re-entered the room, stood glaring at Athol. Athol met his gaze, and spat out, "Spare me dealing with such a knave, at least, until tomorrow."

These last words were too much for Buchan who stormed out. He would never tire of hating Athol now. Athol knew and didn't care. He was a match for any Norman and would prove it whenever and wherever, as he often told anyone who would listen.

Buchan noisily retreated down the passageway dispensing abuse upon his men. Athol, went to the door. Remaining in sight of the boys, and by conjuring out his tongue and poking it out in Buchan's direction, he lightened the atmosphere and brought a smile to the two young faces. The first such expression to adorn their faces so far that day. Morgund asked how Athol had learned of them. He told them William MacRuari having recently enlisted in his service saw them in the castle grounds and informed him.

Morgund, remembering hearing Dolfin say that the new king Alexander was behind his father's death, hoped that this evil rumour wasn't true. If it was, perhaps bad counsel had led the king to believe ill of his family. Athol had no knowledge of it. Morgund told Athol that the King must learn that the name MacAedh could be associated with loyalty and trust. Athol warned Morgund that Alexander was slippery. Morgund didn't want to believe it. He would reserve judgement, he decided.

Unfortunately Morgund did not know that Alexander reckoning the MacAedhs were a threat had decided to kill Morgund and end the worry. However King Alexander did not want it known generally he was, responsible for Morgund's demise, this was at odds with benevolent rule, it was better to appear gracious and arrange Morgund's death to look natural, thereafter to appear suitably remorseful, which hopefully would ensure that no blame for the death would be laid upon him. Alexander did appear good hearted to those who knew him not. Weeks slipped by, and Morgund, who had, by then, spent some time in the castle and its environs, should have taken more notice of the obvious.

On the trip south the king fell into the regular habit of calling to Morgund to ride with him, and was so sympathetic that he made Morgund feel guilty that he had held such a measure of distrust of him earlier. Others had filled his ears with distasteful lies, Athol amongst them. Morgund did not for an instant suspect, how sly Alexander was.

On this journey were men from all over Scotland, highlanders and lowlanders. The highlanders, sharing a common language and culture preferred their own kind. Those of lowland stock eyed them with suspicion, with barely concealed hostility. Scotland was the oldest kingdom in Europe. Celtic since the first High King, Kenneth MacAlpine had united the country in 840. The Celts from Ireland came as conquerors into central and western Scotland. In other areas Angles and Saxons lived side by side with scatterings of Cimbric Celts, kindred in race and language to the Welsh. Other parts of the south being mostly Norse or German. After Kenneth MacAlpine's conquest, the Celts, those whose language was understood in Ireland, until recently, the most dominant of all. Now, by the growth of English power in the south, this cultural dominance was fading.

The Norseman brought fire and sword to the north, and words. Marrying Celtic wives had brought a Celtic revival. As women raised the children, Gaelic was the natural tongue of them until they were older. So these half-Celts seemed no different to their fully Celtic ancestors, apart from a greater fairness, a tendency from red hair to blonde after a generation or two. They admired their Norse fathers but those stories, told by their mothers made them Celts. Additionally, the Norseman allowed many of the original inhabitants to remain, thence, accepting fealty from them therefore the population retained a male Celtic influence. The Celts farmed and worked, the raiders didn't desire to.

To illustrate how Norse became Celts.  A Norse family with many red headed sons became known by the Gaels that lived near them as Mong Ruadhs, being in Gaelic 'Red sons,' who in time became a clan, the Munroes.  So a Norse family became Celtic, this, a notable example, of an almost commonality.

Whilst, the north retained its Celtic culture, the south did not.  The first to turn away from Celtic ways were the conquerors of MacBeth, Malcolm Canmore, and MacDuff, the Earl of Fife.  MacDuff slaying MacBeth therefore earning the hereditary right to crown the kings of Scotland.  Both Canmore and MacDuff lived in a Celtic speaking kingdom one hundred and fifty years before the current King, Alexander the Second.  Morgund was a descendant of King Malcolm Canmore's son, Aedh.  King Alexander was the grandson of king David, also, son of Canmore.

Margaret, the wife of Canmore, was the catalyst for change.  The granddaughter of Edmund Ironside King of England, she intended to marry the king of Hungary to avoid becoming the bride of William the Norman, king of England, and conqueror of her own Anglo Saxon race.  Captured by Scottish raiders before her departure she was forced into marriage with Malcolm Canmore.  To accommodate her, English became the Scottish court's language.  Already many had its use.  Anglo Saxons were a numerous minority in the south.  Just as Gaelic  began to overtake English amongst lowlanders, a new factor swung this process again.  The battle to determine which tongue would dominate, was fluctuating to and fro.

Margaret came reinvigorating English, extending its range, and by welcoming English fugitives to Scotland, of which, there were many after the Norman invasion, added to the vitality of the language. Malcolm made Scottish nobles of the now landless English nobility. Servants must know their masters tongue, they seek to emulate them, so it was in Scotland. It was enough to kill Gaelic in the Scottish lowlands. The country from then on was divided between highland or lowland, each speaking a different language.

The nation over the highland line was thoroughly disaffected with Margaret and her English. The succession to the Scots throne through the century had become muddied by frequent insurrections. Different families ruled and some thought still to, seeing no clear rightful king. Canmore needed something to place him above his rivals and none better than the daughter of the royal house of England. Malcolm also had other concerns, for William the Conqueror was determined to conquer Scotland.

Margaret's children had a better claim to the English crown than William did. Malcolm placated the Norman king, seemingly subservient, promising to surrender, his heirs claims to the English kingship. An undertaking was never formally made, they were empty promises only. Eventually William would demand real action and when he did Scotland would have war with England. Malcolm charmed William for a reason. He needed time to deal with his own succession dilemma. His children might pay for any failure on his part to eradicate the highland alternative royal house, the MacAedhs.

Edmund Ironeside's line, the Anglo Saxon, lived on in Margaret's progeny who later ascended the English throne anew, via James the Sixth of Scotland and the First of England.   As an interesting aside, this episode with Margaret, and her entry into Scotland, brought to Scotland two new families, the Leslies and Drummonds.   Margaret had in her party, as escort a Hungarian with a name shortened and simplified by the Scots to Leslie.  After her capture he refused to leave her side.  Once given lands in Scotland he became a good Scot.  Leslie, had a servant named Drummond, as near as the Scots could make it out.   Although he didn't succeed to lands his descendants gained the trust of successive monarchs and became Hereditary Foresters who shot to fame under Robert the Bruce, rewarded for supporting him.  Given lands taken from those who were on the losing side in the civil war, in the 1290's.

In time the Drummonds became Dukes and outstripped the Leslies, who, when, they entered Scotland, they had served.  As the two Hungarians came to terms with their new country, the Celts, were aghast at what was happening, with foreigners with outlandish ways taking land.

Thus, those, of the old race with the tendency to look back to the glorious past,  sought champions, Lulach, MacBeth's stepson, and a descendant of Lulach among them.   Many others took up the mantle before being hunted down.   The MacAedhs as descendants of Malcolm Canmore's third son Aedh, were an important family and heavily involved.

The two sons of Aedh took upon themselves the name MacAedh to draw attention to their illustrious descent, surnames uncommon in Scotland then, making the reason for adopting one all the more striking. The whole problem of succession and the threat posed by the MacAedh's had arisen with their famous ancestor the son of Malcolm Canmore, Aedh. Aedh who became a priest when his wife died had no interest in worldly concerns from then on. When Malcolm, his elder brother, died, Aedh, next in line to be king was offered the crown. By now a priest for some years, he refused the crown, deciding his greater duty to be to God.

By all accounts he would of made a most unsuitable king. His younger brother David, accepted. Thus, David ruled. Canmore's wife Margaret the namesake of the Margretson line.

When the sons of Aedh attained manhood they were eager to retrieve their birthright there was already a king who had no intention of surrendering his crown. As the Celts saw it, a MacAedh should be king. At the very least, any noble highlander would be a better king than what the south provided. The young MacAedh was granted the Earldom of Ross, in northern sphere, where he and his brother were cast into a cauldron of rebellion. Agitators were drawn to them like winged suicides to a burning wick and being young, no option did they have but to become impassioned. It would have been better to have surrounded them with loyal adherents in the south and have watched them. Ironic, that Aedh with his Celtic name was so taken with his mother's faith to seek Catholicism. The native Celtic Church, was then, the more popular. He eventually became a monk in that Catholic church. Yet his issue would be champions of ancient ways, and a shame that at least one stout strategist could not have won them a decisive battle.

But sons of Aedh, and the sons of Aedh's sons, died with harness on their back, with more sons who struggled on, each generation upon another, dying as they did die, until only one of that name survived, Morgund MacAedh. This explained Alexander's distaste for him, as it explained Alexander's fear of Morgund and the danger Morgund was in.

One day a man rode beside Morgund and Seward, pulling out a flute he played a tune full of sadness and beauty, after he finished, a mouth full of black teeth greeted them.

"Who are you?" Morgund asked him.

Receiving no reply, Morgund turned away. Sometime later he heard.

"My name is John of Loch Lomand."

"Why did you not speak earlier, strange one?" Morgund asked.

"I didn't see the need to. Pardon me if I alarmed you, but as you say, I am strange."

Seward looked disinterested. "Well strange man, we will say good day to you." Seward and Morgund rode off, having had enough of strange men, Duibne had cured them of any need to know such. Seward wanted nothing to do with him. But behind them, they heard, "Seward, I will see you again." It was unnerving, when the voice came low and dark. Both Morgund and Seward moved off, startled. How did he know my name? Seward wondered.

Despite themselves the man intrigued them and they sought to learn more of him, for when he had spoken as they moved off they felt his power.  With the coming of night they met a man who professed some knowledge, his name was Terloch.

"What do you know," from Seward.

"Much."

"Tell us?" from Morgund.

Both young men overlapped each other.  "What is it?" They both said.

"He is  a follower of the ancient God Wicca who some say is Satan's disciple.   There are others like minded, even amongst this army," the man said.

"Who are they?" Seward asked.

"Never mind." The fire threw an unsettling light onto the his face as he spoke.

"Strange this is, it frightens me, leave it be," Morgund said.

"Yes, it is strange." Seward agreed.  Thanking the man, they departed.

"I want to speak with him again and I will Morgund.  I must have it from him if anything is useful to me."

"What use could it be?" Morgund queried, wonderingly.

"Because I believe him only to be strange, but interesting, as well."

"Do not make light of this Seward."

"I still want to speak with him and I will," Seward said. He appeared to speak to himself, saying. "This of Satan is often spoken of, by those who have something."

"What something do you speak of Seward?"

"Power."

"What power?"

"The second sight. Morgund, I believe I am so gifted." The story unfolded of the journey to the bridge which had made him aware of his ability. "I must learn how to develop this, and maybe risk some dangers to do so."

Later that night when Morgund was asleep, Seward slipped away. "I was wanting to speak with you." Seward said when he approached the soldier he had spoken to earlier, the one so knowledgeable of John of Loch Lomond.

"I thought you would." Although the hour was late the man was up long after most others were at rest.

"Why did you not sleep," Seward asked.

"I slept earlier. Thereafter I got up, for I had a feeling you would be back. What would you have done if I had been asleep?" Terloch asked.

"I don't know. Somehow I knew you'd be up."

"Feelings, they have mystery." Terloch smiled at Seward and passed him a hot brew. After speaking for a while about the journey Seward bespoke that which was on his mind. "You are not a Christian?"

"No, I am not."

"How can you turn away from Christian teachings?"

"I do not. Some of those teachings that improve man, I cherish."

"How can you justify this? Do you serve two masters?"

"Not so. The church of Rome is about power and personal gain, at odds with us. It is not about knowledge of God."

"What is your opinion of the Celtic Church."

"It is more holy, yes, but it is a different way than ours."

"Explain."

"Ours is not only a religion. It is a philosophy not about him who suffered on the cross, but about the study of the occult. Learning truths that existed before men became Christians. Knowledge of systems that dwell deep in the heart." He was emphasising how important this was to him by his expanded irises, drawing Seward deep into them, capturing his full attention.

"What is it that you describe?"

"That which is hidden from the rest."

"You would be in danger from the Church if this got out. You would be burnt."

"Yes, but you will keep this secret, that I know."

And Seward acknowledged with a movement of his head.

"Some men who have this gift, join the priests who use it to fool common folk, using the claim that visions of the future are sent from heaven, or worse still, they have to neglect it to the detriment of themselves. A greater circle you could enhance Seward, men like me who believe in Wicca.

"But why do I have this ability?"

"I know not. Some are chosen, that is all."

"What of Satan?"

"Before the fall was he not by the Lords side and his foremost and is not one scorned often lied about."

Seward didn't speak with John of Loch Lomond again until he met him once more, far away in time and place. Terloch who had given Seward this information had a last message for Seward. "That which you wear, will save you."

"That which I wear?"

"Yes, that symbol that hangs from your neck."

"How do you know? You cannot see it." Lines appeared between Seward's eyes.

"As I've said John is not the only disciple of Wicca in this army. One day you will join us."

"No, that I will not do, how do you know about the symbol?"

"We have been watching you."

"Then I must discard it."

"However, you will not." And Seward did continue to wear the symbol of Wicca.

Morgund wanted to know where Seward had gone and Seward told him. He related some of the conversation he had with Terloch.

"My dull head does not grasp this," Morgund's face was bleak. "Have you become a Satanist?"

"No."

"I don't understand."

"Nor do I," Seward replied, "But I will have that which is hidden from me, I will find it out."

Morgund could see nothing good in Seward's preoccupation but knew any argument would be forcefully attacked and so was silent.

———————————

THE DAY AT Runnymead was long forgettable as far as Morgund was concerned, listening to tedious harangues whilst waiting for king John to appear and once he did, nothing but more of the same. During the course of proceedings John deemed it necessary to meet his fellow monarch. Immediately thereafter, John's supporters were presented to Alexander, as in turn, the Scottish nobles were presented to King John. By a lucky chance some Scot commented on Morgund's background to an Englishman who took to those words thoughtfully, which, in fact, would save Morgund's life.

When the day broke up, departing leisurely homewards, a holiday atmosphere prevailed. Alexander planned to visit one of his English estates and requested that Morgund accompany him which delighted Morgund. Alexander's residence was rustic, more of a hunting lodge than a stronghold. Morgund had a room to himself and appeared to be in held high favour as many great ones held no similar lodgings. Seward and William camped outside the castle walls, where strict military guidelines were adhered to.

Even though king John appeared a spent force, they were deep inside England and should be on guard, Athol was responsible. If nothing else, he was a fine soldier who did his best to look out for Morgund but it was getting ever more difficult. He didn't trust Alexander nor many of his confederates.

Alexander said to his follower one day whilst out in the forest, near his estate, "The travelling lantern of the sky, shall be strangled by wet airborne tonight."

"Aye, Sire"

Alexander suddenly looked at him as if to make him privy to some secret. "MacAedh, what do you make of him?"

The man hesitated.

"Do not be faint, speak to me of Morgund MacAedh."

"Morgund seems likely to win your Lord's reprieve for his family's traitorous misbehaviour of years gone by, maybe he is different, he seems a stable fellow."

Alexander was angered, "Blood will be upon his head that does appear so white. He will wear the garment of war against me when he decides."

"Is your Grace aware of something that I am not?"

"I will not remonstrate further. Let us go." Alexander didn't want to make his inner thoughts known to the man.

However on the way to the castle, from his lips did escape, "A curse be on him."

When his companion looked at Alexander, wonderingly, he said, "My dull brain has been wrought with things I wish forgotten - leave this unspoken."

"Yes, Sire."

A steady unpleasant downpour. Riding through the storm, not a drop, did Alexander feel so full of hate was he for Morgund MacAedh. Inside the castle, Alexander's anger caused many nervous glances from those around him, he decided to mask it, returning to that aspect which made Morgund the most relaxed. He did not want Morgund to discover his design and perhaps take some preventative action.

Returning from a successful hunt the next day, the conversation turned to a favoured subject of the king's, the management of plants. "Plants when watered by hand grow haphazardly, or they do not grow. They need to be nurtured by the rain, rain is a better water than that gathered from a well or river."

No one interrupted or offered to interject on the king. When concerning himself with his pet subjects, gardening, the stars or nature Alexander did not need any responses, he merely shared his thoughts. He often did this, and they were good to listen to, for the king had an entertaining turn of phrase, and was knowledgeable in his favoured fields. He was an intelligent man. The conversation turned to Runnymead. Morgund was taken unawares when he was included in the conversation.

"What did you make of Runnymead, Morgund?"

"A dull exercise."

"But nevertheless important."

"Not to one such as myself, your Grace."

"That, I'll not deny."  Morgund's statement appeared to amuse Alexander and he said,  "Tonight, you shall sup with me Morgund, you entertain greatly."

"Dine with you sire, as a favoured guest?"  Morgund was honoured, excited at the prospect of winning favour.

"It is my royal command,"  Alexander answered charmingly.

An event occurred which altered the course of events so that Morgund avoided eating with the king.  Feigning illness he stated he did not wish to put the king at risk of catching whatever it was he had.  A meal was brought to his room, which he did not touch.  He had bumped into one of Buchan's men, a drunken fellow.  The man's mottled face showed the effects of too much strong spirit.

Glistening eyes were cast out from dark brows that showed resentment.  "So, you are to visit with the king, he loves you not highlander.  You dine with him and you'll lead a short life."  Then he had laughed.  His laugh echoing down the passageway that was narrow and dark, lit by torches giving a faint touch of light.

"What do you mean?"  Morgund had asked him.

Raucously taunting him,  he replied,  "You know what I mean,"  and then he disappeared.

The following days which were taken up with hunting and ale drinking. Morgund noticed that Buchan and the king were exceedingly close. On more than one occasion both looked at him in a disturbing way, Buchan with a sardonic smile. Morgund no longer felt safe, even when choosing his own food and confining himself to his quarters. He contacted Seward and William and had them come to him. If ill was planned, he would have his friend's assistance.

With at least two witnesses it might be enough to dissuade any action towards him here and now, and if so it would give him time to find out more about a plot, if there was one. The first night passed uneventfully, so if anything was to occur it would happen this very night, for in the morning they were leaving for Scotland. Should any assassination occur in England and Alexander would find a way to blame it on the English. And a better location to commit it might not occur.

Morgund woke badly from a nightmare. A sword was poised above his head and had commenced descending. He opened his eyes, heart pounding. By awakening he had avoided the sword strike, which if landed, was said to be unlucky. He saw Seward with his head up, eyes alert for he to had sensed danger. But William slept soundly, rhythmic snores escaping him.

"What hour is it?" Seward whispered to Morgund.

Morgund looked at a candle, marked at intervals along its length. As the candle burned down, the time was indicated.

"Just after one," Morgund answered.

"Perhaps I am being foolish, but I feel we must prepare Morgund."

Morgund eased himself up, slowly, he got out of bed, so as not to make a sound. A dog barked. Someone was up. Seward shook William awake. Thereafter, quickly they dressed and armed themselves. Waiting, with ears sensitive to the slightest sound. All quiet. Perhaps the dogs barking had made any assailants cautious. Allow an interval to elapse, then, when deep sleep returned, they would continue, assassins would act so. Seward realised what seemed to be occurring conformed to that design.

Seward whispered to Morgund, "Let us go outside, that will not be expected." He pointed in case his whisper did not carry.

Morgund balked at moving, not wanting to make the danger real but it was, so he eased the door open so as not to make a sound and slipped outside. It was dark and deathly quiet.

Morgund spoke to William. "Stay here. We will go and prepare the horses and find some food to take with us in case things do go wrong. Keep watch to see if anyone comes. At least, I will find out, if they would harm me. We will be back. Stay in the dark of the corridor so they can't see you."

William watched the shadows as time stood still. His heart and breath sounding loud, drowning out all else. The sounds emanating within his own body slowed. Eventually calmer, his eyes drooped ... then ... the unmistakable sound of men moving quietly towards their room very slowly like cats stalking mice. Should he withdraw now whilst there was still time, no, he'd stay to identify them.

In the future, the opportunity might arise to make known their crime and bring to justice, these murdering swine. William could hear several men. Belatedly, he realised Morgund must be warned. Others might be stationed to prevent his escape, they would be on guard upon any disturbance, so he turned and stepped away cautiously. This body of men who stealthily crept were unarmoured for there was no sound of clinking mail.

Nearing the end of the passage, the sound of metal. Armed men blocked his exit. Seward and Morgund must have got by them before they had positioned themselves. He would have to fight his way through. Must act immediately, entering the room soon they would discover Morgund's absence and then there would be uproar. Needing the element of surprise, he quickened his pace but at the same time attempted to move silently so that his presence would remain undetected. Three figures lounging complacently ahead.

They spoke quietly. That they spoke masked his approach and told him he was unexpected. The odds were not so great and he had surprise to aid him. When he was almost upon them a pale head turn towards him, a shocked look, as the man was impaled on William's sword. Crashing over him, he swept right and left, both slashes met by the soft resistance of flesh, anguished cries emitted thereby. Aiming for the white unarmoured, flesh, doing ruinous work. They obviously were only semi-mailed. Shouting started behind him. He was unarmoured so could outrun them. He ran shouting, "To arms, to arms, the castle is overrun!"

The call was taken up by others. Half dressed men ran into passageways. If the gate were closed he would melt into the crowd. The gate was open. Only a select few must be in on this, for the stables were unattended and Morgund and Seward were mounted. His horse was beside theirs. William mounted and they rode out the gates. Galloping forth towards a line of trees, where they stopped briefly.

"What happened?" asked Morgund.

"To the road south and fast, for they will follow." Seward balked William, knowing what had occurred.

Morgund would not be deterred. "Did they come William?"

"Yes Morgund they did," William replied.

"Away Morgund," Seward said. "Later we'll hear all."

They bent low over horses, following the road, this was the best option in the dark. When the first light came they entered a large forest. Camping near water, food was passed between them.

"What shall we do now?" Morgund asked his two companions.

"There is nothing for us in Scotland," Seward said looking at Morgund. "It's far too    dangerous for you to go back."

"For me, it is too dangerous, yes, but for you two, Scotland is where you should go. It is your home."

"Morgund, you know my place is with you," Seward said.

"And William?"  Morgund asked.

"So is mine own place with thee, Morgund,"  Morgund replied.

The three gripped hands together.

"How shall we earn our living?"  Seward asked.

"We are able bodied men.   There will be work for us," Morgund replied.

Seward looked forlorn.   "But with no armour or money to buy it with, the soldier's life is lost to us.

"Perhaps not,"  William said overturning a bag of gold coins.

"Where did that come from?" Morgund's, eyes were wide.

William told of the cave and the gold.   Having recently escaped death, with full bellies, with a large quantity of largess in their possession, spirits took flight.  This would be the start of a new exciting life.  The young men stripped and dived into a large clear stream flowing fast.  The day was hot.   England was a warmer country than Scotland, and so late in the year, such heat, would never occur at home, they appreciated it. Today nothing existed, only warmth and friendship.

Later stretched out near a fire,  Morgund asked William, "William, where did you hide the gold before our escape?"

"Stitched into my saddle bags and in my horse blanket."

"Were you not worried lest someone steal it?"

"Where else could I keep it, and not alert others to its presence? Besides if someone stole it, I could easily obtain more."

It made sense to Morgund. A long night passed in good humoured camaraderie, hopeful futures were explored, asides on Alexander and how they hadn't see his treachery coming, and that snake Buchan and how Athol had misused him. Much laughter. Eventually the fire burnt low and they slept.

Next day Seward walked towards his horse and collected his bow, and said, "I shall return soon. I go to get fresh meat, a stag will do us."

"You will not labour alone," Morgund replied.

William decided to enter the forest and seek game also.

Morgund, who was less confident of coming across a deer said, "I might set a snare for a rabbit for we may as well live on fresh fare and save our dried food."

Each took different paths in their search for the bounty of the forest. Morgund came to a sloping glade with thick trees above and below, to a multitude of ferns. Then leaving ferns, Morgund entered broken woodland where filtered sunlight barely reached the forest floor, the ground thickly covered with strawberries.

The plants were heavy with a multitude of fruit.  He picked up a handful.  Putting them to his lips, he tasted a succulent flavour.  Taking a deerskin from his shoulders he began filling it.   Engrossed in his work, he did not see three figures looming towards him from the shadows of the forest.  Turning towards a sound, he was up on his feet, sword drawn.

"Easy, easy young friend, don't cut yourself.   Is it wise for one so young to carry a dangerous weapon?  Surrender your sword to me, toss it to the ground."  The giant of a man who spoke, smiled at him.

It seemed to Morgund that misfortune did not relent in its pursuit.  "No," Morgund said pointing his sword at them and instantly regretted putting them on-guard.  Nevertheless he sought overcome his mistake.

The man who had spoken was dark.  His tone hard and aggressive, as he said,  "This sickly boy holds his sword towards me.  He couldn't even touch me,  I will swipe a hole straight through your body boy!"

"Oh great giant of the forest I was but picking your strawberries, forgive me."  Morgund walked towards them sword downward, smiling,  "I am lost, and my father would pay a handsome reward to any who would assist me."

The mention of silver money them pause.   His mind quoted Seward's instructions.  When faced with a group of opponents, pick one and cut through him. Stay to one side of the others. They would shield him.   He felt heartened he had remembered what Seward had said.

"Where are you from?"  This from the large one, obviously the leader.

"Only another step or two more," Morgund thought. "Scotland," he answered.

The large one raised his hand. "Hold young man."

Morgund stopped and waited. The giant spoke. "Put your sword on the ground and take ten steps, back, go, move!"

Morgund ran towards them. Deciding he was not giving up without a fight, at least. Good intentions aside he was overpowered quickly. With hands tied behind his back, they walked him out in front of them. They came to a small hut where they gained mounts, thereafter they came to the road and later to the castle.

At the castle, the castle's guardian addressed Morgund. "Morgund, I believed you had escaped us, the king thought as much."

Morgund was drained, defeated, in pain. His head throbbed, his arms and upper body burned from being held in an unnatural position. He was numb. Resigned to his fate.

"I will send a rider to the king and advise him of your return and find out what is to be done with you."

Morgund managed to focus on the speaker, a tall, thin, scholarly type, dark in the French way. He looked down at Morgund bound on a chair and sighed. The man was not unkind. If only the boy had escaped he would not be forced to carry out this distasteful duty.

He had no doubt of Morgund's fate when he said, "MacAedh, whilst you are in my care you will be fed well, and receive some comfort, as much as I can make available in the circumstances."

He could see Morgund was not following him. Ordering his fastenings undone, that he be taken to the dungeon, this, to keep him away from prying eyes. In the cell, Morgund's face was washed and he received a jug of warm milk after which he lapsed into an exhausted sleep. Much later, Morgund awoke and realised he was alive. This caused a sudden elation, which turned quickly to depression. His head hung low. There was no hope, surely they would kill him soon. King John of England's nephew, Arthur, king John had murdered the helpless boy whilst held prisoner. Such a fate awaited the prisoner of kings. Surrounded by darkness he moved an arm. The bindings had been released. There was stiffness but his arms and shoulders felt immeasurably better. Adjusting to the dim, he saw he was in an aperture less cell and alone. Morgund thought a torch must be burning outside the door, for a muffled light there was. The door opened and a guard gave him a loaf of bread, followed by a bowl of soup, which tasted good.

The guard waited silently for him to finish. When he did, Morgund handed him back the bowl and the guard closed the door. The guard left, taking his light with him. It was gone. Morgund could see, nothing. Nothing, only black eternity, no light was outside the door. It had been the torch carried by the guard which gave him sight of his cell. None good reside in the living black, in the dark dwells only the evil creatures of night and death.

# MACTAGGART'S CHURCH

FAR TO THE north, there was concern for Morgund and Seward who had not been heard from since their departure. Some word should have come back from clansmen visiting Edinburgh, but they heard nothing. Perhaps the two were part of the contingent into England, or had instead been captured, or worse. Malcolm and Sienna spoke much of this and had scarcely slept because of it. Malcolm decided to talk to his friend Stony and seek solace from the man. Although he was not noted for his wisdom, however Malcolm's friend was a wiser man than many thought, it was those others, who judged him, who themselves lacked foresight. Dawn was newly broke and the air was crisp as Malcolm left. From a tree covered hill he looked down at an island in a placid loch. Being outside cleared his head, for which, he was thankful. Often lately his nights had been plagued by worry  He saw a neighbour, upon waving, the man waved back.  Work was slack with the harvest in, he decided to visit the neighbour. Audrec who was from somewhere far off in the north, had come to etch out a living amongst them though Malcolm didn't know why.

"How goes it Malcolm?  It is an early start you have to be out."  Audrec's speech was high pitched, being worded differently to that commonly practised in these parts.

"It is early, yes.  I go to see Hamish Stony field."

"Oh, visiting your friend."  Audrec displayed a smile, he was a cheery fellow.  "You must have left home before first light."

"I did."

"Why is it he is named Stony?" asked Audrec.

He might not have heard him say stony field, but he lived nearby, it should be obvious, or if he had heard, just not put it together, it was said of foreigners, that they were notably dense. Malcolm realized he must make some allowances for this.

"He is named Stony because he is not the only Hamish. His fields are stony and that distinguishes him. Another has a ruddy birthmark and so is called Ruad and the third is simply Hamish. Do you like life here Audrec?"

"It is good, I get on well with the folk around."

This was a pleasant respite for Malcolm, a nice change from stifling  walls and from focusing on Seward and Morgund. In answer to Malcolm's worried face, the conversation turned to them.

"Have you news of Seward and Morgund?"

He had dreaded this. "No."

"MacCainstacairt is a villain," Audrec said.

"Yes."

"It is a difficult matter."

This conversation dispelled Malcolm's calm. "Yes, I must be getting on, Audrec."

"It was good to see you Malcolm."

Malcolm walked away.   He would have liked to ask the foreigner why he had left that place he was from, but good manners prevented him.   It was probably a hellish place as most foreign places were.   Up and down, and on, and on, his steps took him to a place where it was said years before a Viking a spear and some helmets had been found.   So, far from anywhere.   Unlikely, he had thought, at first, near to some graves but where no church abided.   However the place was beside a navigable river and this probably explained the find.   A church must have been here once and they had come to sack the church.   Thereafter the church had been removed to a safer site.   He looked out across a stone-flecked peat bog. In the distance slightly higher was Stony's croft, set amongst the stony fields which named him, cows grazing.

His friend met him at the door.   "Come in Malcolm, sit. You're in troubled waters."

"How do you know?"

"It's on you plain.  Speak.  Go on."

"Let me a breath and I will."

Stony kept urging him, "I'm listening."

"I am going to see MacCainstacairt."

"But it is dangerous."

"They might be held by him, that is, if they still live.  They are not heard of in Edinburgh.  MacCainstacairt erected a solid wall of men to intercept them, I fear they did not make it past."

"What can you do?"

"If I cannot save them, at least I can make sure of their fate."

"Do you seriously think you can do anything?"

"I trust I can."  Malcolm was affronted by Stony's comments.

"Do you?"

"Yes, of course I do."

"There is nothing you can do, Malcolm.  Be honest with yourself.  MacCainstacairt is unlikely to admit to murder. More likely he will murder you."

"I may find out what has happened, and put MacCainstacairt in a dungeon for this misdeeds."

"More likely he will put you there and kill you."

"My mind is made up Stony."

"So you have come to say good bye."

"No, to obtain advice."

"Don't go!"

"I will not rest until I have word.  Perhaps some trick will allow me to get close to MacCainstacairt and discover the whereabouts of Seward and Morgund.  I might hear from one of MacCainstacairt's retainers what has happened.

"It appears a sound strategy if you are committed to it."

"But what trick?" Malcolm asked.

"Yes, Malcolm, that is an important question."

"Help me form my ideas, Stony."

"Give me some time to think Malcolm." They were silence for a while. "I have it," Stony said at last.

"What?"

"I hear MacCainstacairt looks for favours from Alexander. In furtherance of this aim he is erecting one of the new Romish churches to bring the highlands in line with the lowlands, so far as worship goes. Nominate yourself religious, seeking enlightenment in Roman ways and wanting to help. You would have the Roman protection and working on the building site you would surely learn something. Many of MacCainstacairt's clansmen will be there and MacCainstacairt could not spend so much money without making many appearances to check progress and to guard his investment against slackness. When you find yourself surrounded by the friends of MacCainstacairt obtain entry to their confidence and learn more. If what you want known is not revealed, kidnap one of his men and force an answer."

"I knew your brilliance would provide an answer. When do we go Stony?"

At that Stoney's eyes shot upward, "Did you say we?"

"Yes."

Stony thought about it. "I'll go with you," he said finally.

They worked out details. Malcolm went home with a more bold step looking forward to helping his adopted son Seward, and of course doing something for Morgund. However Morgund came of unlucky fold who it was hard to help. Most likely poor insignificant Morgund would be the last of his breed.

Thereafter Malcolm and Sienna argued. Sienna was in a state of panic. She didn't want Malcolm to proceed with what she considered an ill made plan. "You are alike to boys playing at a game. This is no game, and MacCainstacairt is a killer. His brain would make two of yours Malcolm."

Malcolm was much displeased with this last statement, and quickly fled her bitter tongue. When she came to find him, he was sitting on a bank near a stream. Malcolm liked this place, she knew. White stones and pale bark of the swaying willow trees gave him a relaxed feeling. They were pleasing to the eye, often he sought them. They were calming to his mind.

"I am sorry Malcolm," she said. "If you must do this, I am behind you, but please be careful. Do you realise how dangerous MacCainstacairt is? I don't wish to insult you, but these things must be said."

"Yes, I do know the danger."

"Do you really?"

He nodded and embraced Sienna when she enfolded him within her arms. She apologised once more and took hold of him tightly, telling him she had only spoken as she had because of the fears she held and because she loved him.

Although winter's blight came upon the land it didn't dissuade MacCainstacairt who initiated steps towards building. Malcolm and Stony toiled away on the building site. Their appearance was commented on hardly at all, for not just a few spectators came to see this new development, some from far away. Workers took advantage of rare silver on offer, there were even masons from England itself.

MacCainstacairt told anyone who would listen about his misfortune in being here, how he could be sharing experiences with Alexander in England, but the church must be built and only he could see to its good management. Constructing the Church in later years would gain him the name MacToisach, son of the Church, in Gaelic. MacCainstacairt, not yet known, as the church builder, was still MacCainstacairt, but building the church that would name him MacToisach. And the name Mac Toisach would be corrupted almost immediately by others into MacTaggart. This became a fairly common family surname, MacTaggart.

MaCainstacairt was solid, tall, with a beard carefully groomed, red tinted in the sun. He bore the airs of a nobleman, which he was not by birth. He had advanced himself by winning the allegiance of skilful swordsmen who admired him for his ruthless ambition, for his worthy intelligence, for his own worthy swordsmanship.

With all these qualities, and more, a quality crucial to a successful fighter, luck, and far sightedness, and perhaps more than far sightedness, unnatural perception. His reputation for awareness beyond the ordinary, was still being formed in the minds of men. Of humble origin, he had seen the path to promotion as being at the expense of Morgund's family. He knew his plan would find favour with the Margretson, the ruling house. Deal with their enemy and enrich himself at the MacAedh's expense.

Malcolm threw himself into work winning renown. Presently MacCainstacairt afforded Malcolm some comments of greeting and one day asked him where he was from.

"Part of Ross, which extends to the coast," Malcolm replied.

"MacAedh's roost."

"But not now, I hear the little scarecrow is no more, which is good. To be released from his line is joyous. Dithering fools who took misfortune with them wherever they went. Ross will be in better hands."

Malcolm hoped MacCainstacairt would enter into a conversation. MacCainstacairt instead watched him closely sorely testing his integrity by closely examining his eyes for a falsehood. Malcolm likewise clever, thought of how he would feel if he freed Seward. This gave outward truth to MacCainstacairt. MacCainstacairt relaxed and smiled, complimenting him on his work. Thereafter MacCainstacairt recalled something he had first noticed in Malcolm's eyes. Malcolm was questioned by some of MacCainstacairt's men, as to his reason for being there and watched.

MacCainstacairt was ever alert for danger, was said to have a sixth sense for discovering it, which contributed to his gaining support  The other workmen kept silent around them avoiding them if they could, and Malcolm felt a pang of nervousness, which intensified when he heard that MacCainstacairt had sent someone to find out about them.

MacCainstacairt was thorough and wise, Malcolm realised, with a well earned reputation for sensing danger. That night, Stoney, warned Malcolm that the end had come. They must leave.

There was nothing to connect the two, few were aware he was Malcolm's close friend, they had arrived at the building site separately, they would learn soon however.  Stoney had a plan.   Malcolm didn't like it, but MacCainstacairt was about to set irons upon Malcolm.  Word was out.  Still Malcolm had to be convinced.

The next day Stony came into camp from the road which led into Ross, thereafter telling someone Malcolm's wife had ran away telling, this fellow Stoney told, to keep the secret, as the culprit was a friend, and he didn't want him endangered. Word travelled quickly and Malcolm got the message by mid morning.   He left in haste and everyone laughed at his departure.   Malcolm's leaving under these circumstances did something to divert attention away from his fixation with MacCainstacairt, whom Malcolm had often talked about.  They talked of the incident and not how Malcolm's eyes had always followed MacCainstacairt.

---

WHEN MORGUND AWOKE, something was different. His eyes slowly adjusted to his new surroundings. The door was ajar. Through blurred vision he saw a man in the doorway, who said, "Your friend has paid me gold to open this door I slipped the key out whilst others slept. When you walk out the door, turn right. When you come to a flight of stairs, the door at the bottom will be unlocked. I must go before I am seen."

Morgund looked through the doorway, to stonework beyond, and to a freshly lit lamp on the wall. Rising, shakily. Walking. Outside, he turned, stumbling into a run. He saw no one. So far he had escaped attention. Luck hadn't entirely deserted him. Descending stairs he opened the door and walked outside. Seward met him, slipped a cloak over his shoulders, pulled the hood up so as to hide him. As a steady downpour started, Seward helped him onto his horse. Then they slowly made their way to the gate. Another group of horseman entered the courtyard at the same time and one of them came close. Lightning flashed onto Buchan's face. "You men, where are you going?" Buchan asked.

None dared answer for it would mean discovery. In a whisper Seward said to Morgund, " You're injured, and on a small horse. When you are through the gates, stay off the road, if you don't, they will catch you. Runnymead is where we will meet."

It was dark but Seward knew dawn was not far. He leaned near William. "I will meet you in Runnymead. Don't tarry William, there is more chance of success if we separate."

Seward rode up to Buchan, kept his hands on his reins so as not to alert him, and kept his head down.

"Where are you going?" Buchan asked.

Seward replied in a muffled voice, in a bid to hide his identity. "We make an early start we are pilgrims."

Behind Seward, Morgund and William made their way to the gate as the rain became heavier.

"Drop your hood so I can see who you are," Buchan commanded.

Seward came on and when Buchan was within his reach punched him squarely in the face dislodging him from his horse. Seward pulled his mount sharply around and sped off. Quickly he caught Morgund and stayed with him.

Buchan's followers assisted Buchan to his feet. "Go after them," he said. "A bag of gold to whoever catches the smaller one." He got to his feet and climbed into the saddle himself.

They were halfway across a field when Seward called out to Morgund. "The hill, go there and then head for the forest, it is as yet, too dark for them to make us out, especially with such rain falling. We will separate. Good luck Morgund. William, leave Morgund. We will meet in Runnymead! Ride for your life Morgund, they are coming." Seward galloped onwards.

Morgund looked behind him. They were catching up. He rode across a bare hill. Beginnings of the forest were not too far. Slapping his horse to gain extra speed he was now amongst the trees. It was getting lighter. He must lose the pursuers for they had come considerably nearer. Racing into a thick clump of timber, dodging around sweeping branches riding through tiny gaps in the trees, he paused to look behind him, slowing his horse.

A symphony of bird song greeting him as he lifted his head up to a sudden sharp pain. His horse was gone. A low limb stretched across a narrow opening between trees, horse tracks continuing on. He had hit the limb. How long he had been here, he didn't know.

Hearing the sounds he least wanted to hear. Dogs, and men. Morgund got up. Ran. He saw a group of men with dogs and changed direction to avoid them. The men released the dogs. He gasped for breath, heart pounding. The dogs were just behind him, almost on him. Running down an embankment, he fell. Rising and running once more. Nearly at his end, each breath wracked in his ribs, heart exploding within his chest, he ran up and over a rise, ran thereafter down headlong, with the dogs ever closer.

Losing his footing, he rolled down a steep descent for twenty metres. Arising, unhurt. He ducked down to get under a low tree scraping his stomach on a sharp rock. Up, for a few more steps, then through a series of falls and risings, until he heard water. A mighty river. Suddenly the ground ended, and he went out into air. This time falling onto hard ground far down. Barely was he able to get up, the fall had knocked the wind and sense out of him, "I will fight," he told himself, "For I have been shown how to."

Saying this was enough to instil the determination to push himself on.  He crawled on, and didn't see the cliff hidden by the long grass, next he tumbled over and over, finally losing awareness of how far he had fallen, before landing in water. Reaching out to the surface of the water far above, struggling to rise with the air that escaped his anguished mouth now shut to avoid drowning.  Coming up, gasping, trapped in a surging current, which, thank God, took him away quickly.

Swimming with the current he heard the sound of water crashing over a precipice.  Suddenly meeting the River God awed by his power.  A magnetic pull fixed onto him, enslaving him, drawing his body to the precipice.   When he fought to break the river's grip, it only fastened tighter, dragging  him down.  This way was up and then, that.  Head above water, for a quick breath.  Then dunked again below the surface.  The waterfall was menacingly near.

Rumbling water plunging over the drop.  For a second he was dead and alive all in the one, and lost.  The fall over the waterfall was almost now.   He was below and above, both alive and downstream, and trapped about to plunge to his death, simultaneously.

In a moment of clarity approaching the falls, he realized there was nowhere to hide!  Even if he couldn't resist, the will to resist was in itself noble.  Somewhere, within him, if only he could find it, he would find a way to affect his fate and live.  He was alive, and inside serene nothingness he calculated what action to take.  For a brief moment he could move, hopefully enough to miss those dreadful rocks, beneath him.  The rocks, were there.  Nothing he could do to avoid them.

Splashing, crashing, landing, torn asunder, white, white, white and more white.  Fear ... relief, as he lived.   Until the river God slackened in the hunger for his life, he must, just, outlast him, and might not he be rewarded for his courage. Surely this ancient entity, the river God, would, as all things do respect an unconquerable will.  Unconquerable will creates, it isn't allowed to die, unfulfilled.  A divine law he was about to test for a second great spill down awaited him.

The rocks grew ever larger, until, he hit them.  Or did he, his eyes were closed.  They were past.  His mind relieving the recent past was attempting to process what had just happened.  Seemingly, unhurt.  Down, driven down by the surging water, water landing on him from above, but by pushing briskly, he was clear.     Swimming with the current through a series of gorges, he came to where two rivers met. The water's tempo lessening he swam to a bank.  Reaching shallows he strode out onto soft sand where he fell.

A girl sitting near the river saw him.  Hiding, watching, she noticed a number of things.  Firstly, that he was armed with a long dagger and wore the clothing of a nobleman and also that he was handsome, and of course, wet through.    Some mishap.    Then, waking up to the danger she decided to get the men folk.  As she ran, excitement grew.  This was special, nothing like this had happened before.   The excitement generated from this would last for days, even weeks, she would tell how he looked when he came out of the water, of him being armed, and her bravely creeping up and watching him.  What else could she add? She would think of something. Returning some time later with her family, to Morgund lying on the sand asleep, it was sunny and warm.  Perhaps this would be the last such plentiful sunlight to fall upon them for summer was almost gone.  The lad must have exerted himself strongly they surmised, for he barely cleared the water to lie down.

Morgund opened his eyes and saw them, three sturdy men, two younger, and the third, perhaps the father, of the other two.

"I told you, he was here.   He came straight out of the river, he did."

He looked at the girl who spoke.  He had nearly missed her, she was so small next to these three sturdy men, his age and pretty.   If they meant him harm, they had had ample opportunity whilst he was sleeping, and they would not have brought the girl, so he addressed them in an easy relaxed manner,  suitable to the occasion.  "How long have you been here?"

"Not long,"  came the answer.  He wasn't sure from which one.

"Greetings young sire."  This from the older man.  Spoken softly, with an educated accent.  Odd, considering his rustic appearance.

"And I return them, to you sir, and your companions.  And you Miss."

"I am Edith, not miss.   No one's ever called me that before.  Father, he called me a name, like a gentry.  My name is Edith,"  she laughed, getting over her amazement at his greeting.  That he could talk was amazing in itself.

This whole event had the touch of a dreamlike quality, shocked as her family to find him here, believing somewhat that her imagination was to blame, for as she well knew, the river and woods played tricks.  She had almost expected to find no boy there at all when she returned.

"My name is Morgund." He smiled at her.

"You're not from these parts." One of the young men addressed him.

"No, from Scotland."

"What brings you here to our forgotten corner?"

Remembering Seward's advice that when answering questions to be careful, he opted for this approach. "To ask for your sister's hand. I have faced many dangers to get here."

"He's lying father. How would he know I was here, only you, and John and Simon go to town. Ah, I know. You have told people in town how pretty I am, and that has brought him."

She went along with this and beamed at him, he was very good looking, after all, she thought.

"No, truly what brought you?" The younger man persisted.

"John, the fellow has been through great turmoil and it is not manners to question, leave him be. He is our guest." In a fatherly tone the older man smiled and came closer. "Morgund, we live close by. Come with us and we will give you a warm meal and find you a change of clothing."

"Thank you. That is kind." Morgund answered.

"What have you heard about me?" Edith said, flirting, as they walked.

"That you are as beautiful as the sun after rain. With many colours that lift the spirits."

"You have heard that." She raised an eyebrow. "Father, what did you tell them about me in town?" She enjoyed the banter. A slight sway in her brows as she said. "We don't often get to speak with strangers."

One of the brothers looked at Morgund. "I had heard that you are all devils with tails," softening his look, thereafter, conforming to his father's wish not to extend ill intent.

"Not I, my mother hid me from the rest being so ashamed of me without one." Morgund asked Edith. "I have heard similar of the English, is it not true?"

"You mustn't tease." Edith scowled and punched his shoulder.

"Your tail is showing, I can see it." She smiled.

It was ridiculously pleasant and warmed his heart, Morgund thought. "Father make him stop," she giggled. "He's teasing."

The menfolk laughed. They were on a rough path crossed with many branching trails that only an experienced woodsman could have stayed on track on, in dense forest. Coming to a cliff they climbed a woven ladder immediately retracted after their ascent.

Morgund asking about these elaborate precautions was told that long ago when Cristo's wife Sylvia still lived they resided in a hut in another part of the forest. Cristo was away trading when group of nobles chanced upon their dwelling, they believed the forest to be solely theirs. Poaching was a crime punishable by hanging.   To live in the forest an even greater crime.  Sylvia hid with the children, but on seeing the intruders prepare a torch, she ran to them, pleading with them that they not burn them out as winter was coming, without shelter they could perish.  She accosted a rider who bent down and drove the hilt of his sword into her face, felling her. Her eldest son, John,   ran forward as the lifeblood spilled thick.

Riders swept past, right and left, leaving their hut burning to the ground, Sylvia diminishing, a mess of broken teeth, her face bent unrecognisable.  John and his brother did their best, but the injury was too great, they couldn't stop the blood. After lingering in pain for a week she died.  A cave sheltered the family throughout winter.  Cristo killed a bear thus saved them from starvation but hardship extracted a toll.   Many times empty stomachs had ached and Edith sobbed.  Those older endured their pain in silence.

"It is a sad tale," Morgund said.

"It is not a tale.  A good woman killed for nothing." Cristo, his voice breaking.  "The woman I loved, still do."

Morgund avoided Cristo's eyes.  Deep emotional scars would rip asunder if faced with an unflinching stare, Morgund knew.  He lived each day appearing to be a whole person when he knew he was not.  He was playing a game which couldn't continue.  These people endured suffering and he felt kinship towards them, understanding.  But still he kept his problems deeply hidden.

The gulf of blackness got deeper.  Cheerful faces he suddenly found disturbing.  Coming over a rise, Morgund saw a small cultivation and a field lying fallow.  Some sheep and cattle grazing in an adjacent field and a large substantial house stood to one side of the fields and the house, he noticed, had a loft.

"Its a fine place you've got," Morgund said distractedly.

"With two fine sons a man can accomplish much."

"The cattle and sheep, how did you get them here?"

"I make a good living trading furs.  Few others risk it.  It was much hard work getting the beasts here.  I bought the calves and lambs at market.  We drove them through the forest, and hauled them up, a process I wouldn't care to repeat.  Of course, it took many trips, as each time we could carry only three.  We require a sure supply of meat and the sheep feed us and keep us in the garments of the town men."

They entered the house.  Morgund received new dry clothes and was fed.  When the time came to tell his story, whilst living through it in his mind, this his latest period of calm broke.  His spirits crumbled.  Tears streamed down his face.

"What has caused your pain?" Cristo asked, comforting hi with a smile.

"A sorrow so great I cannot bear to speak of it." The wetness sprung from his eyes  unstoppable.

"Then don't ... If friends you need, we are they." Cristo crossed over to Morgund and put a blanket around him.

Edith ran over and kissed him, then touched his face. "I know why you came." She squeezed his hand and smiled. "To ask for my hand."

Morgund smiled. The others laughed. It was a good attempt to overcome the pain. He knew he would tell them when he was able to, and that it would help him. Cristo arranged some bedding on the floor, away from the others.

"You will be all right Morgund. As I've said, you're amongst friends. Stay with us, no harm will come to you," Cristo said.

Morgund nodded and was left to think alone. One day hurt might end and perhaps he could rebuild his life.  He could not go to Runnymead. That he could not do. No longer could he live up to Seward's example of bravery and toughness. Hopefully Seward would believe he had not survived. He knew these people had endured great suffering, however, they had each other, that explained their strength. He had no one.

How could he have told Seward of his fears, he was too ashamed to admit to his weakness. He desired Seward's respect, not his pity. Could one so brave as Seward understand his dread, he doubted it, and without Seward to fall back on, his courage was evaporating.

In the morning hearing the swing of an axe and of wood being chopped.  Morgund went out and saw John.  Up and down, another block, halved.  John, had his shirt off, his upper body rippling with muscle as he manoeuvred the axe. Morgund, who had filled out somewhat since beginning training with Seward realised that this activity would increase his size and strength.

Noticing Morgund watching him, John turned to him.  "I've had enough, take the axe."  John's heavy eye fell on Morgund.

It felt weighty, difficult to balance in the downswing but concentrating on hitting the centre of the wood, soon he had the axe there and liked the sound the axe made as it struck, a thunk, little shifts of body weight gave him extra power.

"Letting the axe do the work is the secret of being a good woodcutter," John said.

And Morgund was doing just that, his ability in swordsmanship giving him a head start in acquiring the axemans art.

"That will do," John said.  "Have a spell.  You're stronger than you look and handle an axe well."

"Thank you, John.  It is peaceful here.

John smiled.  Morgund's face was transformed into a look of beauty.  In between the sound of the wood being cut bird song from the forest drifted up to him.   Surrounded by mountain scenery, Morgund could afford to lose himself in simple chores.  He took the axe again.  It was calming to his mind, this, he submerged himself in it.

Abruptly the source of his contentment vanished when Edith called, "Morgund and John, come inside, I have prepared hot cakes."

Work of the day would have to wait, and the cut and thrust of conversation was upon him. He tried to dispel ill humour. Edith meant well and he would be companionable to her. A routine developed the pace of life slow. The days filled with hard work, the nights spent in quiet contemplation, fair fellowship and serenity. As serene and calming as it was he knew he must leave but until he did, must use his time here well. Morgund felt compelled to review his situation and cast about he did for a way to take his destiny into his own hands. Seward told him no matter how long it takes, train hard, forget the goal, concentrate on the small details of it thereby you will attain the goal, wise words from a hardy warrior, a forged path for him to follow. A road to Damascus.

A road of self realization. He could no longer live meek, he had seen power. Felt a dull thudding ache to be a swordsman, as great as any. Better. Godlike. Dispensing death. To be someone they told tales about many generations on.

One day he would fight a crucial fight that would determine his reputation. He knew it was coming and he wanted to be ready for it. Even if he failed, his will, wouldn't. Seward often said the best swordsmen were those who trained longer and harder then anyone else. He was right. That was what Morgund would do now. His quest was investing in himself, creating a new, he. It was the suppression of self-doubt, fear, passiveness.

Morgund realized how he must ensure his life, he must beat his weakness, his fear, and pour his will into his ambition. Morgund, who was prodigious in his application, cut pieces of wood to sword length. In this way he sparred with Simon and John. When defence was breached strikes were pulled, so as not to cause injury. Speed and technique improved together with footwork and judgement of distance.

Seward had instilled in Morgund the importance of unarmed combat. If disarmed one could continue the fight and often when sword made contact you could kick a part of your opponents body, for instance his leg, easily. A half decent kick could be enough to unbalance an opponent for a decisive thrust. The groin kick was the most brutally effective method. Training was realistic and Morgund learned that physical knocks were necessary to toughen mind and body. It was a vital part of the process but requiring moderation. Injuries required time to heal and too much punishment tended to wear down rather than enhance toughness.

After a heavy session bruises were bathed in cold mountain streams to deaden pain and to reduce swelling. The other two, older and stronger should have dominated Morgund but Morgund's commitment was the greater, putting in many extra hours attempting mastery.

Alone, moving back and forth, practising. Coordinating his body. Singing a song with it, slowly building his melody. Seeking to be as perfect as perfection itself. But also knowing perfection was somehow unrealistic, a goal, he would never meet. But endless striving in attaining it made it seem preordained. He was not an ordinary being, even now, not long begun on his long journey.

Having been in constant danger he was determined to be prepared for the future which could hold anything. That wasn't the only reason he trained for now, it had captured his heart. Excellence in this or any art is an obsession. Morgund awoke to this truth. Rest days were important to. On those days he walked down to the river and lay back listening to the flow of the river, the sounds coming from the trees. Today, he was alone with his thoughts at the river. Water splashed over rocks played downstream. In the background the intriguing notes of birds, all relaxing, calming. Cristo joined him.

Morgund learned that Cristo had been a monk. His family entered him in the monastery young, his life filled with long days of boring quiet, a life Cristo was not suited to, which was ironic considering his current situation. Sylvia had been married to an abusive drunkard who beat her.

Losing a baby, she decided then to flee, but beforehand she sought a prayer of protection. Two people seeking an escape had found each other. It seemed so fitting and had been, until that dreadful day, when the hunters came. Cristo changed the subject to avoid spoiling their day.

"If ever there was in a place to avoid strife, this is it. You will see there is contentment and happiness here." He wanted Morgund to stay, for he knew Edith wished him to, it would be the perfect arrangement, for one day she must wed and Cristo wanted her to remain in the forest.

"What kind of happiness?" Morgund asked.

"Listen," Cristo said and turned his head towards a dense thicket, "Harmonies in the background make you want to listen to them, the birdsong. Happy magic, that's what kind and here there is freedom from despicable rulers."

Cristo swished his hand through the air, "Let us put our feet in the river and have its soft rush run across our feet, it will flow through our hearts, it will repair us."

"You show good sense Cristo," Morgund replied.

"Places exist where composure can be found," Cristo said.

Morgund as he sat with his feet dangling into the water felt he had found such a place. Little did they speak, the mood didn't require it. The caress of the water made a cure for melancholy. The sensation clung to their feet long after both of them had retreated from it. But with its loss a change of mood.

On the way home Morgund appeared down, his earlier contentment, gone. "Morgund, things aren't so bad are they?" He heard.

Being betrayed by Alexander left him depressed. Having been trapped into believing in his friendship hurt, made him feel a fool. He couldn't be safe in his homeland. He missed his mother, his familiar haunts. Not yet fourteen, and grievously homesick. All these things troubled him. How could he put it all into words.

"What is it that troubles you?" Cristo asked.

The darkest of his fears was the long term danger ... and now his life was such a misery. Who to trust? How best to restore his fortunes. The destiny of his family was in his hands, there was no one else. Wondering if such a thing was important, knowing somehow it was. Looking into Cristo's eyes, he realised he had to say something and said, "Shadows walk across my soul."

"Not yours only." A sympathetic nod, a step or two, then. "Thinking of past wrongs does no good."

Morgund didn't want to mention homesickness as a cause, he was not prepared to admit to such a childish complaint. "Bitterness of betrayal so tart. Memories so cruel," he said.

"Let them go then, Morgund. Latching onto them won't do you any good. Perhaps after a while torments will relent. They do, you know." Cristo realised, as one who had experienced it, that a great wrong had been done and it disturbed him.

He also guessed correctly that it was in part homesickness and mother anguish. "Scotland," letting the word play upon his mind, "Broken wastes, full of wild men, strange beasts, winged serpents, and it is said that Scotsmen drink the blood of Englishmen" Cristo's attempt to cheer up Morgund failed for Morgund only heard him indistinctly.

Cristo spoke on. If Morgund heard him Cristo didn't know it. Morgund did hear, he thought they were sounds without sense. These words didn't improve him. But Cristo's friendship was a thing of value and he was willing enough to realise it and be thankful for it. Once inside, Morgund felt better and after talking with the boys and Edith, for a time, better still. They always lightened his spirits, they were his best tonic.

That night Cristo sat up and talked with Morgund. Cristo knew Morgund didn't like to talk about his upset but he also knew that if given the opportunity and showed enough friendship, he would talk and that Morgund would improve, thereby, so he forced his way on verbally explaining his theory.

"You have plummeted to the depths of despair and have come back to lead a normal life."

Morgund liked hearing that he seemed whole and sound.

"But you are contending against inner matters that are threatening to overwhelm you.
"Yes, my mind plays upon hardships."

"These memories will lose their sharpness and you will learn from them."

"How?"

"By using them as a tool for growth."

"Explain what you mean."

"Morgund, you feel lacklustre now but you will not always feel so."

"But how will I learn?"

"The answer will come from within."

"I would like to be restored to a normal condition, with regard to my nerves and confidence."

"You know how best to rectify it. It is too much you've been called upon to do when too young. All men in danger come to a threshold of distress thereby losing harmony. Conquering and overcoming leaves a shadow, but also leaves a strength as well. You know yourself better now, which is a decided advantage."

"My mind dwells on death, my father's and on others. I have seen many. My own death seems imminent and it is frightening. It is a plague on me."

"Your appointment with death is quickening to its moment, with this realisation, you've passed into manhood. Rest and strengthen, be sound enough to face your next conflict, for something tells me it will arise."

The candle had burned low by this time, the signal they depart to their beds. Once there Morgund thought long about Cristo's advice. Appreciating Cristo's intelligence, his willingness to help, he decided to take each day as it came while continually preparing for threat and pay back in whichever way he could, Cristo for his kindness. Cristo possessed a wealth of knowledge.

This new life felt temporary, here would never be home, however he appreciated it, for now. One day he would stride forth back into Scotland and face whatever fate held for him there, or be tormented by his lack of manliness till his dying day. Until then, however, it was pleasant.

Each night brought new topics. Morgund learned much about the world, its history, generals, great battles fought in the past, all well told. The croft filled with tale telling and debating. Information from the outside was especially pleasing, and covered from every angle. They had not been to town for many months so any news was old. Cristo stocked with winter furs decided they would travel to town and catch up. One of the boys would stay behind with Edith.

She did not like this, complaining bitterly. "Father that is unfair."

"The next spring you can come with us, Edith," Cristo placated. "We will camp in town for a few days and you can see shops and buy clothes."

"I want a sword on this trip" John said.

Cristo turned to him, "What is this? Are you planning to leave us and become a knight? What do you want a sword for?"

"I want one too," Simon chimed in.

"I thought this sword play was mirth, now each of you want a live blade. It's an expensive piece of equipment, I can't buy you both one, not straight away, at least."

Simon looked at John. "John, I'll toss a coin for who gets the first sword."

"A fair way to decide. You toss, I'll call," John replied.

John winning, spent the rest of the night imagining his sword, eagerly anticipating this trip to town three months hence. One by one, the days gained themselves on, by and by, it was three months hence. The furs were good, so well laden, they travelled to make trade, to the city and to find a smithy. They watched him work, made comments, were fascinated how a metal object gradually changed until it become a thing of beauty and of nobility, a sword. The smithy handed it to John. Holding it mesmerised with rapture, he didn't speak but his face said it all, if only those who loved him would have realized the danger he was in. John was now a part of a sacred brotherhood of soldiers, knights, even kings. The sword was their symbol of power. Those that held it were to be feared.

That these men were feared because they could kill or get others to kill escaped his notice. He held a dangerous misconception. Back at home John allowed no word to betray him and his life continued much the same. Only his eyes changed but no one noticed.

One day Morgund looked out at the distant green, the cool beauty drawing him. Unencumbered by duties deciding to descend the ladder and see it up close. Taking a bow and a quiver, intent on practising his archery learned from these Englishmen. If he shot a deer it would feed them, venison was always welcome. At the base of the cliff threading his way out to the sand bar near the river. A ford allowed him passage to the far bank. Reaching the place he'd started for, which had looked closely hugged by trees, in fact it contained numerous fields, thick with flowers.

He couldn't explain the treeless openings, different soil perhaps, or, or, what? He wondered over their existence, although not coming up with a solution, enjoying them immensely. They gave views of open skies allowed warmth from the sun to bathe him. Kept on walking, taking in changes, trees some bent, fallen, in shadow, some light.

Open spaces began to restrict with the land becoming thicker in forest, not totally obscuring the sky yet, but if the trees continued to close in around him, he wouldn't see five metres, let alone the sky. Further on, trees tightly interwoven so that with each few steps he had to take to them with his staff to make a way through.

Abruptly entering a clearing of lowly vegetation Morgund came near a hillock with a large broken conifer.  He went there.  Continuing walking passing a while without incident, growing bored with the sameness of it all when a stag appeared, noble beast only slightly too distant to expend an arrow at.  It disappeared.  Firstly it had raised its head from beside a sapling.  Thinking it might still be on the other side of it Morgund moved cautiously forward.  Passing the small tree he saw it again.  The deer had resumed grazing, it had leapt the log as he had thought.   Whether it was unconcerned or unaware that danger was present Morgund was unsure.  An unmistakable feeling that the deer had seen him, it was preposterous of course, but nevertheless he felt this.  It raised its head again, this time appearing to gaze closely at him.  He stopped and the deer moved off a few strides.

The wind changed and blew from his back.  The stag must get his scent and flee.  It did not.  He was intrigued.  Hugging the earth and creeping towards it, whilst it was below his line of sight, he gained on it, until he could hear it.  Then there it was just ahead.  The hackles on his neck rose.  He surmised the animal was unfamiliar with man therefore it did not feel threatened.   Deer were notably curious and it appeared this was the explanation for it came towards him.  *How close would it come?* He wondered.  It stopped.  Looking startled, head up, and its nose testing the air.

Whatever had disturbed its peace, no longer did, the head went down, it began to feed.  Morgund unslung his bow and slipped a dart next to the notch.  Slowly he took the bow up until he aimed his arrow at the deer.  Suddenly the animal unleashed a burst of speed and was gone.  Morgund smiled.  He had imagined the creature possessed of unnatural intelligence.  He had almost expected it to speak.   His mind was open to superstition, he realised.

In a glade, dimensioned of narrow width he stopped and sat. As Morgund thought about the deer and the landscape, he was thinking how he would, forever, remember this journey, this beauty and calmness he had experienced. Long, hungry now, he wished he brought the deer down, his stomach pinched. To his right clustered a group of fir trees, evenly spaced, or nearly so, the ground here, heavily strewn with pine needles. Morgund passed between a gap in the branches. He trod into shadows, and through low hanging vines. On the soft footfalls the scent of pine was delightful. Another wood, where the conifers were interestingly shaped and high, their bark, dense and rough.

When he was in the full sunlight again, swaying limbs and the sun low on the horizon. On a gradual rise parkland grew less and the forest thick. The quality of the trees deteriorated scrappy saplings in poor soil, impenetrable thorny bushes so care was needed to negotiate through. The lower ground cover here was prickly and dangerous. His footing was unsure as the ground was precariously interspersed with furrows and logs. He thought of turning, but had come too far to do so, so he persevered and was rewarded by coming out on lower slopes hardly forested at all and kindly proportioned. The hour was late and darkness stalked. Morgund ran downhill to the river and back towards the ladder and finally arrived home in darkness. He felt a special appreciation to be indoors and sheltered, basking in warmth, safe, partaking of food and company. Edith questioned him on his journeyings and he told of the places he had seen. Subsequently, he took her with him on trips, not too far, close by and it was good for them.

Each day now backs were bent working to dislodge weeds, from their vegetable garden, they worked hard. On this day it was midsummer and hot. Edith fussing over them, took them out drinks. When they came back inside after the working day a cup of cider was taken. Each afternoon they savoured it.

Edith poured Morgund's, as she did, she winked at him boldly and he winked back and laughed. Morgund decided then to stay here. One night, he had his first kiss and a promise was made.

Morgund and Edith sat on a haystack behind the house. "Ask what meal you want made and I will prepare it for you Morgund. You know I am a good cook. I will make a good wife, you know that."

She prompted him when he didn't reply. "You know that? You know I will be a suitable wife for you. If I made a wish it would be that I could marry you, my dearest wish. Answer me. My wish is to marry you. Do you agree that we should be sweethearts?" Her eyes were huge. He could almost hear her heart beating within her chest.

In reply, he kissed her. No greater contentment could Morgund have had  Joy swept every particle of him. Only she existed. They spent hours entwined together lying hidden in fields sharing their closeness feeling swept up in the power of their passion. This idyllic journey would fade but the awe he felt at her beauty would never leave him. It brought a smile to his lips years later whenever he thought of it, of how much he had loved her. Everything about her fascinated him. Scotland seemed far away.

All went well until she saw another young man. She accompanied them all into town trading furs. Edith allowed herself to fasten her affections onto another boy, a young townsman who sought to turn her head and succeeded. She wanted a dramatic turn to her love. She was young, she wanted Morgund to pine for her, to win her back. She didn't understand the gift she had. True friends, true friends who suited each physically and in temper. When they got home she appeared to pine for the townsman, seeing what Morgund would do. Morgund saw it for what it was and he thought they'd be close again, but events changed all.

There was not much to do after planting so time was on their hands. John still the only brother with a blade had become quieter and more thoughtful since. Cristo falsely believed that he had achieved some measure of maturity. None were aware that he had lost touch with reality, that he possessed a disturbing idea. They would learn what he thought and that day would come soon.

The three young men set off on a trip of long duration to a place where the forest was open, and trees were wide and majestic. It was a royal place. It should have dissuaded them from staying there, for no doubt it would be the haunt of noble men. On the very edge of the forest, they were.

Deciding on a foot race, after marking out a course, they lined up. They were off, feeling young and fit and strong. When one got ahead of the others he slowed taunting those behind him. Their yells dominated the forest as were the sounds of other men swallowed by their noise.

"My father's old dog can run faster than you Morgund," yelled Simon.

"The race isn't over yet. If you could run as fast as you talk, you'd already have won," Morgund shouted back.

They tired, and the talking slowed.

"Nearly finished," thought Morgund, nearing the finishing line.

John won. The air was muggy and hot, and the sound of their breath heavy to their ears as it started raining, fine refreshing rain. The cool mist felt good. This green wonderland would become a cauldron. Walking with hands on hips, trying to regain his breath, it was Morgund who alerted them. "What was that? Listen."

The rain was heavier now, it was difficult to hear over it. Trying to listen above the sound of pounding hearts and the rain, none spoke. Soft ground and their talking had failed to warn them of approaching horsemen.

"There." Morgund pointed. "Horsemen! Run."

Riders broke through the undergrowth at a gallop. Morgund knew the consequences if caught. Being in largely open country the chance of escape was slight. John could not bear the thought of running. He was armed, so he would fight. He turned. Morgund could not believe his eyes. John must be sacrificing himself, for them, slowing down the mounted men so his two companions could escape. After another few steps, he turned also, determined to convince John to run with him. John was taking an erect stance. "Come on you bastards, I'll kill you."

This was madness, surely he was aware he had no chance. Running towards John, Morgund saw John take a swing at a swordsman, then saw an enemy bending a bow, firing. And too quickly, the arrow came, hitting the mark, piercing John's neck. John, gurgling, grasping the arrow.

A frothy red muck was gushing out from his open mouth. John sunk to his knees, his face deathly pale. He spoke between gasping bloody breaths. "May God forgive me for my arrogance," he said and died.

Morgund, surrounded held his sword ready prepared to sell his life dearly, he thought to perhaps get in one strike before it ended. However, it was very disheartening to see what had just happened to John.

"Not him ... hold." A richly dressed man addressed his archer who had Morgund in his sights.

He spoke to Morgund. "There is nothing more you can do. He is dead, drop your sword and you may live. If you attempt anything foolish one of my archers will kill you." Morgund dropped his sword.

"What about the other one, the one who ran away?" asked a young nobleman.

"Forget him. This is Morgund MacAedh, a rival for Alexander's throne. King John will be pleased. Bring him a horse," he said to a man at arms. "He is noble."

One of the men at arms dismounted and offered Morgund his horse. The man at arms walked beside him. Suddenly Morgund's life had taken another unexpected turn.

The richly dressed man rode at Morgund's side. "Morgund I saw you at Runnymead, do you not remember me?"

"No."

"I am Sir Clifford Montgomery, I am a loyal subject of King John. One of the few remaining. King John has spies everywhere. He knows Alexander tried to kill you. That man is no friend to my king, do not mistake he will hold you dear Morgund. With you he can topple that foxy swine Alexander. King John will put you in his place. Of unlucky a fold I am told you are, but some luck abounds for me to find you here in so vast and unexpected a place."

"You know much of Scottish matters. Were you looking for me?"

The man smiled at Morgund. "No. But lucky in finding you sweet boy ... amongst us you will be royally treated as befits one of your position."

"What is expected of me?"

"Never mind all that, all will be explained. I'm sorry about your friend. I had no choice, he would have killed one of us."

In the dim grey light of the little glade, Morgund remembered the glint in John's eye. He closed his for a moment remembering, prickly, brave, bustling, John, Morgund should of fled, it would've been the wisest move. He should have taken more notice of the change in John.

Montgomery spoke, "The farmer doesn't leave the crop in the field to rot." Morgund looked confused. "Some men learn the way of the sword and have courage, but alone it is nothing. One must choose the right companions. If one is permitted to. A man can befriend kings."

Morgund should have listened more for he would grow to react to what was brought rather than bring on what was best.

---

IN CANTERBURY THEY found the king and learned that civil war had begun. It was brought about when king John fell out with many of his nobles to the point where the only solution as they saw it was in overthrowing him. Alexander was involved with the rebel forces. Morgund as the only Scotsman in the hall was singled out by King John who spoke to him. "There is a Scotsman amongst us, what say he?"

"Only this Sire, that as a king he is unworthy."

"What am I to do? Tell me that."

John beckoned Morgund forward and indicated he lower himself. Bent low, Morgund received a fatherly pat on his shoulder.

"I will tell you." John said, to Morgund quietly, to him alone. "He will die." Then the king stood. His voice boomed. "That so unworthy a head should wear a crown is wrong. He shall wear that crown."

John pointed at Morgund. His eyes bored into Morgund searching him closely. The eyes were small, sharp, glistening with intellect but became filling with wash. He turned to the assembly. "I shall have his head."

Momentarily unsure whether he referred to Alexander or Morgund, they didn't know what to think, for king John was still pointing at Morgund, until responding to their uncertainty, he said, "Alexander will die."

The audience rose, applauding. King John continued. "Alexander's head I shall hold in my hand."

The words were spoken with compelling venom. The king shook uncontrollably as his emotions overcame him and his hot tears burned, this ungovernable temper taking him unawares. A strained gasp he let out, of utter pain. Tears erupting. These seizures happened often, struck without warning. With difficulty he sought to suppress them and go on with important matters. But Alexander would not go from his mind, bringing on tortured torment, freezing out all other thought. He lapsed into stillness. Finally he walked off, shoulders slumped, appearing white and sick.

His mind had degenerated into a disordered mess and he needed time to dispel his mind-demons. Morgund saw John for what he was. A dangerous man. To be angered beyond sanity was frightening in any man, and particularly in a king. Later Morgund asked someone what he made of it, and received the common sense reply. "A Plantagenet can be whatever he is. We onlookers must not see, or worse still speak, of that Morgund could cause us harm." A measured look brought home the danger. Morgund remembered those chilly eyes, and immediately felt intimidated. Morgund wanted very little to do with King John, and thankfully wasn't to see him often.

King John resolving to invade Scotland intended to use Morgund as his puppet. Supporting Morgund's claim to the Scots throne would enable those Scots opposed to Alexander to rally to Morgund, once Alexander had fallen, Morgund himself would fall. But until he invaded he had no use for him.

Morgund who must be kept in readiness, was assigned a keeper, a man to be responsible for his safety. Richard Talbot, a swordsman, a flatterer, a schemer, ruthlessly ambitious, engaging when the need arose, he cultivated Morgund's friendship, and caused no disharmony to occur between them. Before they had parted King John had given Morgund a sword, finely inlaid, carved with Damascene carving, the blade of the finest Toledo steel.

Morgund missed Cristo, Simon, and Edith. They were his surrogate family and his sweetheart even if she disputed that, he thought with an odd smile. He knew he would have gotten her back. He knew how she really felt about him. But another thought he had, of his mother, he could not bear her absence. It was his responsibility to protect her to see to her well being. He wanted to ensure nothing untoward affected her and how could he do that away from her ... unable to do anything.

Morgund passed time with monks in Canterbury learning how to read and write, all the while being jokingly chided by Talbot for seeking to engage in these unmanly pursuits. Scribes were thought of as being beneath the knightly class. Knights were at the apex of mediaeval society. Scholarly monks made up the second class. The third class, traders were thought of as nothing more than up-jumped peasants, yet, they were not permanently placed, for sometimes wealthy merchants changed position, a grateful monarch might ennoble a merchant, or, as sometimes happened, they married into the nobility - the English De La Pole family became Earls of Sussex after starting out as money lenders.

Morgund thought all knowledge was worthwhile and learned all he could from whomever he could and his development in arts undesired in one of his class developed at pace as did his swordsmanship. Talbot knew that one day Morgund would be an extremely proficient fighting man, which pleased him, for it was his responsibility to train Morgund - he would gain credit for it.

The kitchen was Morgund's favourite place where he had warm food and relaxed company to pass the time with. Seward told him that the heavier stronger man possesses the edge in combat, so Morgund consumed much, gorging himself when he could. Thereby he who had been small for his age grew thick limbed. This was not a disagreeable life but he was missing his friends and his homeland ever more as time passed. The itch to return was beginning to become unbearable. If he knew what was to occur in Scotland he'd have had no peace of mind at all. Alexander had returned to Scotland ill humoured. He had heard of Morgund's whereabouts and that King John was his protector. He summoned MacCainstacairt.

"Yes, my Lord," MacCainstacairt said, on bended knee before him. "I want that nest of vipers done over with, those who are supportive of Morgund MacAedh."

"Tell me what you want and it shall be done Sire."

"Burn them." A king planning to kill his subjects is not a pleasant sight. Not that MacCainstacairt was a man to speak for his heart was black also. Many were his misdeeds, yet he thought that he's not seen a more evil look.

"But I will need men to add to my own, and arms Sire."

"Certainly you shall have them," Alexander replied.

The men lent to MacCainstacairt were accompanied by a lesser known supporter of Alexander's, only a minor castle knight, nonetheless competent, Sir Bernard Renshaw. This servant, Renshaw, was a relative to the Comyns. His task overseeing of the king's men to ensure they were used wisely by MacCainstacairt. Allow MacCainstacairt his way but to keep him within guidelines set by me, the king had said. The matter would be dealt with suitably as Alexander wanted it dealt with, Renshaw would see to that. Renshaw was in addition given licence that if any conflict arose with MacCainstacairt to overrule him but if no such an act occurred, MacCainstacairt was to believe his was the leadership.

Therefore Alexander could blame him for it all. The plan was for his soldiers to be arrayed as highlanders so it would seem an instance of highland affray. Alexander imagined the heady feeling of importance, MacCainstacairt would feel at leading such an important mission. His Celtic vanity was his weakness and laughable, he was in fact so typical of his race. Massacre seemed imminent. It was not to be. On the way some of MacCainstacairt's men rather than disguising their intentions, made them clear, whether out of pity or stupidity, none discovered. Warned in the village, chaos ensued. A few, ignoring the warning, suspending their belief were viciously set upon, others who were more astute, and in the majority, made it away clear.

Far away to the south, Morgund meanwhile toiled unsparingly in fields of summer straw giving his body nourishment through fierce labour. By this activity he grew. The following spring when Morgund sought out Talbot in the ale house he found Seward waiting for him.

Gripping hands firmly, they smiled at each other as true comrades. Seward saw that Morgund had grown, and told him so. Morgund was pleased to hear him say so. Then his own story. William had returned to Scotland shortly after leaving the castle, but Seward refused to go, deciding not to leave England until he had found Morgund. Not knowing where to look, he had cast a leaf in stillness. A slight breeze blew giving him a direction, a completely wrong direction as it happened. They laughed at that. He had finally heard a rumour that a young Scotsman was a ward of the king in a southern town. He knew southern England well, now having laboured from town to town looking for Morgund. Whilst this was going on, Richard Talbot eyed Seward suspiciously.

Seward could make Morgund difficult to control, even persuade him to leave Canterbury. Better to make the newcomer gone. But how? This was awkward.

Talbot questioned himself, looking for an answer, and thought. It was best, surely to pick a fight and kill him. In no other way could he ensure he was not thwarted in any purpose opposed to his own. Talbot remembered Morgund commenting on Seward's prowess as a fighter. This did not concern him, Richard Talbot was one of the premier swordsman in England. Surely he could easily dispose of a semi-barbarous Scot.

"Seward, I hear you are something of a swordsman."

Seward did not like the look on Talbot's face when he said it.

Morgund interjected, "Seward is the very best."

"Best where?" Talbot snickered at Seward, curious to see how he'd respond.

"Best anywhere." Morgund replied.

Talbot's eyes never left Seward's as he said, "Is that so Seward?"

Not liking the man, deliberately casual, Seward said, "It is not some small skill I possess."

"You are high handed man Seward."

"I merely make a statement of fact. You asked me a question and I answered it. If answering a question here is highhanded, forgive me, but we have simple ways in Scotland."

"I like you not, Scotsman."

"Despondency does cast over me at that."

Talbot raised his voice, "Have you cut down English women and children on our borders? Perhaps this is where you've gained this great skill you say you have."

Talbot was insufferably arrogant. A crowd gathered, smelling blood. "Do not let fear make a captive of your tongue, Seward." Talbot sneered.

"Is this Englishman your friend Morgund?" Seward had a worried cast to his eyes.

"He is friendly towards me, but no, the only true friends I have are MacRuari, MacSwain and yourself." MacRuari was a friend he had left behind in Ross. "He wants a fight Seward. Give him one."

Talbot was blustering again his insults crassly provocative. After addressing the tavern crowd he turned to Seward. Seeing a lengthy tirade of loud speak coming, Seward caused its halt, or more correctly, averted it, with a look of the direst menace. "Enough Talbot, or I will split your sickening tongue."

And by then a sword Seward held. Talbot drew his own and the lamplight reflected off the blade. "Outside, where innocents will not be harmed," Talbot said.

Seward nodded. Quickly, warily, as Morgund watched his back, Seward dodged through the crowd to torch lit grounds. He waited as time rolled sluggishly by. "What is Talbot doing? Finishing a jug of ale?"

The man was making a fool of him. Morgund watched, concerned for Seward. Morgund knew Seward couldn't ignore such insults. How could he lie down and ignore Talbot but Talbot was much renowned. Perhaps it would have been better to fight inside where confusion and obstacles might have allowed Seward a better chance to overcome Talbot. Seward's own advice on facing a superior foe.

As if hearing his thoughts Seward said, "I could not fight inside amongst innocents, we might have cut somebody who has no part in our contest."

Talbot burst through the door suddenly cutting the air in a figure of eight missed Seward's nose by a mere hairs width and nearly caught his head again moments later. Caught unawares Seward nearly died there and then. It was instinct and training which allowed him to survive. He had the relaxation and trained reflexes to maximize his defence. Having ducked the whirling metal he came up with his own. Taken to his hilt was Talbot. Seward's sword was blocked in his chest, stuck, like pinning soft cheese the blade wobbling slightly. Standing on Talbot's chest to withdraw his sword, an escape of air occurred and bright red blood spilled shockingly disturbed from its common paths. Seward and Morgund didn't tarry long, they rode away quickly. A slight breeze chilled them.

"Life so stable, was a dream, as easily disposed of, as a candle blown," Seward said.

"That was neatly done," Morgund replied.

"He brought about his own death," Seward sounded defensive.

"Yes, of course." And Morgund continued on, in case Seward felt unjust in the taking of a life; Morgund knew Seward would never do so lightly. "He did, cause his own death."

"Of course he did. He had no cause to be so. It is good it was done to me, another's recourse could only be to die on defending."

Morgund remained silent. From the distant inn he heard a dogs barking. A mournful fading yelp. At least Talbot was mourned, by one, at least, occurred to him. Eventually it was drowned out by movement as they rode off. They stopped to rest and eat, then pressed on.

The next day they made camp, intending to seek fresh meat, on foot, which would allow the horses a rest. That night, with the fire going warmly, Morgund looked up into vast space filled with swirls of cosmic light.

Morgund risked a sentence, for Seward's close brush with death had disturbed him, had made him silent and morose. "This outdoor life is good. Townsfolk never realise it."

"Do you really believe so Morgund?"

The facile way Seward said this required a like response. "No, not all the time, only when I'm bored and stuck for something to say." Morgund ventured his opinion again. "But seriously Seward, it is good, until the rain washes you."

Seward disagreed. "There's ever something, constantly, wasps, or bugs, and rain and cold, it's never good. Better a warm bed."

"Seward, you sound old and dull."

"Not filled with youthful nonsense you mean," A small smile exited, however, Morgund couldn't see it.

Obviously Seward had not regained his full measure of happiness, Morgund decided. Looking into the abyss of death was to know what lay beyond, which was nothing, a blank shroud, a doorway into black nothing. Having come so close Morgund knew, and he knew the thought caused anxiety. He believed this was the cause of Seward's change. Seeing Seward made his heart quicken, then his pulse slowed for he had learned self control. Self control was at the centre of mastering the swordsman's art and Morgund had learned a measure of it. Morgund was determined to be content with things, life was good, or mostly, it was, at any rate. To enjoy life to the full most, that was his aim. However vain the effort, he thought to himself.

"Still in a bleak mood Seward?" He would prick at him, to allay boredom.

"The hunting is scarce, not even a partridge or a quail and we have no coin for food," Seward replied, ignoring Morgund's teasing.

"What are we to do then?" Morgund asked.

"It is dangerous to stay. Both the rebels and king John would hand you over to Alexander if it suited them, or kill you themselves. I have heard John lost his treasure in the sea. He is in dire need of funds. Alexander may have contacted him about you."

Seward proceeded to tell Morgund that king John had taken his treasury with him. On attempting a crossing of a tidal estuary, had lost it, the advancing tide caught his baggage. A most disagreeable event for this benighted king. John had no luck, and had earned the title 'Lack land', lacking sense, lacking friends and lacking funds.

Seward gestured at surrounding fields. "Not even these are tilled, with war sweeping the land. We two must fight to earn enough to live and equip ourselves. The northern rebels are like to win. As common mounted esquires, our identity will not be known and the armies are full of foreigners attempting to earn by the sword, no notice will be taken of us."

Good coin was being paid for experienced fighting men, it was true. As they sorely needed money, they rode into Durham and signed to fight alongside Sir Walter De Vesky against king John.

---

BEFORE THIS WEEK was out, many living would be dead. Morgund was about to undergo his greatest test, his first battle and was silently tense. Seward, older, now an experienced fighter, surveyed the men around him with an almost detached sense of serenity He recalled the stories of the gods of war from his native land, of Thor and Odin, and their great deeds of martial valour. Morgund not long turned sixteen years of age, looked to Seward for confidence, and found it within those coldly glittering, killer eyes.

Confusion reigned amongst the rebel forces. Morgund questioned their wisdom in remaining warlike, awaiting the catastrophe that could only occur to an army without morale or readiness.

In time, however, an order of sorts emerged, the natural leaders taking control of number of men at arms and those more inclined to follow instruction were thankful for the opportunity to do so. Finally, a powerful host, numbering in their hundreds and thousands, they marched south. Near Bedford contact was made with the enemy. These contacts involved the scouts only, to discover size and disposition.

However, with an inexorable and fateful slowness, the two main bodies of the two forces drew upon each other. In the growing dark of a clouded afternoon they stood mutually in full view at a distance measured in hundreds of yards. The darkness of night was encroaching quickly, and with neither side seeing advantage in night fighting, an unquiet truce was established. Until the full light of day, it seemed, nought of significance would occur.

The next morning the sun rose through a smoky haze, the colour of blood. "An unkind omen, Seward," Morgund said, jittery.

Seward looked amused. "As much for them as us."

Morgund's hand played upon a magnificent sword given to him by King John. A work of art, in carving and in inlay, perfectly balanced. He had trained hard, parried, blocked and swept up and down until both man and steel had fused together in splendid synergy.

To Morgund, it seemed to have a will of its own, deftly directing his hand, at times an extension of it. He became dynamic and was driven to lightning speed and adeptness, impressing all who saw him.

From his own personal perspective, he felt like a spectator looking down upon himself watching the exploits, not the swordsman. It was some other great being, so skilled. Not until he sheathed his sword and resumed his former station did this feeling cease. He kept to himself, this elevated state of awareness, deeming it an important secret, and, a key to his success. However, paradoxically he also regarded it as an embarrassment, an admission of wrong-headedness, a strangeness.

At an early stage in his swordsmanship Morgund believed his dexterity and deftness with a blade may be particular to his own personal weapon. However, upon switching weapons, he found he remained equally adept. Constant and fatiguing practise had redesigned him elevated him as if he was borne aloft by wings upon his back. He was scarcely the same Morgund MacAedh, son of Kenneth, who had ventured forth so long ago.

He had once been un-noteworthy. Now, he gave off an aura of danger and readiness. Yet his swordsmanship had been learned in a vacuum, his skill with a blade honed in training sessions where the risk of harm was incidental, and the probability of death nigh on impossible. This, however, was to be a trial by battle a baptism of fire where no sage voice would correct him on the proper swing of a blade or reprimand him for undue recklessness. A battle was unpredictable to all but the most learned of generals and even then it was far from a tame beast.

No, on this field his correction would be a bloody wound, his reprimand a stab between the ribs. He looked over the serried ranks around him and spurred his horse to ride beside Seward who was cantering ahead. His contemplations deserted him when he saw the amassed forces of the enemy.

Morgund, holding the high ground, looked down into the massed ranks of the enemy. They were battle hardened mercenaries, pikes thrust forward. Well positioned in neat orderly squares, and awaiting the events of the day, just as Morgund and Seward were themselves. Morgund and Seward, dismounted. The boggy ground unsuitable for large numbers of horsemen meant today they would fight on foot.

Flocks of ravens, known, as the gallows birds, took to the sky, the carrion birds circled high above knowingly. These black winged, harbingers of death had learned that large numbers of men meant fighting, and the opportunity to scavenge flesh once it was done. They wheeled blackly in the sky on unkind wings, their screeching sickening the men below. They followed expecting to feast on the corpses provided. War, the ravens knew it well. Morgund thought they symbolised all the dark foes who dwelled in the minds of men, set forth in a vision of Armageddon. The End Of Days ... Now, it would be, the End Of Days for many here. The ravens screeching above them didn't seem like earthly birds. Nor did these men, these enemies, men, of this earth. Morgund, neither sought their salvation nor condemnation from this other race, the men he would face in battle, were just that: menacing, alien, and apart.

Morgund and Seward pushed their way closer to the front line on foot. There seemed a particular calmness, or at least solemnity, on the part of the enemy forces, much apart from the jostling and sauntering amongst their own. Morgund and Seward wondered alike, would this be another learning opportunity, or would it be their own end, a blood drenched annihilation.

Hushed tones. The noise of the wind. If he shut his eyes he could think himself alone. It was difficult to believe this calm-quiet, would end. Morgund cast his eyes down at his foes. The rising morning sun illuminated a multitude of faces. Pennants waved in the breeze. Obviously a well trained army. One of these very men he gazed at might kill him. They gazed back at his army with neutrality almost boredom.

For the moment it seemed no battle might occur. That they were simply two large assemblies of men warming themselves in the sun, peering at each other. For now, just peering. A very precious now, the now of peace, so very nearly at an end. Morgund looked at some of the men beside him, many had curiously relaxed expressions. Whether they were acting a part or beyond caring, he couldn't decide. How must he look to them? He wondered. Like a frightened child, no doubt. He knew well enough by now, to reside within a shell of bravado. Might not some of these very men be thinking of slipping away, but remaining here, because others beside them, did not slink off. They were brave the men who stayed and he was one of them. A sudden terrible thought. Now and forever condemned to the earth many men now within his sight. They knew, as he did that great numbers of their own number presently within sight would be condemned to bleed the earth red.

By virtue of endless effort Morgund was well ready. A litany of priorities went through his mind, the first, that his sword still hung by his side. Morgund felt for it. It was still there. He thought over what Seward had told him. To read men was essential. To read intention, to anticipate correctly, essential.

To affect men's thinking and overwhelm them before a blow was struck; essential. That particular maxim redundant in this particular contest where nothing was certain except uncertainty itself. For a master swordsman must not merely match his opponent in skill or speed but excel in will. And, last of all, die like a warrior be proud in death and do honour to the heroic tradition set by those who had gone before.

Whilst sparring one may take his time, attempt to wear down his partner in order to exact a coup de grace stroke, a glorious killing strike. Everything he had learned might count for nothing. Upon the battlefield a duel must be quick, decisive. To allay would surely see an enemy chop into an unarmoured back or hack at him from some other angle. A rarity possessed by only the best of men, to exist in a state of nothingness and be emotionless and effortless and fearless, be as one with the sword know another's thoughts by reading their body, by having the eye and reflexes. To be faceless. To be nothing but the sword. To be a master of the blade one must also be a master of himself.

To grow, a swordsman must fight. Today, Morgund would prove whether swordsmanship counted in a large battle. At least, although, he felt fear, but with it a certain method of thought. He had Seward to thank for that. What a lesson this situation gave him. He was looking through a gateway into another world. It was a rare place to be, offering rare perspective.

A single drumbeat began, like the beating of an immense heart. Looking back, Morgund saw a rebel banner dip. There was a general movement towards the enemy lines, sluggish at first, but with the sense and then with the reality of, a landslide.

Men ran, like waves rushing to shore pitching long, strong. Swords, held high. The drum beat from the hill behind them, drowned out by screaming war cries. Suddenly the waves stopped by a wall of pikes. Within moments Morgund's shield was reduced to splinters and blood, his or another's, blinded him. He was badly shaken by the ferocity of the charge and defence, which nothing could have prepared him for.

Morgund was swept along, grasping his sword firmly, lest it become dislodged amidst the crush. He thought he might be wounded, for he felt nauseous and his vision swam with grey stars. Finally his sight cleared. Thick masses of men were coming forward. Pushed back by the enemy, trying to stay afoot was a near impossibility.

Pressure from behind as men surged forth into battle. Morgund almost collapsed, but somehow retained his footing. Charging again, forcing. Falling meant certain death under foot or at the end of a pike. The sheer stress of the situation unhinged minds. Affected men emitted shrieks, or low moaning sobs. Those surrendering to panic lost their lives immediately. Morgund pushed the panic from his mind as the crowds pushed him. To stay upon one's feet meant to live, at least a while longer. Morgund was among the stalwart.

The relentless crush caused disruption, upon the separate enemy detachments. The first enemy square, followed by another, sagged. The king's soldiers were tough and determined, however. They key factor affecting the course of the combat that the rebels had numbers against them. They withdrew sluggishly, remaining in their contingents and maintaining their martial discipline slowing the rebel advance.

The bulk of Morgund's rebels had flattened the first line of defenders. The king's men were stout and the next line continued to withdraw in good order. To Morgund, it was akin to hacking into an impenetrable forest. After the initial collision no cohesion could be maintained. There was no end to the slaughter, nor low acts. Captured men had their eyes cut out whilst still alive. The young men attracted by trumpet and bright pendant alike came to realise their mistake.

Morgund with no choice nevertheless. To give him the courage to face his enemies, with grudges to repay, Morgund could easily see MacCainstacairt in the men before him. He saw the face of the man he hated which kept his sword arm rising and falling. He felt a severe pain in his head. Had he been hit? His legs were weak. Crouching down, he gained a few minutes of rest but soon thereafter he was one of many who were fighting for space and life. Morgund saw no point in the fierce resistance of his enemies. He could see, as could all, that for them, this day was lost. Yet fight on they did Hired outsiders, the kings mercenaries, knew what that if they were broken into small numbers and spilled into the countryside they would suffer cruelly. Having cut a destructive path through these formerly green and productive lands, defeat would deliver them into the hands of the people they had molested.

The protracted fighting and close quarters combat sapped away the strength of men on both sides. Morgund could feel his strength draining away, as surely as if he was drained of blood. He was jostled remorselessly, battered from side to side.

At one moment he could see the ground, splashed red with blood, littered with the dead and dying, and parts of the dead and those who would die, all being ground under a stampede. To fall was to die, and Morgund almost lost balance when he trampled over something that moved. Then his eyes were skyward as they were dragged thither by raven's wings.

Those black birds wheeled high above, patiently waiting for dead flesh. His vision was grey again, the pain in his head intense. The smell of blood and sweat was overpowering. The shriek of a man impaled on pikes. By his side, a comrade lost his hand, at the wrist, and held it with his one remaining hand. The man's sword fell to the ground at his feet, along with the hand. Defenceless, he was cut down. A wave of nausea flooded over Morgund as he breathed in the mingled smells of the flesh torn asunder, life blood flowing freely, the earthen smell of loosened bowels. He vomited violently, coughing and gagging.

Then, from the thick of battle, Morgund was cast into gentler waters, from darkness into light. Men moved alone or in small groups, and he was assured at least of not being trampled. Fatigue settled heavily on him like a lead cloak. Struggling to remain upright, having fought his way through densely packed men, he thought he had survived the worst of the melee.

One of the king's soldiers raised a shield and Morgund saw a glint of metal in the man's hand. Morgund's feet wouldn't move. Morgund finally lunged out. Cold steel met flesh, and another of the enemy fell. A greater lull developed. He stood in a sea of tranquillity, alone, on an island bare, none close by

He was temporarily reprieved from the frantic haste. Morgund looked down upon a pale, glum, face, its owner, knowing his end was come. The man who had lately been a foe was now just a man succumbing to death. He gasped loudly, his gurgling expiration a fountain of bright red froth. Morgund tried to avert his eyes but fascination pulled his eyes back.

The soldier's eyes rolled crazily from left to right before his expression settled into a sad, mirthless smile. Was it a glimpse of heaven, or a memory of his mother, that made the smile. The question weighed on Morgund's mind as the mans lips turned blue. It made him remember the blow which caused this. He had almost forgotten that he had cast this man into death. Looking down, the seed of decay was already on its course, for the blue was not a living shade and the fallen enemy became as grey as the sky. No longer in immediate danger he felt momentary grief. Loud thunder rumbled overcoming the clatter of war. With a jolt Morgund noticed for the first time the steady rain which had been falling for some time. Then he felt a sudden terrible sadness for the man he had killed, an impulse to fall down and beg forgiveness, which as quickly passed. It was war men died. He noticed all around him men were fighting, bleeding, dying. He remembered then where he was so held his sword tight, and concentrated. His tongue and mouth ached. How long it had been since he'd last drank? He knew not. He went for his hip flask. Unfastening it, a few sips, then quickly put it away.

A knight descended as if from heaven, gleaming sword in hand, reaping heads like a harvester out and gathering, but instead of wheat stalks, heads, he took. He galloped past Morgund, the horse almost crushing him. He swept down with his blade, in an arc, whereby, he caught an arm, sprayed blood onto a number of faces, the surprised looks made the knight laugh. He came straight at Morgund.

Standing in his saddle high with his weapon ready to strike, by staying nimble on his feet Morgund managed to avoid the attack and the knight rode on seeking easier game. The knight had taken a huge risk riding alone, on mud. He must be a valiant man.

The energy to avoid the knight was Morgund's last. Every step was exhausting from here on and his instinct for survival had become dull. Each step seemed to grind him into the ground. He could eternally, sleep, just sit down and close his eyes and be banished from this cursed field. The maltreatment of battle had him cursed. It was a sobering experience to kill a man, he thought. He looked down at a superficial wound on his arm, already it had stopped bleeding.

Perhaps he had killed many in the burning melee, he had seen the bodies falling, had bypassed them, but he didn't know positively, perhaps glancing blows he had dealt, or, his sword didn't land at all, they had slipped, or rather than been killed by others, or were still alive. There was no way to know with certainty; all had transpired in that fearful, blood soaked haste where Morgund could scarcely single out anything. But that poor man he had watched die. That poor last man, had died most assuredly, at Morgund's hand. Now that the invigorating humours of battle lust were draining away from him, Morgund reflected and mourned.

He sought to clear his mind, but the battle's hardship was far too much. It was as if he was dreaming, a prolonged nightmare of insanity, with murder, and bloody wounds, crisis upon crisis, men slaughtering each other like beasts from the bowels of hell. So much hinged on luck. It was hard to tell friend from foe and it was certain many died at the erring hands of comrades.

Thinking all this whilst his feet still moved taking him across a muddy patch of ground. Then he saw the clarion flash of naked steel thrusting out towards him. Too late to deflect it, a burning pain entered which replaced all other sensation. A knight entered the fray, mace in hand, struck down hard. This blow saved Morgund's life hitting the soldier who was about to kill him. Somehow Morgund managed to come to his feet, but he was splattered with blood and trembling, staggering.

He saw open fields, close. A series of measured steps, in a topsy-turvy world, the ground and as sky one. Despite the ground moving his feet stuck to it. Intending to live, but why? The question was beyond him. He sought an answer and sought and sought, though as much as he struggled to find a solution no answer that made sense came to him. Suddenly not too far away a wonderful thin strange light came from the sky like a descending silk ribbon. It's strange beauty held him fascinated. The light moved off. A call came from far away; his mother's voice, and the soft light threading down were one. If he could grab this light he'd reach her. The light, catch the light, so simple, but it was just beyond his reach. Leading him on to safety, was his mother's voice, and her loving simple heart. So he walked, and saw a vision of two outstretched hands as she called him on ... and music, the quality of the melody, exceptional.

He had a sore ear which muffled it but it came from that direction with thunder and fighting. "Follow the song." He heard her say. He must get there one way or another and far away from the battle, to life and to the song ... and then someone else was near. Cold grey eyes, an enemy, of evil rankness.

But the eyes weren't real they were a memory. Or were they? If the man before was real he was dead. He had nothing left to defend himself with. The sword he held, he couldn't raise. A vile mess was at his feet of his making, he wiped his chin, saw men, walking on him, felt their feet, heard trumpets, saw banners, heard the maggots feasting on him.

The man standing before him was gone. Had he ever existed? He sought to focus on his mother, who was drifting away. There was soft light. The soft light, he must get near it again. That was where his mother was. She defied earthly laws. She stood aloft, in the distance, high. In intimate contact with God she drifted above the earth's surface. Was she beckoning him to follow? If only he could follow her to heaven. Once he caught up with her he would ask about this state of grace. Losing all touch with reality he rose into the air and rain and electricity. As he floated skyward ... the battlefield far below, he realized he had died. The bad luck or bad judgement he had seen befall others, had become his own. He looked at his dead body far below. Now ascending to heaven where was his mother? He had expected her to be here, might not his dear father be here, to greet him. Sucking in an enormous breath, he was back on the field of battle and still upright and alive, a wonder to him.

For a few moments he didn't know where he was until slowly taking in that he was on the battlefield. The sky was brilliantly captivating and he saw the clouds racing orange hued from the sun set. Those few mercenaries still in the fight sought not to impede him seeking only to disengage and flee. Morgund just wanted to find safety. He took his tired feet, and made them move. One of the enemy finally decided to prevent Morgund's escape. Whilst Morgund was unable to act the man blocked his path, blessing his luck for finding a defenceless foe, Morgund saw.

Morgund tried to reason with the man. "Cannot we go in peace?"

The soldier ignored Morgund. His sword would speak for him.

Staggering forward, it took all Morgund's strength to lift his sword. Meanwhile the man in front of him brought his own sharp edge speeding downward. Morgund deflected it. Collapsing underneath a second down-strike. Was beneath the 'corpse maker', as the attacker liked to name his favourite killing stroke. Morgund's assailant brought his sword up preparing to bring it down. Morgund lay helpless on the ground awaiting the next blow. A sword struck deep between his assailant's ribs. And, once again, Morgund was surprised that he still lived. He rolled out from near his now dead opponent and arose, again his feet took him forth. He was not alone, someone was beside him badgering him onward. A nuisance really, the man was. Morgund wished the man would take himself off.

Morgund's throat burned, he was sick, semi conscious. From the vile taste he knew he had vomited recently. The man who had saved his life lifted him up and took him to a stream. There, they quenched an immeasurable thirst. Morgund lay on his back. How he came to be here, he couldn't recall. He was as hot as molten lead, and thought, there was something he must remember, but what? In the sky he saw a single rain drop as time stood still. His mother had been up there in the sky looking down at him? A blessed feeling. She was still somewhere and loved him.

He tasted blood. Where did it come from? An opponent had fallen on him, it came from him, he realised, when his enemy had died and spattered him. Perhaps not. Many shared in the battle and it could have come from one or more of them, blood drifted down from his head, he felt the pain of a wound that grazed his ribs, another wound and another mystery, he searched his memory for this moment which escaped him.

A sour taste, in his mouth, that arose from the depths of his gut, he swallowed it. Blood trickled down the back of his throat. His nose was bloodied. A metallic reek encased his nostrils - blood.

The rebel soldier who stood above him, spoke, "I can't lift you again. Get up or I will leave you. You don't want to get caught out here in the open. We must go to that hill, amongst the trees, over there." With his last strength, Morgund regained his feet.

Amongst the trees, protected from bleak heavy rain and fog, Morgund watched in fascination the leaves and branches forming the canopy that sheltered him from the rain, stored tiny points of wetness. Droplets of water rolled, collected and fell, big fat forest leaves glistened like diamonds. The beauty and peacefulness a balm to his turmoil. An occasional sprinkling of rain struck his face, slid along it, and moved down. Above, many of the droplets held by leaves and branches elongated, threatened to fall but held firm. Seeing loveliness, so contrary to the quagmire of destruction, he thought, benign and blameless these lovely spheres that clung to the trees. Here was God, he thought. A robin called, the battle slipped away and he felt the forests closeness. Aching muscles and wounds felt painful. He shivered.

The other man produced food and they ate. He couldn't remember where the other man had come from but if he was an enemy, he would be dead by now. Neither had the energy to speak, nor dared to, for they might return to the subject of the hell they'd escaped. Parched throats required further quenching so they returned to the stream where a group of rebel soldiers came upon them.

"The battle awaits you. Good men are dying whilst you are at rest."

A speaker was in Morgund's face, menacing him, posturing with his sword, drawing close to him. Cuffing him. Morgund who didn't have the strength to resist, turned away. Here was a man who didn't know pity and Morgund felt totally powerless in his presence. He had been extended a permit to admonish, was suited to it, revelled in it.

Morgund wore a coat, stained red with the blood and valour. Clearly he did not deserve this, in his weakened state, Morgund was easily set upon. It strengthened the cowardly accuser's worth to smash down another, for he was a plunderer of good men's strength.

To survive and be struck down by one of his own seemed a sad irony to Morgund. Nothing could save him, he saw. Then his guardian intervened to save his life again. "Hold, Harold, hold. It is a bad thing you do here, ill conceived. He fought well, is wounded and exhausted he could not stand, let alone fight."

"What of yourself Edwin?" These two obviously knew each other.

"I'll go with you to fight now."

Edwin disappeared with them. Not wishing to risk another such episode, Morgund returned soon after to the tempest. He saw a patch of light being smothered on the horizon, it was a mirror of himself, he thought.

The battle moved away, the threat diminishing with it. Men fought further away on the hills. Morgund battled to stay warm, felt overly ill. Sitting down he inspected his arms and armour then saw that his helmet was heavily dented. This he felt sure had contributed to his loss of surety. Alternately he felt cold then hot and could barely walk.

Seward found him semiconscious and babbling incoherently. "A knight, hacking heads like wheat, he threw heads at me, he threw heads at me." Morgund thought he was dying but said. "Glad I am, to have been able to endure the difficulties associated with the battle."

Later he managed some ordered thoughts. "You're a good friend Seward. I can trust you. Did we win?"

"Yes, we did."

"How did it happen, and where did you find me?"

"I searched the battle field and luckily you were afoot and drawing attention to yourself by speaking senselessly."

Morgund laughed and Seward found that Morgund had retained his calm. Seward admired him for it, and took some credit for showing Morgund the face to put forth. A broken bone when mended is said to be stronger. When he thought of that, he thought of Morgund.

"The battle, how was it won?"

"Through luck and the courage of good men."

"And where was Seward and what happened to you?"

"I was part of a solid mass, he said. "After the battle began I couldn't say who was beside me. The fleeting combats scarcely lasted a moment but took all my commitment. I was surprised how much stronger I was than others. I easily bested any who clashed with me. Yet I remained workmanlike, and careful, in case my superiority made me careless. The closest call I received was when a pikeman behind me tripped and nearly thrust me through."

Seward then took Morgund into a cold stream, and cleansed his wounds. He found them both, shelter, built a fire, and wrapped Morgund in a thick blanket. Sleep descended like a hammer on them, swift and sure. The next day Morgund felt a great deal better, enormously sore but whole in mind and body. He was elated that he was in fact, still alive and relatively intact. As the story unfolded of their different experiences, Seward's face reddened on hearing of what Morgund had suffered at the hands of Harold.

"This Harold I will track down. We shall see how hard he is."

"What?" asked Morgund.

"I am going to find Harold."

With that Seward was off. He walked far but eventually he found the man he was looking for. One particular Harold fitted the description. Seward approached him.

Coming closer, he knew he had found the right man. Small piggish eyes darted out of his hate-filled face, as Morgund described. "Did you threaten a young man whilst he was wounded, and surrounding him with your fellows?"

Harold thought himself safe and risked an aggressive comment. "Yes I did and I enjoyed it. Depart Scotsman, whilst you can."

"No, I am not finished with you yet," Seward replied. The breeze cast Seward's hair askew, making him look wilder.

Harold, tried to intimidate Seward, "Go, before I send you to hell, where I should have sent your boyfriend."

He was an angry man who needed to be taught a lesson. He was intemperate of others, so therefore others must be intemperate of him and pay him in the same coin. Seward was just the right man to do so. Harold didn't see the smile that his comment made for he had turned towards his slovenly laughing soldiers, laughing with them. Obviously he was performing for them.

"Allow me to test a theory I have," Seward said. "I believe intimidators are also cowards. Are you a coward? Let me test you with my sword. Will you fight me?" Seward's eyes were hard and cold and his hand rested on his blade.

Harold's self confidence took flight. This blonde giant was outnumbered many times over but still was spoiling for a fight. Harold's voice became sulky, taking on something of a whining tone. Seward thought he was like a little boy, a spoilt evil little boy, the kind who enjoyed being cruel, who liked taking the wings off insects. "I am Harold De Taunton, trusted servant of Sir Richard Cressingham. He would hold it a grave matter indeed, if any harm were to come to me."

"He is no fighter like yourself. It would be murder."

A nearby priest hurried over to the confrontation, and placed a restraining hand on Seward's shoulder. "The Lord looks graciously on those of us with a gentle spirit. Spare him."

The priest was distraught at the prospect of violence. Seward held his blade, but not his tongue. "You are a worthless wretch De Taunton. A pathetic scoundrel, a coward, and such cowardice is unfit for a man."

Turning his back, Seward heard the priest call after him, "Thank you, in God's name. May God bless you."

When Seward left the ruffian's eyes filled with hate again. No lesson had he learned. More men would come to suffer at Harold's hands and it would have been good if Seward had killed this brutal fellow who spent his life destroying the lives of others.

Upon his return, Morgund favoured Seward with a warm smile.

"Did you kill him?"

"You know I did not. I couldn't kill him in cold blood. That De Taunton was too cowardly to face me.

"What happened?"

"He warned me of his protection, when that didn't work he nearly cried."

"Was he very badly frightened?"

"He was, yes.  He is a terrible craven."

"That he is."

"I learnt something today ..."  Seward paused, reflecting.  "Something a priest told me.  God looks kindly on those of us with a gentle soul."

"That is true."  Morgund replied uncertainly.  Those words, coming from the mouth of an experienced killer the likes of Seward, confronted him strongly.  Involuntarily, Morgund said, "Seward, his face haunts me still."

Seward knew of what deathly face he spoke, for a little earlier, he heard Morgund on about him, to himself, mumbling about the man he had watched slowly die.

"In battle, men fight or die, don't blame yourself.  You chose to live, the only choice.  Let us go and help the wounded.   Action is the best antidote for troubles of the mind."

Morgund felt a queer sense of rebellion against Seward's prompting.  After all, he was the last surviving MacAedh Earl of Ross, whereas Seward only a shipwrecked serf.  By what right had Seward the killer to tell him to tend to the sick like some old hospice nun.  He would not relinquish it so easily.  "A knight rode on horseback he cut down panic stricken men like a wolf amongst sheep.  That way of fighting is good, is useful for our purpose."

"What purpose?" Seward asked, sensing the shift in his friend's behaviour.

"To rouse the highlands, to meet King Alexander in battle and defeat him."

"A fatal curse that has greatly reduced your family. The MacAedhs have been fighting it for a hundred years without success. Hide away in the mountains. He'll forget you, Morgund."

"But I'll not forget him."

"Morgund, you're probably the last MacAedh alive. Stay alive and carry on your family name."

"I am descended of kings, I shall not hide. Besides, they have done too much to me for me to forget. He contemplated uneasily and Seward could see him grinding his teeth. "I can't let things be."

Seward walked off with more ill humour than was common with him, fearful lest his quest to keep Morgund alive should fail. Morgund caught up to him and stopped him.

"You have committed a gross act of impertinence to a future King of Scots," Morgund said.

"You will never win!" Seward shouted.

"No, he will lose. He will lose," Morgund's voice was rising. "Alexander is wise in the ways of stealth but not the ways of battle."

Seward scoffed. "How can you be sure?"

Morgund in his zeal ignored Seward's words. "Alexander killed my father. His great grandfather captured mine, put his eyes out and killed him. There must be an end to it, one of us must die so the other can live. Whilst I live, I risk any future he has. He killed my father. Ill be avenged."

"Or dead. He is King he commands all Scotland and he fight you, a man with one retainer."

"He fights me, a son of a noble house who is the right claimant to the throne, and you must support me. If you don't, you are a not the friend I took you for."

Morgund's look changed then and he caught Seward's wrist. Held it tightly. For a moment Seward doubted Morgund's sanity.

Tears filled Morgund's eyes and Seward finally knew, why Morgund was taking this course. His shoulders heaved. "He killed my father Seward! He killed my father."

# THE WITCH QUEEN

THE DAYS FOLLOWING the battle ushered in October. The injured either healed slowly or died, the bodies of the fallen were looted and buried or burned. Biting Autumn gales from the mountains brought not only a fiercely penetrating cold sleet but discordance among the assemblage. A messenger, half dead with cold, arrived in the central hall of Rochester castle to bring news on bended knee. His words were few, but portentous. "The rumours of an army are true. Already they advance upon the castle."

Within a day a great trebuchet was casting massive stones at the towering fortress walls. All those within the castle knew, should only one small section of wall come down the king's men, vastly outnumbering them would pour in. The only relent to the devastating fusillade was for the enemy to launch the occasional corpse at the besieged defenders. With a grinding inevitability the great wall finally buckled and collapsed in an avalanche of stone and wood. A brief futile attempt at containment was overcome. All was lost. Greatly disheartened the rebels resited, but to no effect. Seward and Morgund joined the unrelenting confusion.

"Our only hope is to seek concealment and remain hidden and tonight to slip away." Seward shouted.

"Seward, I leave everything to you including my finely inlaid sword. Use it well." The sword a gift from King John. To Morgund it was like no other the sword, so finely balanced so beautiful. It felt like an extension of his arm. Morgund looked jolly. "I don't deem I will need it, hereafter."

Noting his composure, Seward wondered if anything did worry him. Considering, if the events of the battle had left Morgund in a permanently unhinged state of mind, or whether his friend had developed an extreme sense of fatalism, believing himself destined to overthrow Alexander. They climbed castle stairs, only to discover the path densely packed with men. "Another way we must find. We must go," Seward said, grabbing Morgund, "Quickly."

"Pray there is another way." Morgund replied.

Seward knew of a passage leading to the dungeons. Darkness might protect them. "Follow me!" he shouted.

A group of the King's men reached the passage first and met them. Seward and Morgund unsheathed their blades. To resist this many skilled warriors was tantamount to suicide. Surrounded, Morgund shouted a warning. "I am a ward of the King. If either myself or my companion is harmed, you will answer to His Majesty!"

A knight stepped forward "Hand me your sword and I will take you to him."

Morgund surrendered his sword. Seward doing so with a sneer. The leader among the troops ordered them bound, a command fulfilled with little regard to Morgund and Seward's welfare. Their arms were fastened behind their backs, the cords painfully tight, and were urged along with the occasional prod of sharp metal.

"Almighty father protect us," Morgund whispered. He looked at Seward. "In prayer lies our only hope.

They entered a large central hall and there were made sit. John engrossed in other matters appeared to take no notice of them. After a while he ordered they be brought over to him. King John intended to carry the war into Scotland and needed Morgund's help to divide the Scots. The King pointed his sword at Morgund's breast and said with a profound sense of gravity, "What shall I do? Kill you with this sword or, knight you with it?"

This was unexpected, John must be gaming with him. Morgund had anticipated protection from the King. Not the offer of knighthood. The King was serious. To be granted passage into the realm of knighthood was utterly unexpected. Morgund looked to this king. Likewise he knelt, hands bound and under duress, but wore a charmed, serene smile. Morgund felt an odd, sense of revulsion. "Knight me with it, of course!"

Morgund, kneeling and still bound, held his head high. As if in defiance of the king. Morgund gazed into John's eyes as an equal, heedless of the sword poised to either elevate him or bring him low. John's supporters, and John himself, were taken aback by the young man's impudence. The court waited expectantly in silence for the King's response. It was well known that King John could be mercurial. The sword was raised, and not once did Morgund's eyes waver.

Many were to later say that in all the time they knew him, only this once, did they see the King laugh so heartily. John addressed Morgund. "A brazen boy. A very brazen boy, indeed." His head rocked back in laughter. "I can identify with that." Then with a more serious tone, "You shall be rewarded for your audacity." John touched one shoulder and then the other. Arise, Sir Morgund MacAedh."

Morgund felt the grace of knighthood. That it happened so quickly and unexpectedly stunned him. Morgund was cut from his bindings. As he stood, an almost palpable lightness of being. All at once he could do great things and felt indebted to John. He was a product of his age and knighthood was honourable in the extreme. John handed Morgund a chalice full of wine. "Your young squire shall share our wine," John said.

King John assessed Seward, his face displaying pleasure. Of late assured of his success in battle. That worked to Morgund's favour, and now it seemed, to Seward's. "He is a good looking fellow. Looks like a hardy warrior, Morgund."

"That he is, sire," Morgund said.

King John smiled good naturedly at Seward and motioned that he accept a cup of wine. Here was a very different John; engaging, placid, mannerly. Could he finally have come to terms with his tormented soul? Whilst Morgund savoured his new title and trappings, Seward remained sceptical. The fact betrayed by his suspicious expression.

Only later, was Morgund to realise that it was like a sunny day in winter, appreciated, and persuasive in the hope that the night would be pleasant. But soon to discover when the night came and with it misery and bitter cold. Winter nights were always thus, always.

John was a dangerous man, and in time would revert to his true nature. The reprieve from the caprices of his harshness was nothing more than a whim.

The days passed and two courtiers of note beset England's court, Seward and Morgund, who were determined to avoid to king John's attention, as much as possible. All dreaded John's temper. Seward was persistent in reminding Morgund of this fact, and that Morgund had surrendered his allegiance all too willingly to a man untrustworthy. In time Morgund would see the reality of his friend's words, for the King's cruelty was becoming all the more apparent.

Morgund was kitted in the trappings of a knight. Thereafter, the owner now of shield emblazoned with the ancient boar emblem of Scotland, white on silver, which he intended to carry into battle against Alexander. But the anticipated invasion of Scotland never eventuated. King John died suddenly of an unknown cause. Poisoned, many thought. Morgund was again fates hostage. King John left behind a son too young to rule. William Marshall governed in his stead.

Morgund had an audience with Marshall. "I have no wish to pursue a tangled game with Scotland Morgund, sanity must prevail. We need peace. You will be kept in safe custody until King Alexander advises us what he desires done with thee." Marshall said to Morgund.

Marshall's voice sounded like so many blades to Morgund who visibly sagged, if only briefly. Morgund wondered why his life was one endless series of confinements and captures, hopes and disasters. His eyes reflected this, but something else also, toughness, a swelling pride. He pulled himself together quickly and looked at Marshall unflinchingly. It was the same look he gave King John on the day John knighted him.

It disturbed Marshall so much that he softened his attitude. "You'll suffer no ill treatment, close confinement perhaps, but your friend shall share it with you, if he will. No dark dungeon, it is a river you will see if you've a mind to." Marshall couldn't relent further. Affairs of state had to take precedence over a troubled conscience.

Seward and Morgund found themselves conveyed to the Tower. There, kept in captivity. Fed well, treated with as much dignity and respect as their station allowed. Neither Morgund or Seward knew much of Marshall, and did not know what to expect. They did know, however, that if they fell into Alexander's hands a swift execution would be theirs.

The jailers admired Seward and Morgund therefore, their vigilance, inconsistently prompted, and reinforced by their superiors, did not last long. Prisoners couldn't escape from the tower, so why watch them too closely? The only one way out which was to fly from a high window, an oft-told jibe spoken by the guards. Such a leap and subsequent survival, was of course an impossibility.

Practising leisurely eating habits, plates and knives were left behind with them and when they were, they were hidden. Salt air had loosened fastenings on the metal grill to their cell. After two weeks working on them, they weakened. One good reef and the whole grill would come out making enough space for a man to crawl through. Complaining about noise coming from the cell above Seward and Morgund learned that this cell above was vacant. The cell above was to carry them onto a section roof not too far away.

Waiting upon a dark suitable night for their escape. Two weeks on, such a night came, and their attempt was made. The grill was levered out. Balancing on a ledge, Seward wedged a knife into a gap in stonework, above. Seward was on the outside of the building. Going up, using more knives to extend his footholds. Seward the stronger of the two, ascended first to achieve the difficult task of wedging the knives. Having seen eroded mortar on the facing walls, they judged that similar would be above ... they were right. Seward pushed the cell-grill, bars and framework, into one such. He had twisted bed linen into a rope, weighted down at one end with a brick, carried it on his shoulders.

From outside his jail-cell, onto the wall higher, Seward threw it, trying to catch on something above. The weight snagged. Seward held the sheet fast testing to see if it would hold him. It did. He pulled himself up onto a piece of battlement. From the battlement he sent the rope out again. Again, the rope caught tight. Then back and forth, swinging and kicking off the walls to get further along to a skirting wall, a footway. There, on the footway, he was. With his final objective sighted below him, the roof of an outer building, next to the river, he ran swiftly and threw himself ... landed nimbly quickly and skilfully.

Seward signalled to Morgund that it was his turn. A series of grips as Morgund followed in Seward's wake until his feet stopped. Morgund looked across at Seward who was beckoning him to continue. This was hard work for Morgund who found he had a terrible fear of heights. Discovering his breathing fast. Holding the wall all of a sudden Morgund stopped moving. Morgund recoiling at the horror of it couldn't move.

Seward told Morgund to stay calm, that he was coming back for him. Seward's call alerted a guard who raised the alarm. Seward would either return, or escape. Morgund was readying to climb back towards his cell. Out of the corner of his eye he saw Seward with the rope coming for him. Morgund could see his friend would return. They would be captured together. Morgund couldn't let that happen. He closed his eyes. When he opened them he ignored the cries of men-at-arms, and climbed.

Reaching the knotted bed sheet, thereafter, across Morgund went, and landed well on the battlement, but it had been sickeningly stressful. Although, beset by shaking legs, Morgund leaped onto the building Seward was on. Seward didn't notice how badly affected Morgund was. "Come on hurry, we must find a way off this roof," Seward said. "The guards know we are here."

So sapped of energy was Morgund that he sank down on his knees. For moments only. He resurrected himself as he had done so many times before and as he would continue to do until his life's end. They believed, there might be an easy way down, but there wasn't. One way down only 40 or 50 feet into the river. Winter and the water was freezing. They agreed to hang from the building, to gain, if only slightly, a shorter drop, the length of their body. Hanging from the stonework looking down, it seemed a frighteningly long way to Morgund and he felt to certain death. He shrank from it, there was such an impermanence to life, these last moments he wanted to savour.

After a time Seward asked. "Are you letting go?"

"No ... not on this fine day. "

"You're going mad, Morgund."

"Yes, but I'm not going down there, not yet, a least, and you can't change my opinion. Its still a fine day."

Another few moment of maddening exertion.

"What are you doing Morgund?"   Seward said.

"Hanging on, until I can't."   The exertion was starting to make Morgund's voice low.

"Then what?" Seward asked.

Morgund looked down, thereupon his face grew whiter. "Hanging on longer,"  he gasped out,  "until I can't."

"This I know Morgund.   Cowards die a thousand deaths not one."

Seward looked too serious, Morgund couldn't allow that. "At least a better phrase than such tiresome nonsense?"

"Its something we all know Morgund."

Morgund smiled. "Yes, it's true, but if I hold on a little longer what difference does it make?"

"None."

"You're a good friend Seward."   Morgund said and let go.

Morgund plummeted downward, arms and legs flailing. The water was visible only in part, shrouded by a thick blanket of mist. The river rushed up to meet him, it seemed, and the very moment before he hit the water. Morgund felt the jarring impact and the icy cold of those chill waters. The confrontation was sufficient to force the air from his lungs, in a pain wracked gasp that left a wake of bubbles. Seward hurtled into the water, feet first, narrowly missing his companion. To an observer above, the pair had simply let go, fallen, and been swallowed by the fog. No wave nor wake through the veil to reveal the evidence.

The layer of vapour filtered the first of the morning sun's rays through the miasma depths. That very same fog cloaked a small craft, it's oarsman stroking in silent obedience. The boat was empty save for one other figure, who stood impressively tall, despite its crooked back, gauntness and air of antiquity which not even the voluminous robes could disguise. The figure twisted its ancient head from side to side, glaring at the waters surface. Eventually it extended a gnarled, talon-like finger to point. "There, I see a face above the water," the ancient crone croaked, and the colourless slit of a mouth twisted into an approximation of a smile.

She scowled at the oarsman as the boat neared the unconscious, floating form. "I spoke they should be here." She reprimanded him in a voice that sounded like old parchment being unravelled. "And ye had the gall to doubt me." The hooded oarsman making even strokes made no reply. "Thee doubted me." Her ugly head shook releasing a slobbering cackle.

She had an agent in the castle but didn't tell him that was how she knew they'd be here, she would have him to believe it was by means of supernatural power, which, although he'd like to scorn, he could not totally discount.    The boat drew nearer to the two figures drifting.    With difficulty, they were dragged aboard.

---

MUCH LATER, SEWARD awoke under clean, stiff linen, to the pleasant aroma of cooking food.  He knew not where he was, but at least it was as far from drowning.  He was indoors, the room's small fire illuminating Morund in a nearby cot. Seward's observation of the room was cut short by movement. Seward closed his eyes so nearly as to imitate sleep but yet remain with sight.  He watched as a girl entered the room bearing pitchers of hot, rich soup.  She set it down and approached Seward cautiously, as if fearful of waking him.  He remained as he was, silent and feigning sleep.  The girl was pretty, with red hair and grey eyes and could not have been more than fourteen or fifteen years.  Silently she touched Seward's cheek before moving to Morgund.

Seward watched with something akin to a pang of jealousy when he saw the girl touch the cheek to only to stoop and kiss Morgund upon his resting lips with a reserve only enough to prevent him waking.  She obviously admired the sleeping form.  She admired the youthful but powerfully aligned chest, with its downy hair, noble head set upon shoulders well-toned, even in slumber.  The sleeper had strongly defined arm strength.  He met her every standard of beauty.  His head hair fell in a way that kept her staring at it.  All of him was good.

The shape of his lips so kissable. He would be hers in every way and soon, she would see to it. Disturbed by a noise outside, the girl shied away from these thoughts. Mixtures she administered to dampen inner cold. Although a young girl, yet, with those eyes they said she had felt her loins from as early an age. A beautiful smile. He smiled seemingly responding to her. Morgund's teeth, they were as perfect as his perfect face. Her morning duties over she intended to sit near a fire and enjoy thinking about the beautiful young stranger, yes, that is what she would do. First, to pass on information on to her mistress. In the fog between sleep and waking, Seward drifted off again into a profound slumber thinking only of falling, water, and a girl with red hair and grey eyes.

Late afternoon brought conscious movement and a peeling back of eyelids. The room was clean and light, flooded in through large open shutters. The day allowed a hint of warmth before spring. A deep sense of well being filled them. When they were both awake they ventured a few words.

"I didn't think to wake up, Seward." Morgund sighed. "Have they moved us to another part of the tower?"

"No. Hear those noises from the street? We are no longer within the tower. But soon word will get out that we've escaped, and like as not a reward will be posted for our capture and these people who hold us, will turn us in." Seward said. They ate what they could of the broth left warming by the fire.

Later an older woman, ugly but seemingly, kind, entered. She watched them sleeping. Turning, a door, closing it, silence.

Neither could move as pain assaulted them at each small suggestion of it. Whatever fate awaited them they could not now avert it. Accepting this, they lay back and soon slumbered. The next morning a physician arrived and began testing, prodding, poking. The doctor asked them many questions. Finally he advised them that no permanent injury existed, and rest, a great of it, would restore them. When he left, they fell into that state where the body is refreshed and the mind enters another world, free from conscious cares. The, deep sleep. The old crone had accompanied the physician.

Somewhat later, she told them kindly, "You are very safe with me. I know that you are escapees from the Tower, but I do not care. Many innocents are unjustly lodged there." She was cross in her disproval and said, "I will protect you." Her direct gaze dispelled ill humour. Her eyes were convincing and as they were in no fit state to attempt another escape they chose to accept what she said.

Nothing untoward happened. The days passed easily. Meanwhile the hag waited, summoning them, they would come. Magic would ensnare the two. In a room nearby, insulated from the bitter February weather Seward and Morgund were content to wait it out. Thereafter, they intended to be away. Their main diversion, every day the beautiful young girl came. It was obvious to both that he held a fascination for her. It was not a case of being smitten by his good looks, although she admitted to herself, she had been, initially. Far more existed than mere looks, her soul opened up to his vulnerability, to his warmth.

This was a deep need to know him and be close to him. He was her first thought in the morning, and last at night. Every contour of his face was visited in her mind, and of course when her duties spared her the time it was to him she turned. He made her supremely jubilant.

It was impossible for Morgund to be forever unaware of her feelings, for she made them obvious. Morgund however was too uncertain of his own to commit himself and he doubted if he could give her what she wanted. Coping with hardships robbed him of a softness and an ability to surrender himself. Needing all his resources to survive left little. For now, such giving was impossible and there was a second reason. He admonished himself for becoming distracted from his purpose, which was returning to the highlands and rousing them against Alexander.

An English girl would find it difficult in the highlands. That way of living was beyond her. And, should he fall in battle, she would be stranded far from her loved ones with no easy way ever to return to them. In the highlands she would suffer, he saw, so he distanced himself. As an excuse Morgund told her that he did not allow anyone, other than his trusted companions to become close to him. To them he owed a debt of loyalty so had to make allowances.

But in an unguarded moment he told her of his famous ancestry and the turmoil that had plagued him since the day his father had ridden out to meet the King of Scots. This he let slip, "I will not sleep peacefully until I have made amends for that killing." His voice was fraught with even greater tension when he said, "So treacherously slain was he I loved. It was an ignoble end to a noble life."

So swelled was her heart with pity for him that her eyes glistened with tears.   And a secret voice whispered inside her head, "By kindness I will make up for his past."

   Though she tried, her efforts to change his attitude towards her were to no avail.   With time realising that his secret soul would never be hers, she decided on an act that would effect a change, a love potion obtained from the physician who first attended Seward and Morgund.   Her love for him made her, act thus, she told herself.   If she could not capture his heart at least she could have a memory of his physical love and hopefully something of his for hers, a child containing his blood.     One night she stole his cup away, adding an elixir to it.   She waited.   Meanwhile, Seward and Morgund were separated.

   On the following day Morgund felt his resolve towards her weaken.   Through dull clouded eyes he returned her long looks.   His eyes searched for hers, his head followed her movements, loving glances made her way.   He had allowed himself to be ensnared in her closeness.   He reminded himself that one day he would leave and miss her.   Though his befuddled mind failed to comprehend fully, she knew despite his reticence that her presence with him one night, would purchase her desired outcome.

   She knew he was ready, his love escaped every pore of him,  "His son will link us," she told herself.

He was awake when she came to him. She wore a thin mantle that she slipped easily from her shoulders. He gasped. She was radiant, young, flawless. His gaze became transfixed on slight breasts with little pink nubs that were erect and suckable. Below them was a slight tuft that little covered her rounded inviting opening. Noble was her skin and she was shaped exquisitely. She entered Morgund's bed then fierily and longingly she buried Morgund's manhood deep within her and thereon every touch was sacred. Whatever the future held, these moments were theirs, she told herself and she crammed into them all the unsparing love she could. All too soon dawn arrived and the majesty of their shared union ended.

The elixir's clouding effect upon his mind dissipated during the day. His sole goal was to be avenged on Alexander, this girl was a distraction he did not need. This he realised, finally. Although her friendship and body were welcome, it saddened him to think of the added complication his life now held. And she realised that by her actions she had incurred upon him yet a further injustice. Hopes that they wouldn't drift apart seemed to be in vain. Even as a new life quickened inside her, destined to be nurtured lovingly as a descendant of kings, she told herself often whilst patting her belly in composed contentment, "His love is within me."

Long after he had left to fight on the braes of Scotland from her lips passed the words, "Morgund is not now the last of his kind."

ONE NIGHT AN oddly tasting broth they were served affected them.   Their limbs felt heavy and sleep beckoned remorselessly.   Stupefied, Morgund and Seward slept where they fell.  A raucous laughter above finally wakened Seward. He looked at the sudden light that entered the room.  The hag stood at the open door.  By a winding stair, she led him up. The stairs became narrow and straight.  The house was large and it would be easy to become lost in it, Seward realised. They walked towards a patch of light, noises coming from the other side of a door.  Seward's ears pricked up, detecting the sound of a ruckus.  Both walked in.  Seward's pupils quickly took in images of naked cavorting women, dancing brazenly, displaying themselves, in shameless ways, their cursed bodies filthy and stained in what looked like blood.  Turning to flee he found his feet rooted to the spot.  He tried to loosen the bonds of drug induced weakness, to end the confusion and make sense of this, but couldn't.  Worse was to come.  In the middle of the room was a pot.  Protruding from it was a human arm  soft and white and covered in a sour griminess.  An overpowering sickening stench dominated the room, and the pot, its source.  Seward retched violently.  Here,  was a room awash in infamy, morbidity, the ecstatic, gleeful celebration of evil and horror.

He started for his sword, but was unarmed.  He was powerless!  In horrified disbelief Seward, saw a group of women greedily consume a bloody substance from the pot. His spirits sank and sickened.  He gasped.  The wizened old hag stood in before him, shirking her robes to reveal her shrunken, skeletal frame.  Gazing penetratingly into his eyes, the crone, their saviour, their benefactor, told him she ruled this coven, by her will.  By her will alone, this macabre festival occurred.   Seward found it impossible to avert or escape her. She seemed to see beyond his skin into his heart and soul. In his mind she screamed, she screamed, *"Look at me!"*

She did not avert her gaze. Instead she burrowed her very presence into his head. He wondered how he must look with his anguished ashen face. Her eyes and lips crackled with amusement at the sight of him, a wolf-grin. He got out, *"Help me."* But the voice which said it wasn't his. It was her voice.

*"You approve me not."* She stared at him amused at his discomfort. "I read minds, too. And I can speak through your mouth, if I chose." He wasn't sure at first if she truly spoke or he heard a semblance of her. No words could be given to anything as horrible as this.

Her withered lips moved, her rasping, ready voice filling his ears. "It is a human they eat."

He couldn't abide her eyes. If only she'd look away. Deep inside his mind, he screamed to himself, squinting his eyes straining with effort, compelling himself ... "Look away look away!

"I'll *look* as deep into your eyes, as I like."

So, she could read his mind. Then, there was nowhere to hide.

"That poor weak fool mocked and resisted me, and now here he is. Food. As you will be if you doubt me. You will be my humble servant and with time become one of us, for I claim you Seward. You are like us, your soul is ripe for the taking. Consider it taken."

Seward frozen to the spot, watching.

The witches continued their insane dance. The occasional intonation and animal-like grunt was accompanied by the rattling of horrible necklaces, bracelets and corded belts, replete with the bones of small creatures and human teeth. Others bedecked themselves in feathers, or strange symbols painted upon flesh in human blood. Seward saw the girl. Who had assisted him, and who had grown so very fond of Morgund, prancing wearing nought but sprigs of woodland plants tied around wrists and ankles. Then he noticed they all had a metal coin, or medallion, on a leather thong around neck or belt or tied painfully tight around a thigh. It was the very same image he had received mysteriously, after he and Morgund's encounter with Duibne. The cackling crone before him wore it too, on a very long cord of tendon that dangled between empty, sagging breasts. Unconsciously he reached for his own, and felt the blasphemous image under his fingers in low relief. For now he knew the significance of the beast who played the played the cracked flute in clawed hands, prancing deer-like upon hooven feet. He knew, by some dim seat of reasoning more subtle than speech or thought, that the figurehead of Wicca was none other than Satan himself.

Now he knew the significance of that symbol and knew who played the flute, those great dangerous eyes on the figure intruded, they spoke inside his head, telling him, "I am Satan. Fear me not for I am all glory and power." The voice which told him was male, it was not repellent, it was seductive, sounded, mesmerising. "I am the Anti-Christ. The soul keeper. The soul keeper."

The terrible dawning of that realisation settled upon him, as ravens upon a corpse. Satan spoke in his head.

He wanted to hear that voice again. It remained silent however, allowing him to return to the horrified realisation of where he stood. The noise of the witches supping broke him from his thoughts. They were drinking from what might have been a flensed skull.

"Surely not.....not inside this house, not here." He said.

"Forget that and listen to me Seward. He still lives whilst we eat his flesh." The crone pointed her claw like finger to a darkened corner Seward had previously overlooked. A man, or what was left of him, lay there. His limbs were gone hacked off. The stumps were bound tightly with cloth and cord, the ends ragged. The man opened his eyes and looked at Seward who immediately fell upon his knees and vomited but he could not keep his eyes away.

It was true, for unbelievably moment the eyes of the man had flickered open, as if on command. "What an ugly, vicious hag you are," Seward croaked, spitting strings of vomit and saliva.

The darkness swept in overpoweringly. In one horrifying moment Seward saw the moment of his death and knew its hour, an arrow would pierce his chest to kill him. He saw the future, irrespective of his efforts to divert it. She wanted his mind on this moment. His mind focused on the manner of his death, because his earlier premonition that an arrow would kill him meant he would survive this night and escape this room. His true vision returned though he remained paralysed through sheer terror whilst she implanted deep controlling thoughts within. Rarely did it fail. Seward appeared totally submissive, crouching as a craven before her, his self-will gone, and hers to bid.

His only purpose was to serve her, so he must. As would his companion, Morgund, who someone got and he then underwent the same terror the same enchantment. Although not possessed of any advanced psychic ability Morgund was needed to bind Seward, close to her. Reading Morgund could help her find what Seward thought.

Thus, the two were robbed of their free will by the collective power of the coven and suggestion and shock. Morgund, so well beloved by the young witch, disappeared and in his place, a stumbling husk. Morgund performed humble chores; cleaning and carting wood, delivering messages and being subjected to the grand witch's temper, which often resulted in a beating. Morgund cut vegetables like a lowborn scullery maid. He dug out weeds in the vegetable garden and stood sentry a living scarecrow in the field over her produce - she had an acre of land. Morgund the scarecrow rooted to the spot, seeing off the birds. Seward, took part in rituals of spell making. She had Seward, delving into the lives of persons whom she thought it well to know things of, to influence events and profit from the knowledge. Having Seward close brought substance to her own particular predictions, enabling her to grow formidable amongst the Wiccan community.

Acts of depravity amused her and both young men served her hungry orifices and those of her favourites who were as sluttish as she was. Pretty boy toys what lovely toys to play with, those who sought favours from her, often sought those very playthings.

She could at any time, in a fit of drug induced rage kill either or both of them. At times she was wary, her thoughtfulness as frightening as her cruelty, for death was never far from her thoughts. Often members of her household disappeared never to be seen again.

Seward frightened her. With his gifts might not some other purveyor of the black arts exploit him for themselves, thereby dictating her ruin, or if he escaped, seek vengeance on her, himself. He so favoured could end her days and she knew it well. Morgund she especially hated and he endured her taunts at his noble ancestry and how his family had sunk so low.

---

Morgund awoke in the dark. He was needed on the kitchen. Soon after, making bread which when ready he was to take to his mistress. A day beginning like so many others. His feet felt heavy. Malnourishment, harsh treatment and potent brews he was forced to drink kept him weak of mind and body.

She also knew how to undermine whatever sense of self worth could enable a moment of clarity, by overwhelming him with a sense of her superiority and fear of magic. Nor would he leave without Seward, who was her slave. It seemed they never got to speak alone, someone was always, watching. They slept separately, Morgund, in a lean-to, locked outside like a dog.

Morgund served bread and cheese, waiting to be noticed, so she could tell him to withdraw. Mirium was also in attendance, sewing under the watchful eye of the grand witch, who was all knowing, she who must be obeyed. Mirium suffered the penetrating ruthless looks, and biting sarcastic jibes on how hopeless she was at sewing.

Morgund, waiting, found himself yearning to have this over and be away elsewhere. "Please God, have the ugly hag notice me!" The hag's eyes darted across to him. She was good at reading mannerisms, it often made her seem a mind reader.

"So, now to you, Dog." She had taken to calling him Dog. "Dog, was it once I thought you a boy worth feeding. I tire of you. What say you in your defence. Are you worth feeding? Or, will I sell you to those seeing value in a boy's body. Catamites would give you the fucking you deserve. Some, others, would like to torture to your death. They love to see the blood flow. It relieves the boredom of the days. I tire of you. I might join in turning the blood out of you."

"I have a better idea." She produced a vial. "There's a poison I wish to test. Those who drink it, I've been told, die within a day. Girl." She addressed Mirium. "Get me a cup."

Mirium too frightened to do otherwise, complied. The hag filled the cup. Smiling seeing Morgund with his head down, tears in his eyes. She thought him very entertaining. The cup now full her head rose to Morgund.

"Come here and grab this Dog. And, Mirium stop looking so woebegone, or you will have it, too."

Morgund did as he was told, and took the cup. Mirium choked back her fear. She shook. The hag missed nothing, and found particular enjoyment in the girl's distress.

"We will test this friendship between you. A full cup is deadly. Less, produces mere retching and sickness. Your life, Dog, is in your hands. Do you understand, drink half a cup or less and you live? A sip will do. Let Mirium test the rest, this poisons potency will kill her and a sip will do you little harm. Her sewing deserves no less. ANSWER ME YOU SON OF A WHORE!!!"

Morgund nodded.

"Answer me. Speak instead of looking like a witless whore son. Answer me, or two full cups you will drink, each."

"I understand."

"Drink it up. Whatever you don't finish is for the girl."

Morgund nodded. He drunk the entire cup.

"Now go away and die, like a Dog. But before thee does lay the bread and cheese down on that table." He did. "Now depart this room, and your short life."

Morgund did as he was told and Mirium watched his departing back.

"The morning's entertainment is at an end, girl, back to sewing."

Mirium bent her head and sewed. Morgund fled to his cot in the lean-to where he expected to suffer unto death. He was wrong. Morgund laid back resting feeling very sick when the door burst opened. It was she.

"Get up and get back to work. There in the corridor outside my room, find the broom and sweep it until every particle of dust is gone, and then, die." Slamming the door behind her, she went.

Very wearily Morgund got himself up and step by wearying step took himself to the corridor and swept, beyond caring if he lived or died. Thereafter, Mirium heard the grand witch talking to the cook directing him to lace Morgund's food with a sickening agent. The cook and his mistress, loved every moment of it. There was no poison, however. The agent within the food would send him to the privy and wrack his stomach to emit all its contents. Put him in dreadful pain. He would think himself dying. Morgund about his sweeping was given a small bowel of food by the cook and told to eat it. He did. Thereafter he couldn't sweep anymore. All he could do was run to the privy.

This was but the start, Mirium realized  No doubt he was doomed to die. Mirium could foresee a day when there was actual poison in the vial. Morgund tried to save her life by swallowing all the vial of what he thought was poison, himself. Mirium must act to save Morgund. But the witch kept them apart. She knew Morgund and Mirium had enjoyed a special closeness, and was having her watched.

Two mornings later.  The grand witch had Morgund before her.  Mirium was in the room, watching.  "So, Morgund the poison was second rate.  I should of tested it on a rat and not a dog.  I heard that thee was very ill of the flux, your insides falling out behind you.  What say you?  Dog, answer me!"

"What I say is it did cause me much distress," Morgund replied sullenly.

"I heard the stink of you was rank.  No matter.  I have a suitable remedy for you to help with your ailment.  I would test it on a dog.  A medicinal.  I would have you well enough to do you duties without evil rank smells emitting from you."

She produced a flask, it looked much like the one before. "Now a return to health."  She handed the flask to Morgund. "Drink."  Morgund hesitated.  "Come, Morgund.  Does thee not trust me, me, who has been so good to thee?

Morgund's memory of how sick he felt mired his feet to the floor.

"Now, Dog, have sup of my good will, or will I summon another poison for thee.  I will you hold you down and you be made drink it.  Morgund step forward, and get it over and done with.  Take thine medicine like a good dog."

Morgund gulped it down.  It was like swallowing bricks.

"Now be off and be thee anchored to the privy for thee has been the victim of a bitch, as thou will be forever, until thee dies.  A Satan's blessing to you Morgund, son of an Earl.  I have it my mind to use thee even worse, have my man servants ride thee, till thou is hollowed out like a gutted pig. Out of my sight, dog."

Morgund immediately felt the bile rise to his throat and hardly made it outside the room before his mouth filled with vomit.

The sound of her voice followed him through the door. "Take thy vile self off. Pray for death."

Morgund fell to his knees gasping for breath. Pain wracked his entire body.

"I will have thee bark like a dog from now on." He heard her call from her room.

Morgund lay in his own vomit unable to move.

Inside the grand witch's room, Mirium fretted worriedly. "Madam do this more and you will ruin his constitution. He could die."

"I will kill him."

"My Lady is he not a man who deserves some human kindness." Mirium begged.

"No! He is a block of wood for chopping and I like to chop."

"Would Seward not miss his companion?"

"I have decided he is more to my liking without this companion, I feel he holds back my total domination of Seward."

Hearing this from outside the door, Morgund knew then he would die.

The ancient crone emitted a guffaw. "I have plans for him. None good will come to him. Next time I'll bend him over and shove an enormous phallic rod up him. The flesh will rip asunder. Truly then, he can ask me for kindness."

The cruelty of it forced Mirium to act.    She rushed to Morgund, but he was beyond listening. Mirium fled down the corridor. She must act quickly, her mistress would hold her to account and prevent any help she could give Morgund. She went to Seward.

When she found Seward alone, she told him,    "It is untrue, the man in the pot, it was a trick to bind you to influence your mind. Some potions were used additionally to achieve the effect. It was done to humble you and deceive you and to make you a slave."

"You're lying," Seward replied.

"No I am not."

Grabbing Seward and gripping her hands onto his shoulders, she related the story, of the cup Morgund had dunk, of that which he thought was poison, and the grand witch laughing with the cook over the lacings in Morgund's food. How sick Morgund was now.

"Morgund can expect no mercy from the grand witch. "She will kill him."

"She is a cruel demon."

"Double so, for she has spoken of ripping him asunder with a blunt object cast into his behind in an act of perversion."

"Where is Morgund?" Seward realised he was so under the grand witch's spell that he had forgotten to think of Morgund.

Mirium could not go to Morgund lest it draw the wrath of the witch queen. So she bid Seward on. Seward found Morgund was confined to his cot, too sick to move lying in his own foulness. Seward saw to his care, washed him and had him drink water.

Making Morgund as comfortable as possible he departed to find Mirium. Finally he caught her alone. In a corridor. Seward spoke quietly. "This witch has the power over us."

"She has no power at all. She has us believe by fictions."
I can prove it to you."

"Do so."

"I shall. Meet me tomorrow morning before first light, near the stone wall. If you value your freedom and possess any small light of awakeness in you, you will come."

# TO THE FOREST

THE NEXT MORNING before dawn, Seward forced himself to think about the impending day. He still didn't know if he would have to courage to do as Mirium sought. If he was gone for a time and the grand witch found out about it, his life was forfeit, and Morgund's, and the girl's. A storm sounded overhead. Rain provided less chance of being discovered with fewer people outdoors. There was the slight warmth of early spring, despite the wet. Before long, Mirium stood before him. By now having been broken to following instructions automatically, he followed her without emotion to another large manor house. Once there, hiding behind a piece of shrubbery whilst she entered the house. Shortly thereafter reappearing, Mirium. With her was the very same man he had seen in the pot, alive and well who, cutting some larger blocks of wood into smaller and stacked her cart. She brought it with her wheeling it back the way they came. As she passed Seward she nodded to him, beckoning that he follow.

Mirium led Seward by the arm as she said, "See, her tales of what happened to the man in the pot nothing but lies."

Seward looked intently into her eyes. "We must escape with Morgund. She will try to stop us from leaving. We must think this through."

"No, time is short."

"To act hastily might be our deaths," Seward said.

Mirium replied. "If the grand witch finds out what I have done she will kill me. I am afraid! I am frightened, what if she has already discovered our absence? She will do something dreadful to Morgund. I am so scared of her. She will cut me entire. We must run."

A very determined Seward: "We will go back to the house, collect Morgund and be away before she realises what has happened."

Meanwhile, Morgund felt dispirited in the extreme, drained of energy, without emotion. He had a deep seated fear that ticked away, washing over him, eating him away like a cancer. He imagined his death, and how meaningless it would be. Life had no meaning. Nothing had meaning. He would fade away in a whisper, all that he had worked for and aspired to, not to be. Even if he stood his ground and defied her, only with words, at least he gave worth to himself. Today was dreadful but there was always tomorrow. What could he expect but more of the same, or worse.

Weighing up how things stood caused no joy. And he pondered the unfairness of life, that he was here at all. What had he done to deserve his present condition, many others were worse then was he, and yet he was as cast down as far as almost as anyone could be whilst others went about normal lives.

An hour later, Morgund dreamt himself torturously trapped in a narrow tunnel without a way to extricate himself. Imagining reversing, but knew going back would only end in a deep sided pit where he could not escape. Perhaps forward there was light and life and freedom, so he pushed with his knees and elbows, into the darkness.

Each push along the tunnel in inky blackness meant exhaustion and pain. He stopped exhausted and cried and cried, but that did nothing to alter anything. He compelled himself to continue whilst there was life left in him for staying put would only end one way, a solitary agonising death.

Thirst, would come first and his throat roared to tell him so. So he moved forward. The tunnel ended with a light ahead, illuminating a pit and a ladder that led up. He opened his eyes. Awake, he felt sweat all over his body and his heart beat rapidly. He wondered if the dream was a sign that there was a way out.

Morgund detected a difference within himself. His mind was clear. He had not felt like that since first arriving. The witch thought she had him beaten. But by being cruel to him she had given him a great gift. Despite his shaking hands his head felt clearer than it had for weeks, the drugs she had used on him had left his body renewed through his constant vomiting and flux. Feeling weak but triumphant. He would stand up to her. He had told himself this earlier yet stood before her totally under her command. Morgund had been under the influence of her drugs then. But not now. He knew clarity of mind. None of the substances she was accustomed to drugging him with were left inside him.

Thankfully the grand witch let Morgund be, this morning, and no others came to disturb him. He could rest, regain some strength. Seward had left him some oat bread and milk which he ate. He would maintain the demeanour and expression of someone, beaten, uselessness. Whilst she was under this impression and her guard down, he would make use of it to his advantage.

He did not know how but he would take her into death, but a chance would come, when and if his moment came to do something other than be subject to her will, he would cast her down. She was old, he would just advance upon her and kill her. Her terrifying, hypnotic eyes, would not protect her this time.

There was nothing stopping Seward and himself walking away. Just then he thought of Mirium and it gave him pause. Perhaps escape would not be so easy. Thinking of her made his stomach queasy. The door opened. Had she read his thoughts and come again, to do him an injury? He was relieved to see Seward and Mirium.

"Morgund get up, we are leaving," Seward said.

"Where to?" Morgund replied.

"Anywhere, anywhere at all," Seward said.

Morgund looked around anxiously. "We never shall escape."

Seward stood defiant. "These powers of hers are not so great. They are largely a falsehood. The oarsman still lives, I saw him. He was alive in the pot, the muck was offal. It was all done as an act to affect us. To fool us so she could have control of us. Rise up Morgund."

"She will catch us." Morgund felt sick. "We can but try." Morgund, drawing upon a reserve of defiance. "Waiting here is nothing but waiting for death."

They would need some provisions and went inside to find them.

An eerie whistle vibrated through the house, Morgund imagined that the witch queen knew what was happening, her spies could be watching from the shadows. "Hurry, let us go," Morgund stated.

A wind somehow not of this earth shook the house. "Mirium, she awakens." Morgund said to Mirium.

"I heard that wind too Morgund. She may soon wake and think to send for us." Mirium looked frightened.

"Think of the pipes Morgund. That will calm you, hearten you." Seward said.

Morgund came to a decision. "We are going to Scotland. Noting, can stop us."

"We must have provisions," Mirium commented.

Seward acknowledged with a tilt of his head. "We will get them and go."

Raiding the kitchen they put food in a sack. Now, to upstairs to get warm clothing. Quickly and silently they obtained whatever scraps of warm apparel they could from Seward's room. So provisioned, the trio headed down the hallway, its creaking boards protesting underfoot. It was as if the house itself had turned upon them. They neared the doorway that led to the Grand Witch's quarters. The glow from a fire within cast the shadow of one of those contemptible handmaidens who stood inside the open door. Whatever ministrations she was acting out were now done. Seward motioned for the others to back into a darkened corner of the hall, for not only was a figure leaving the room, but she was turning towards them. Morgund felt hatred rise up.

He had suffered the humiliations and depravity of the coven, for how long his drug-ruined mind could not say, and Seward had suffered. They remained in the pitchy darkness, the handmaiden merely feet away. She appeared to be no older than Mirium, and was bare save for an iron amulet shaped like a snake eating its own tail. The girl paused, staring into the darkness where they hid, the faint light catching suspicion in her eyes. The shadows failed to conceal them completely, and before the girl could scream Morgund reached out and clamped a hand around her mouth, twisting her so he bore her in an inescapable hold. There was a muffled gasp, a brief struggle and a suppressed but distinct crack. The girl twitched, like a young deer shot by an arrow, and Morgund let the body slip silently to the floor. Shaking, Morgund motioned them forward again.

There was stirring from the crone's room, so they hurried. Nobody had challenged them when they reached the rear door and drenching rain. They must get beyond London. There was a yelling behind them. Whether they had eventually been detected, or somebody had stumbled across the body of the girl they did not know, for all their efforts focused upon escaping. They never looked back.

Morgund felt born again. The rains intensity increased as they found shelter under an overhanging roof. The rain hit over the top of them, like waves at sea, like waterfalls descending, angels curls aglow, this liquid loveliness touched a deep chord within Morgund and he felt like walking on in the rain forever, thereby being swept clean by a thousand brush strokes. Perhaps the rain could wash away this taint. Thunder rumbled, cobblestones sparkled; he noticed them clearly for the first time. Shadowy moistness, and a distant cold grey sky.

A charging spilling of musical tones, heavier, lighter, suddenly turning into a pelting clamour drowning out all else, diminishing, until heard again with fury, a point on the ground, jiggling like water boiling in a pot.

Finally Morgund spoke to the young woman beside him. "You've given me back my life, how can I thank you? By showing Seward the oarsman lived, it broke her spell."

To never leave me, she thought. That was what she wanted, but she knew his wish was not so, remaining silent therefore. The partial control she had over herself slipping. Her emotions overwhelming, she ran, unable to speak. A future without Morgund was too desolate to bear. She ran, not knowing if her heart would break from physical exertion or from sheer suffering. Remembering trying to convince the grand witch to leave Morgund alone. Her courage had failed. The memory of it wracked her conscience.

Morgund caught her. "What is wrong?"

"You will leave me. Yes? When we are away to safety, outside London."

A look of confusion from Morgund.

"Yes."

A slight acknowledgement.

"But I love you Morgund."

He held her close, it was only out of pity, she thought, but this embrace felt good nonetheless. She treasured it, longed that it would never end.

His eyes told her much. "You only feel sorry for me."

He didn't answer but pulled her closer. She was partly correct; in his heart compassion but not possessed of this alone, there was something more, a withered spark given life by the joy he felt at being free, by the need for him she displayed, he revelled in her love, thought that he had been a fool not to notice her for what she was - his friend.

She owned a piece of his heart and always would. He held a belief that things would turn out well for her. It was important to him now that they did. She must be safe, it was his responsibility. There was a ripple in his heart, but not yet did it overcome his reason.

"Take me with you," she asked. "Wherever you go."

"I will not leave you behind." Hugging her, thinking to disperse her anguish but not really meaning it. He could not take her into the highlands of Scotland, to war.

"Thank you." She tried to be happy, but read in his eyes that it was not his design to take her.

Morgund nodded. Tears burned her eyes, they were mirrored in his own. He realised then that he too was in love with her, and that was why he cried - because he loved her.

A hopeful look. "Do you love me?"

"Yes," he replied, surprised at himself and how the words, spoken aloud, made him feel.

Lips met, passionately. He cradle her by the small of her back, Mirium, relishing the closeness and sense of security imparted therein. Her lips parted from his and she breathed into his ear her voice quavering with a mixture of emotion. "Morgund, I am to have your child." He did not answer. "I will bear a baby if all is well with me and child. Is it well that I do?"

Returning to Scotland, settling the score with Alexander seemed to have moved far from him. He was both buoyant and disturbed at the same time. Did he want this child? He was not sure, but he would protect it and nurture it with whatever ability he possessed.

Seeing his concerned look, she asked, "It was just that it happened."

"It happens," he replied, "like that I mean, often, unplanned."

"What do you mean?" Mirium's voice expressed her hurt. "Is it not well?"

Too much had happened too quickly. This child was of his making, his mind clumsy floundering. He had spoke thoughtlessly, now, even more so. "How does it concern me?" Her face whitened at his comment. Holding her in his arms, he said, "Don't mind me. You are mine and I want to marry you I adore you. Our babe, I look forward to us having it. He patted her stomach, softly, gently, using his fingers in long strokes. "It is lucky indeed to have the protection, of ourselves."

Time prevented him from showing the full depth of his feelings. He would, when they had gotten far away into the countryside beyond London. Seward was with them and he hadn't spoken for a full ten minutes. Seward could wait. He looked at her again, savouring the thought of being with her for a long time. Their tongues collided again as love's fire rekindled.

Seward ventured, "Now we wait until the rain stops, then we rob someone and steal a horse."

"Only one horse?" asked Mirium.

"It will be easier to waylay one man. We can obtain another later." Seward replied.

"The first thing we do on leaving her house is commit a wrong on another?" Mirium said.

"Fortune's wheel must turn. We be atop, presently, but to hesitate, is to risk the fall to the bottom. She! May have horseman out to find us," Seward said.

"I won't steal a horse, Morgund. It is wrong." Mirium said this to nettle him, and she tried not to smile, so as not let him know she jested. Then her mind took in the seriousness of it all. "But I can't walk to Scotland. I am with child and such a difficult journey might badly affect my babe." She was proud of her child and wanted Seward informed.

"What?" Seward's mouth dropped.

"I am pregnant," she repeated.

"I thought you said that. God be good."

"Were you not listening earlier Seward?" Morgund said.

"I walked off and gave you privacy," Seward replied.

"I did not notice," Morgund said.

"I know, my friend, you were otherwise preoccupied."

Morgund said. "Enough. It is best we address the issue of our escape and later about joyous news. We need to be away. We will talk more later, about the child."

Seward was unresponsive, as if he had slipped back into his haze. He was staring at them both.

"Seward, we need to be away urgently."

"It is best that we go," Seward finally replied, having regained his voice. It was not, however as it once was, one shock too many, this day. Seward's confusion eventually lessened. Seward thought about the morning. The beat fell different, the Grand Witch didn't hold the stick, that felt good. Whilst waiting to put their plan into action Seward pulled Morgund aside. A sudden realisation springing to mind. "Should we die in Scotland there will be no one to protect Mirium and the babe. Your grandfather had his eyes taken out by a King much kinder than Alexander. What might Alexander do? She cannot come to Scotland."

"Mirium has my promise, Seward."

From Seward. "If ever you set foot back in Scotland, from that moment you will be hunted until death. Can you think of your safety and hers so little, and think, not to protect a babe. To return to Scotland a dead man walking."

"Cannot we take to the heather and hide? If all goes wrong," Morgund replied.

"Morgund, think of what you say. You know that would not work."

Finally, Mirium spoke. "Morgund, stay, here in England, when our babe grows enough to make for itself, then take to Scotland."

"I have been too long away neglecting my responsibilities. My mother could be in danger and might need me. My clansman must know they have a chief. Alexander. I am ready to cross swords with him and have payment for the wrongs he has done to me. I will go as soon as I can. I will test his mettle. When it is safe, I will return for thee."

"And what will I do?" Mirium asked. "Wait? Look into the fire wondering if you will come, or I am abandoned, or widowed?"

Morgund didn't reply, silence engulfed them a long uncomfortable silence.

Mirium finally said. "Who would I stay with?"
.
"I have friends who would take thee in. When it is safe I would return and have thee with me."

So it was decided that Mirium would stay in England until it was safe for her and the baby to come to Scotland. Mirium resigned herself to her predicament much reduced in happiness, realising where she stood in his priorities. Her attempt to meet his eyes and resume the discussion met with nothing, he looked away. His mind was elsewhere, he regarded the matter as over and decided.

Mirium walked the forest path. It led north, and was the route to avoid the major highways where word of their passing could reach any pursuers. Mirium well sick of looking for comfort from Morgund, knew he regarded her as a liability. A pregnant girl she thought herself a liability, not wanted by anyone. The tiring day came to a close. She looked towards Morgund seeking to draw some comfort. He gazed beyond her intent on the greenery. If Morgund didn't want her he would not have her. Halting to attend to a call of nature, she traipsed off into the green-woods.

Whist Morgund and Seward waited, she pushed further in. Mirium did not become frightened until darkness began to settle over the woods. In the fading light, the trees began to take on unfamiliar and menacing shapes. There was movement in the shadows. She felt hunted. In a panic, she ran. A sudden wind blew, shaking water from the branches drenching her. Wet tendrils clawed, discomfortingly. Low-hanging branches barred her path, and rain-sodden leaves trailed wetly across her cheek. She could hear sounds behind her and kept quickening her pace, until she tripped over the exposed roots of a massive oak and sprawled headlong into the dark. She lay very still, but heard the unsteady echoes of her own breathing and brambles and broken branches stirring in the wind.

"In the forest you may find yourself lost without a companion." It was her mother's warning from long ago.

Her mother had once warned her thus as a child to prevent her wandering far from her, amongst the woods to get lost. A mother's love was the only true love. A man's love was selfish, it could not last. Her mother had said that to, as in so much else, the wisdom of her mother prevailed.

A great lot of good Mirium had done herself, she thought. Withal, she would have to wait here till morning to try and find a way out. Life seemed so hard and unfair. She had been a pretty child once. Now, she lay destitute, and unloved on the forest floor. In an agony of discomfort wet-through, tortured with unpleasant thoughts. Closing her eyes shivering from the cold, she heard … "Mirium where art thou? Mirium?"

It was Morgund's voice, and further away Seward sang out, calling out, "Mirium? Mirium?"

"Morgund, I am here. Here!" She kept calling to him drawing him closer until he found her. She shook. She was soaked and cold, lacking the fortitude of spirit to continue alone having spent many hours laying on the wet ground and being rained on.

"What happened?" Morgund said breaking through the undergrowth.

She lied. "I must of walked too far within the forest. I thought I'd easily find my way back and become lost."

Morgund sounded angry. "We have been searching for hours."

"Are you very angry with me?" she asked challengingly.

Morgund hugged her. "Of course not."

He gave her his arm and led her away. She knew little of what happened after that, only that she was sheltered and before a fire, and very soon asleep. It was well into the morning before they again walked the road. Being unaccustomed to the heavy exertion, Mirium's body grew sore quickly.

The young man sat high in the saddle, imagining what a fine figure he struck. Handsome, tall, and lithe was Edward of Linwood. A fortunate life he could call his, born; into gentility, not too rich nor too poor. His family were known in his shire as notables. He rode without a care, having never suffered a serious misfortune, nor did he ever expect to meet with one. At a turn in the road he saw three figures, rustics who must make way for him. His servant Giles would give them short shift and bid them stand aside. He cast his eyes to Giles, with a commanding air. Giles knew what was required.

The rain was lessening as they continued on the road. Morgund and Seward both eyed Edward as a cat may a bird with a broken wing. Not only was the man, of evident, if not extravagant wealth, but his physique and demeanour identified him as one utterly alien to ways of the blade. The both bore the merriment of character and lack of articulation Morgund and Seward associated with complete stupidity. By providence or mere luck, proceeding towards them was an opportunity far too good to miss. The pair adopted the station of beggars, their hands open, outstretched and imploring.

"Sir, I beg you to stop, we seek charity. Two starving men and a girl who is also so," Seward said.

The young horseman rode up to the two. "Be off with you ruffians," Edward said.

Seward grasped his reins. As he did, his voice became threatening. "Dismount, we do not seek to injure you, but we need your horse, so get off."

"How dare you!" Unaccustomed to being touched by one of the peasant class, he was in shocked that one would dare to touch him.

Resisting, suddenly he found himself unhorsed, relieved of his purse and as an added injury, roughly pushed into the mud on the side of the road. The dandy, disorientated and fearful and equally, unused to being covered in mud, attempted to come to terms with his situation. His servant, Giles, likewise grounded. Now saddled, Morgund and Mirium, turned to wave before disappearing behind a turn in the road.

Edward and Giles, in somewhat elevated spirits from their earlier sampling of wines, took a somewhat pragmatic approach to their situation and began their long, if not unenjoyable ramble back home. Edward of Linwood was not a particularly dynamic, intelligent or energetic man. His hereditary title and estate allowed him to live comfortably enough, but the meeting he had in the woods with Seward, Morgund and Mirium marked by far his most exiting adventure, to date. Their lives had been at stake, undoubtedly. An hour later, Edward walking easily moments before, coming to the gate to his manor began staggering. He had to be stood upright by men in the yard. The incident on the road to London grew with each telling.

Edward embellished the story of arriving home in his mud-spattered attire, throwing off the men who held him up, and bravely making the doorway, alone.  He failed to mention not drawing his purely dagger when accosted.  Firstly, straight after the incident he had given obliging thanks to God above that he still drew breath.  But in safer surrounds the unarmed assailants and a girl metamophed into a dozen armed and dangerous assailants who fought Giles and Edward, until they were overwhelmed by sheer numbers.  No one who knew either, Edward or Giles, believed them.

Mounted, with Seward leading, and Mirium clinging to Morgund, had made good time, pushing themselves far north. That night a small wood sheltered them. Fish caught from a stream cooked on the open fire, sated them.  They laughed heartily, recounting their robbery on the road, of the dandy and his shocked man servant.

The third day found them too weary to travel.  They spent the day in a field.  Tall grass and flowers seemed to drink in the spring sunshine.  That day brought the most peaceful sleep Morgund recalled since leaving Scotland.  He slept well, knowing he was heading home.  After so long, his mother, he would see her once more.  The day next they spent some of Linwood's money in a small town, helping themselves to fresh bread and cheese.  Mirium, made herself pleasant.  Morgund and Seward did their best to entertain her, and succeeded.

Later in the day Morgund grew silent.   Mirium considered him.  Weariness crinkled his brow.  Morgund must be very tired for he, more than any of them received dire treatment from the Grand Witch.  Then there was the question of the future.   His intention to leave her with strangers was an ungallant act, unworthy of him.  He was better than that, and he would see that for himself.

To Morgund, each league brought him nearer to his reckoning with Alexander. Mirium would be safe. He would return for her. She must wait for him. All his training was leading to this moment. Alexander would find payment for his actions. Nothing else mattered. Nothing. To take up the leadership of clan MacAedh ... That was the station he was born for. Mirium must see that. An abandoned barn sheltered them for the night. In the morning they were away again. A forest skirted their horizon, ahead.

"Is that where we are going?' Mirium demanded, the forest looming closer.

"There? Yes," Morgund replied earnestly.

They travelled to a isolated section of the dense woodland, its forest paths, hillocks and streams familiar to Morgund. It was the woodland estate where Cristo and his family had sheltered Morgund for a season of recuperation. After an hour picking their way through the trees, two men, Cristo and Morgund, met again. They shared a heartfelt embrace. Cristo, however, was somewhat solemn in his disposition. Cristo told Morgund disappointedly, Edith, had become somewhat wanton in her attitude since Morgund had left. In her caprices Edith would steal away to town alone and spend time with whomsoever took her fancy. Edith found it both exhilarating and soul destroying in equal measure. The years had been unkind to Cristo, and he had aged beyond what Morgund expected. The greatest cause was the taxing circumstances of his daughter, and the realization he could not control her. Also, the tragic lose of his son, murdered by nobles in the forest, as had happened to his late wife which had done much to disturb him.

Perhaps Edith would not have been beset by waywardness had she married Morgund. If married to him she would have been with someone who had conquered her inner being, both spiritually and physically. What existed between them in a sense was gone forever, never to be recovered yet in another sense it was as strong as ever. Close proximity renewed the attraction. Morgund felt it. Mirium saw it in his eyes. And, Edith definitely felt the power of their mutual attraction.

That revivified fascination was with him every moment. The fact remained that Mirium also had his heart, which made him introspective. The situation was unfortunate for all. Mirium asked him about Edith. He reflected of their time together, and seeing the look on his face, she did not ask again. Edith fought animosity towards Mirium as did Mirium her own. They were in each other's presence daily, toiling together, giving them no release from the stifling anxiety. Edith was quietly supportive of Mirium and helped her, but she was torn, her compassion made her want to help Mirium yet whenever she thought of Morgund her heart raced, it antagonised Mirium beyond measure. Mirium noticed every little look Edith gave Morgund, and he her.

This atmosphere brought about in Mirium a progressive fall. She could not withdraw from the vacuum of the depression she found herself drawn into. Things went on like this until the first thaw when Seward and Morgund set out for Scotland. Morgund was too young to understand. He thought she was using feminine guile to prevent his departure, by appearing so despondent to guilt him into not leaving, or was in sorrow at the thought of it, which was partly the cause, a matter he could do nothing about.

The night before he left he told her. "I have to go, to restore my fortune. I cannot be dishonourable and skulk in England."

He sounded very young saying that. The recollection of his words would bring a smile to her lips in years to come, but as much as she loved that image, she would expend much effort trying to forget it, for immediately after the smile came the moment when she remembered her subsequent actions. But presently, Mirium acknowledged that he had to be true to his conscience, though it didn't lessen her hurt. Her eyes, as he rode away very grey and desolate.

# MORGUND MEETS ALEXANDER

THE RENEWAL OF spring fell across the land. The freshly fallen rain giving a vibrancy and glistening sheen to all that lay beneath the clouds. The air was refreshed too. The hands of grace were outstretched, and resting upon open places the new season's glorious bounty. The two riders on horseback approached a fork in the road where the northward path bisected.

"We shall take the low road Morgund," Seward declared.

Morgund scoffed aloud. "I'm taking to the high road Seward."

Morgund took off with a dash. Seward, realising belatedly he was being challenged to a race, dug his spurs in. In places the two roads nearly overlapped. Morgund's elevated trail leading him slightly above Seward. Seward's horse was much faster. He expected to surpass Morgund easily. The two paths came very close together as Morgund and Seward sped on. What was the fool doing now, Seward thought. Distracting him? Balancing in his saddle, Morgund leaned forward, then climbed up on the horse's back. Pushing himself off, Morgund sailed through the air and hit Seward squarely, dislodging him from his saddle. Together they tumbled, joyously rolling over the earth. At this moment they both felt completely free. The ground, softened by the rain, had been warmed by the sun's rays to a comfortable soft rest. They sat near a stream that twinkled enticingly.

The water came from the hills nearby, caressed by boulders on the way down. It sang happily, and by the action of plants and the movement of rocks, the water was purified. They could taste the clarity and purity of the water, the crystal stream cleansed their palates.

"At least you didn't beat me Seward."

"I still might," Seward replied, as he had his hand closed into a fist in feigned threat.

"I fell. It was an accident and you just happened to be in my way. Sorry." Morgund couldn't subdue a smile.

"It was quite a feat, catching me like that."

"Aye Seward, you are the biggest fish I have caught."

"You told me it was an accident."

"It was," Morgund argued proudly.

"Morgund."

Morgund protested, "It was, I." He was at a loss for words, "I, umh, I, umh." He laughed.

Together they fought their way up the hill. The ascent was tougher going than first impressions allowed. Nature's harmony and serenity however, calmed them. They talked easily, enjoying themselves. Later that day they crossed into Scotland and their jovial spirits were almost immediately quelled. Trials of strength ahead lay, Morgund and Seward hoped they were ready for them.

Upon crossing into Scotland a dismal rain set in. Irritated and growing colder and wetter by degrees. Seward remarked upon the rain in the negative. It rained, every second or two, Seward felt cold. "It's raining," he said. "Again!"

"Yes," Morgund replied. "You have said that, already, often."

Morgund gazed heavenward. The falling rain grew heavier, the dark, rolling clouds unburdening themselves upon the earth. The sky, Morgund noticed, seemed to have a life all its own. Morgund continued to stare at the clouds, and wondered perplexedly wether his introspection drew apparitions forth from the sky or if the firmament above was haunted by giants and spectres which sprang there by God's will. To the north, a great bearded face, whose contenance divided slightly before dissolving. A group of boys racing. The fleecy blankets parted for a moment, the lighter patch of sky formed the perfect outline of an axe. In time a dark woman with long hair in a drifting halo around her head took flight on great feathered wings. Morgund, in his daydreaming, thought of the effigies that graced the prows of ships, of whispering giants conspiring, of princess and godesess. The growing intensity of the rain eventually rendered the sky a uniform black, with an occasional lightness where thunder light up. He felt chilled and shivered. With no shelter nearby he and Seward pulled up their hoods.

"It is supposed to be spring, Seward," Morgund muttered gloomily.

"In Scotland the word means little."

To Seward it seemed as if this weather had taken issue against him personally, and he'd like to settle it somehow. Yet with nothing to do but gaze at the sky. The rain slowed. The light improved, and the clouds parted in the western sky. The blue, a blessed relief. Morgund looking up, saw nothing interceding between them and the far up stratosphere. Then the clouds rolled in again. The wet being overtaken by sun and the sun by rain. The clouds looked wispy at present as if they would flee, but he were not taken in by appearances. For he knew to keep his eyes closed for a short time and open them again all would change.

"For how long I wonder will it shine?" Morgund asked, to breach the silent monotony of their journey.

"I don't know," Seward replied.

Soon bleak quilty layers smothered the sky's blue and wetness glided down. The horse's hooves made splashing plods on the sodden earth. Morgund wished to be in front of a roaring fire. The atmosphere, cold. Soon mighty blows came down upon them in the form of bitter hail.

"What a day," Morgund complained. "It would test the patience of a Saint."

"Welcome to Scotland, Morgund."

"Just as well I don't believe in omens," Morgund said.

"Perhaps you should," Seward replied with an arch of an eyebrow.

From the breaking cloud cover narrow corridors of light, bridging the divide between heaven and earth. Morgund and Seward focused their attention upon the glorious spectacle. But as they rode on, the divine display of light and colour fled from mortal sight.

"This day is as moody as a woman suffering her monthly predicament," Morgund cursed.

"It does not pay to mock the skies, Morgund. The issue is not their wrath, but our stupidity in being out in it, for we are not made to dwell in it, as well we know."

In a sheltered clearing they set up camp. The pair claimed warm, dry lodging, for within the trees the rain had scant opportunity to reach the forest floor. They slept poorly, disturbed by insects and the noises of the woods. The next day as bleak as that before. The day following however brought fine weather. Food was scant in their possession so they went searching for it. Fair pleasant place this was, furnished, with soft ferns and wild grasses. With the odd gnarled tree. Reminding Seward of a landlord, watching over his tenants. The smaller growing trees, each half-acre, a multitude, thereof. A wide view containing many of them yet only one large tree, seemingly a guardian to his smaller brethren, a curiosity of nature, pleasing to the human eye. They came to a stream, with flowering vines hugging the higher bank. Downstream, bulrushes. The woodland bore a multitude of hues from the high vaulted canopy to the saplings and shrubbery. Yet, what of game? No doubt this was its habitat, but they could see no beasts and their bellies scolded them, at the scarcity. Seward followed a narrow path.

Something caught Morgund's attention. A bird made its way across the sky in a relaxed rhythm. It swept away in an arc. The wind unleashed a steady stream of debris, this, the reward for Morgund's steady gaze. Morgund had a nudge from Seward, "Come on."

Morgund followed his friend on the game trail. The close trees and branches he pushed aside took him thither. Occasionally Seward paused and Morgund would follow suit, listening and alert for any signs of game. The path led to a quiet glade and ahead they could see a hill of ancient forest. Surely the towering trees in this section of the wood were the progenitors of the rest. They stood tall and proud, like ranks of disciplined soldiers.

They continued. Decaying leaf matter and crackling twigs betrayed them as they walked. Amongst the leaf litter and scattered logs mushrooms grew. They collected handfuls and shortly after, found a partly dismembered deer. The deer was newly killed and some of its meat untouched. Dogs, close by, began growling. Morgund sent an arrow to disperse them. Once he did this, the meat was theirs, and they cut it into long strips.

"Mushrooms will be good to eat tonight with this," Morgund said.

"Aye. Maybe on the way back we might find some more. Perhaps even a live stag," Seward replied.

"That is my hope Seward."

But they did not see any live game.  Seated, they looked out at the terrain.  This was an odd place, picturesque yet unforgiving.  Seams of granite encrusted the hills, and the peaks were adorned with great boulders, like alters to long forgotten gods.

"Here, I sit beneath this tree, with a fire going and water boiling.  Soon to quench my thirst with a mint tea."

"I didn't have you marked for a poet Morgund."

"Nor did I, myself," Morgund replied.

Seward prompted.  "Tell me more."

"When I think of more I will.  Today has magic to it.  Most days aren't like this.  I wish this day could go on forever."

"What about Mirium?"

"If she were here.  Perfection."

"It is good to feel full again," Seward declared.

Seward nodded with smile.  "Aye, indeed."

Once night fell, their eyes fastened onto the roasting fire.  A short period of conversation was followed by an exhausted sleep.  Morning came, and amply provisioned they continued.  The weather remained fine.  Scotland's climate did not consist of many clear days, thus, those few that occurred were savoured.  People living in cold climes do lust for them; the rays shining down made for easy travel.

Riding along, wheat fields waving their fluffy hands at them.  Later they came to a patchwork of fallow fields and the remains of hovels put to the torch.  This was the handiwork of the English raiders.  Some of the crop survived but this was poor land.

Then the cool green shade of woods enclosed them briefly before dense forest cast them in deep shadow.  At last, an end, the open sky,  which they had not seen for long.  A thin white apron hung drawn across by an unseen brushstroke in the heavens and at one end leaving a distortion on the blue a transparent smudge.  Soon dark trees surrounded them again. This an offshoot of the main forest. They were looking forward to leaving it and regaining the pleasure of the sun.  A little spring sprang to their sight.  They took their horses down to drink. Sitting themselves down.  Sunlight streamed down past outstretched branches, like silver fountains cascading.  The undergrowth made a comfortable bed.

They built a fire and a concocted brew of roots.  A slow-paced interlude, where they drank often, and enjoyed warm concoctions.  Then they began organising their departure. Thereafter, riding on.  Ever more the woods became more peculiar, and eerily silent.  Morgund could not help recalling it was in a similar forest, a place fit for kings, that he had been captured by king John's henchman.  Notwithstanding, though, they were far from that forest.  He was sure, like that forest to the south this would also be the haunt of noblemen.  Seward thought there was danger.  The watchful silent forest had them on guard

"Morgund, someone with red hair comes this way," Seward said.

"A red haired man," Morgund observed, spotting the intruder from a distance.

"With an affinity."

There sounded the galloping of horses, the baying of hounds and the blast of the hunting horn.

"Yes Morgund someone this way, comes."

"Let us into the forest and tether the horses, hide them well," Morgund said.

It was done. With the horses far in and tightly tethered, they blackened their faces and put green sprigs amongst their clothing. They crept to where they could see.

Hooves pounded the forest floor. A wild boar, the evading dogs, scampered up the track. Horses ever closer. And then there he was. Alexander. Still slim, still wearing that pointed red beard. Still, the fox, as king John had so aptly named him. The irony that "the fox" should be the hunter was not lost upon Morgund.

Alexander rubbed his eyes. The hunt had been going ... too long. The night before he had over indulged in wine and revelry. He looked around him. Mud. There was always mud. Sticky mud on his new boots. The treacherous ground strewn with timber tested the courage and ability of the riders. Alexander enjoyed these forays, for he found the galloping through the forest as equally entertaining as the chasing of the deer or boar. Many were the days he spent like this; drenched with mud and rain, exhilarated, laughing, in flight between the logs and thorns, turning and chasing his prey and spearing it.

Admired, for just who he was, the king. Breathing the aromatic, resinous scent of pine, and feeling relaxed. His cousin, Cospatrick, Earl of Dunbar was his friend and sworn man, and these were his forests. Cospatrick had a very tenuous claim to the throne, as did many, yet too tenuous to have any real validity. His most serious rival, Morgund MacAedh, not heard of for many years, was widely thought dead. If Alexander died, childless, the succession could go to his impulsive cousin somewhere away in the timbers. His wife, king John's daughter, Joan, had born no child, nor ever fallen pregnant. If God willed it a son would rule after him, if not, others would. The churned ground caught his eye. Mud, always mud. On days like this it froze and never dried out Sticky brown glue, where did it come from this bog, everywhere. He was thoroughly sick of it. A fire sounded good.

Cospatrick was a boon companion, yet he was often headstrong. Whether by the man's nature or because of his close ties with Alexander, Cospatrick, Earl of Dunbar, behaved recklessly, often daring those amongst his retinue to the same feats of bravado or hot-headedness. Any battle Cospatrick fought would be his last for he had more courage than sense. Alexander thought Cospatrick reckoned the providence that made Alexander king would rub of on himself, and protect him both in terms of body and diplomacy. Alexander, however, did as he felt fit. Had Cospatrick encouraged the others of his retinue to acts of foolishness that led to a broken neck, Alexander would have laughed heartedly at them. But for now Alexander managed to evade his entourage, to seek some solace in the woods to clear his head.

Nonetheless, Alexander's bodyguard would be replaced. The man had become distracted by the hunt and carried on without him. As much as Alexander appreciated the solitude he saw the danger. Alexander had eluded him very easily. Presently, the fact was of negligible consequence. However, one day it could prove deadly. A king who lost his companions could be killed. Many of Scotland's kings had met violent deaths, and Alexander was not about to join them. As if in answer to his thoughts there was a rustle in the undergrowth and then Morgund stood before him.

After a long moment of shock Alexander recovered enough to say, "The MacAedh risen from the grave!"

"The fox, it seems, has been caught," Morgund replied.

Alexander looked around him nervously. "But by whom am I caught? It is just yourself I see, only."

"Don't be alarmed, fox, I have only a companion, but a companion armed with a bow with an arrow pointed at thine breast."

Alexander could see another man to one side of Morgund, no doubt the bowman.

"And if you shoot me my cousin Cospatrick will be king. He would love nothing better. It helps thee not."

"I would kill you for your treachery, for what you did to my father."

Alexander played for time, he knew his bodyguard would soon notice his absence and return for him.

"I did what I had to do," he stammered, trying to find his confidence. This was laboured under the burden of his predicament. "You're a highland miscreant who won't come to heel."

Alexander moved his horse away slightly. Just then he heard men calling his name. The undergrowth moved, Alexander ducked down, expecting an arrow as he furiously rode away. Alexander thought he heard, "We will meet again, Fox."

But it was faint and could have been his imagination. Only four men rode to meet with him. Alexander sent one to alert the others and sent the other two after Morgund. The remaining bodyguard abiding by his side. Neither of the men sent forth into the undergrowth wished to be skewered and moved just out of Alexander's sight and sat down, waiting. Alexander was safe out of target range. Meanwhile, Morgund and Seward had regained their horses and escaped, a brisk gallop and some hastily concealed tracks forestalling any pursuit. Alexander sent out search parties to hunt down them down which met with no success.

Morgund silently brooded on how close he'd been to killing Alexander and Seward let him have his thoughts. Morgund and Seward broke free of the forest sometime in the afternoon. They rode with focus and determination. Suddenly, all energy was spent, it was as if the woods, the birds and beasts therein and time itself had been stilled. Now they were exhausted from spurring their horses fast, and the horses themselves shone with a glistening of sweat. The forest had provided some cover from pursuers. Now, in open country, but far from any pursuit they allowed the horses and themselves to rest.

Coming to the midlands, it was late afternoon and still warm. They gazed at the sun. The fiery beacon dying in motion shooting reddish pink across the sky, then, with one last red-yellow peak, it was gone and night descended.

---

THE MORNING WAS one of gold; the early sun warm at the horizon's edge and the rolling fields below were populated by stalks of ripening wheat bowing under the burden of heavy full heads.

Morgund said with wonder. "If it were somewhat warmer, I'd say it could pass for Italy here. Where we are? What do you think, have we escaped Scotland to be there? I remember the forever rain of Scotland. Are we in another land, the land of sun?"

"In pockets, where wheat fills the land, aye, it seems so. In bog lands and broken dwellings where English raiders have put abodes to the torch, I'd say no. Hereabouts it could be Italy. If there is such a state," Seward said "They say Italy, looks not like Scotland. There are no soft dreary rains and it isn'a always a'blowin, like here."

Finally Morgund spoke on the matter preoccupying his mind. "I should of slain Alexander when I had the chance, Seward."

"I agree," Seward replied.

"Is that all you can say Seward?" Morgund said.

"At least my behind is not rain sodden today, Morgund."

"Please tell me what I could of done.  It happened so fast, so unexpectedly," Morgund said.

"I'm sure if you make battle against him, you will meet him again.  Seek next time to kill him then, surely he will seek to do you to death, Morgund to.  And you will both be content."

Morgund didn't look interested, he was looking for a way to get under Seward's skin, a remedy for his frustration and what he saw as his failure to act meaningfully upon meeting Alexander.

Morgund said.  "Good biting winds that's what Scotland is noted for.  The Latin's know that, I bet, as we know sunny or wet, we wouldn't swap our Scotland as it is a better home for us, than anywhere."  He hadn't finished yet although Seward wished he were, because he didn't want to hear such nonsense.  The unspoken hurt with Alexander was not a subject Morgund or Seward wanted to discuss, this but, a distraction, an irritating one Seward thought.  "Although  more of like sun would be to my liking" Morgund finally concluded.

Seward cast a hard gaze at Morgund.  "I enjoy brightness as do all.  But judge this? Never think the sun more pleasant in Italy, the sun would burn our like to cinders.  We are not made for it.  This our home and there is nowhere better than that surely."  Then Seward said, contrarily,  "I love Scotland to but wouldn't it be grand to see scenes unlike any we know."

Morgund put words to a quickening heart.  "This land, the land of my forefathers that begat me  is the only place for me. You weren't born in Scotland.  It is understandable."

Seward remembered the expression Morgund had displayed a couple of days ago when it rained. He wondered what his opinion would be if it was pelting rain. Seward knew it would be different.

Morgund was at it again. "This land a better one than any."

"Aye Morgund, if you say so." Seward had enough of distant lands and the comparisions with hereabouts. Seward was thinking of what they might find when returning to the land they had called their own, the MacAedh, inheritance.

Horses advancing at a rapid clip, looking at the expression on Seward face, Morgund said, "You're many miles from here aren't you?"

"Yes."

Seward cast his mind to Alexander and the change in him since they had last met him. Alexander was in his mid twenties now, and taller. Seward continued on having his flighty thoughts for he didn't want the peril he was heading into to make him anxious. He was thinking of how neatly trimmed Alexander's beard had been. Alexander looked quite gallant, like a king. Morgund was replaying the meeting with Alexander. Morgund imagined himself as king, and determined he would be equally, if not more regal.

"Mine are?" Morgund said, looking like a wistful poet.

"Are what?" Seward asked, finally leaving his private world.

"Good thoughts. Concentrating on these fields of plenty."

Wheat fields stood ready for the knife.  This was a part of the land that produced most of its wealth, however only the elite benefited by the richness of the soil.   Peasants lived simply by running cattle and sheep, or both, on small places. Game and other natural foods supplementing  their diet. When conditions were favourable life was good but in less promising years they barely subsisted, or worse, starved.

Family relationships were the interwoven strands that held these people above despair.  In adversity, they made haste to assist each other.   It was often a hard life but they were not alone.  Gaining the harvest and planting was the tenants' due, which they did without complaint as they raised in arms for his Lordship in times of war.   Morgund couldn't help but think of how many men the lowlands could provide - many more than his highlands.   Morgund brought up in conversation with Seward on the vast resources Alexander could call upon, so much more than their own.  Seward did not seem interested. Morgund let the matter drop.

With the full import of their intended endeavour brought home to them, they practised their sword craft long and hard that same day.   The realistic bruising encounter they welcomed as a distraction.   Afterwards, whilst nursing injuries, they talked  tactics, going through various useful methods slowly and carefully.  They analysed themselves and confidence began to burn.  If nothing else, as individuals they were a match for all but the very few who, like themselves, were extremely gifted in the art of swordsmanship

The sun had dipped low on the horizon when Morgund and Seward chanced upon a man, being dragged behind a party of six men by a rope tied around his neck. When the captive collapsed, as happened often, he would be kicked and harassed until he clambered to his feet again to continue his humiliating pilgrimage. As the day grew darker the men stopped, and tied their prisoner tightly to a tree. Morgund and Seward observed the men preparing a meal from a distance. The captors did not share it with their charge despite his protests.

Seward snarled at the injustice, and Morgund knowing his companions mind had a like disdain. The two of them had suffered and been dealt many injustices of their own, far too many to simply witness another being tormented and to not intervene. Without a spoken word, the pair decided the prisoner must be released, and that his captors had a grave case to answer. They rode down the hill towards the shameful sight.

Pulling their horses to a stop, Seward and Morgund, watching. The captors sneered indignantly at them willing them to react, confidant, amused at their anger. Morgund's eyes were snakelike, deadly passionate. It was a foolish man indeed who took him lightly as these men now did. Outnumbering them, the soldiers expected Seward and Morgund to be apprehensive. But they weren't, they ached, yearned to attack. Seeing this, one of the keepers advanced on his prisoner with a hot stick pointing it out obviously intent on burning him. Looking across at Morgund and Seward daring them to action. Morgund advanced. He would not permit this to go on. Coming close to the held man one of the soldiers moved to intercept Morgund.

"This concerns you not."  The swordsman who blocked Morgund's path stated matter-of-factly.

There was the shrill noise of a blade drawn quickly and expertly from a scabbard, and a keen flash of steel.  Morgund swung the blade with force and precision, and the man toppled over to his side in a kind of weak, ineffectual cascade.  A fount of crimson erupted three feet from the man's truncated neck, the head attached by only the scarcest of sinew and skin and staring backwards at his companions with a quizzical, stunned expression.  It was several seconds before the remaining partly members realized what had just transpired and stirred to adopt any semblance of defense.  Morgund, too, was shocked.  Those seconds seemed like days, and he felt the blood rush through his dilated arteries, felt his heart pump blood to his muscles and his hands tighten on the hilt of his sword.  He let the rush fill his mind; whereas it would befuddle the minds of most he would use it to his advantage.  A final, glittering spurt of blood came from the twitching body on the ground, awash with gore, the growing stain forming a slick on Morgund's boots.

"We are tenants of Cospatrick, the Earl of Dunbar," Thomas, the leader of the men declared.  Seeing the unconcerned expression, Thomas, added, "The great Earl no less.  The great friend of the king.  His Grace's Chancellor."

This leader of the guards, taking his role seriously, expected this to resonate significantly.  It would come out, that Thomas was not a man to trifle with, as the agent of Cospatrick, he was dangerous.  Confronting Thomas was a stupid move which the intruder would realize before too long. Coming between Morgund and the prisoner, Thomas.

But the intruder had taken leave of his senses and was hot in anger. Cospatrick's servant saw a smile. Seeing how the man looked he was bereft on how to proceed.

Morgund was mildly amused at the man's attempt to use Cospatrick  as a shield.  The fellow, persistent if nothing else, said, "Stop, in Cospatrick's name!" Distressed that his plea did not have the desired effect cried out,  "Fellows tell him what is at stake here."    Ordinarily Thomas treated his men with contempt, and they would have loved to see nothing better, than his head beside the other one on the ground.

"Don't become confused," Morgund told him.  "Numbers will not serve you. Leave the prisoner to me."

Still Cospatrick's nagging servant, Thomas remained defiant, "Let us do our duty."

Morgund felt the urge to burst into action and almost struck the man down then and there.  He made the effort to restrain himself.  "If you desist from getting in my way, and obstructing my purpose of freeing this fellow you shall live if not, you will die, make your own decision."

Thomas must stay in possession of the prisoner to keep his fee, he could not afford to lose his fee, or Cospatrick might even kill him.  Knowing the man's famous temper that was certainly more than a possibility.  The second thought made his face redden  Desperate, he said. "This man is a felon. If you go now, we will accept my friend's unfortunate death as an argument gone wrong."    Trying to ingratiate himself still further, he went on,  "You will not then face justice."

"As you should for treating him so," Morgund reproached Thomas. He would not accept further balking.

The futility of Thomas's appeal was evident in Morgund's expression. Thomas held up a hand, his own countenance betraying a combination of frustration, fear and resignation. Seward stepped forward, blade unsheathed, and deftly cut the prisoner's bounds. The man's shoulders slumped exhaustedly, but despite his condition he armed himself with the fallen man's blade. Equally thankful and weary, he took his place by Morgund and Seward's side. The revelation of liberty and personal desire for revenge, granted him a combative spirit.

"He will go with us," Morgund stated. "And we shall take your horses so you cannot follow."

It was done. Cospatrick's men did not accost. They accepted that the situation was beyond rectifying and were engrossed in seeking a plausible explanation to pass on.

Morgund, Seward and their newfound friend rode. Their companion introduced himself. "Paten."

"Seward."

"Morgund."

"So what did you do to incur the wrath of Earl Cospatrick?" Seward asked.

"Disturbed the king's peace, or really Cospatrick's peace, for to do one is to do the other."

His story unfolded.  As an orphan he was taken into the household of a noble.  This nobleman's daughter kidnapped by Cospatrick whilst still only a small girl to be forcibly married to Waldeve, one of Cospatrick's sons, who then held her estate.  When her aged father died, Cospatrick, would be entitled to all.  Though, of an ancient Celtic family, Cospatrick was as shameless as any Norman in seeking self-aggrandizement.

Unfortunately for Cospatrick she died without issue, meaning the old man could will it to another.  The nobleman decided to give it to a distant cousin, but only by virtue of the king's authority, for the cousin was distant enough that the law dictated the king rule on it.  The king could take it as his own for the discretion was his.  Cospatrick paid the king to ensure he would be the beneficiary.  Not useful to Cospatrick thereafter the old man was abused in his own house.  Waldeve, had mistreated the daughter.  He mistreated her father.  Cospatrick himself didn't, he was ruthless but not sadistic.  Cospatrick's son would have murdered the old man if not for his fathers wishes.  Paten took exception to Waldeve and told him so, whereupon he was soundly thrashed.  After this Paten caused trouble everywhere he went until he was waylaid, his captors informing him he was to be taken to Dunbar castle to be hanged.

"Do you regret your actions?  You can't go home now." Morgund queried.

"I have no home."

"What of the old man?" Seward asked.

"I can't help him." Paten replied.

The day next, the best four mounts were kept, the rest sold cheaply to a trader who asked no questions.

---

GORMLAITH WALKED IN her fathers garden, filled with the most pleasant roses.  Her companion sought her attention and quite possibly a smile or a pleasant word.  Thinking to impress her John MacGauchie told her a long rambling tale, one he thought in part humurous, about his family's origin.  In ancient times a battle had occurred near here.  The Norseman besieging their citadel looked likely to overrun it.  The anxious MacGauchies called all the young men from nearby who marched with their farm implements, their women with makeshift banners coming up behind them.  Farther away, the closer men called out threats.  These factors, giving the appearance of a major army, this generated enough confusion in the Norse ranks that they retreated.

"It is a fascinating story to someone who has some interest in it."  Gormlaith sighed.  "Unfortunately I am not interested in your supposedly elevated origins.  Are not those armed with pots and pans better of as cooks?  If thee had a coat of arms no doubt a pot would be proudly displayed."

He was offended but kept his temper.  "A title won ... but MacBeth persecuted them and most of my family fled to France, and those, that retuned, the Hays, are now nobles leaving us in their wake.  Lords of Hay."

Gormlaith did not reply, but something about her gait through the garden suggested impatience. Similarly, John MacGauchie fell silent. Though he regarded himself, and informed those who would listen, that he was brave, eager to prove his mettle in the field of war, he bore every physical trait indicative of the opposite. MacGauchie was a short man, somewhat squat and rotund of aspect. His face, replete with an inelegant line of receding hair, doubled chin and somewhat low-set eyes, giving him the appearance of mild cretinism. Coupled with his rather flaccid persona, for he was a man docile in both his speech and ways, despite his claims of bravado, MacGauchie held little attraction for the village maids His chances of obtaining a mate were remote. This was true even of Gormlaith; though one of the more attractive girls in the village, she had become insular to others and cold to male admirers since Seward had left years ago.

John MacGauchie's tireless devotion reminded her of a dog. Even though he bored her, his family had some riches, so she tolerated his company, even to the extent of letting him put his arm through hers when it pleased her. She talked to him on those days amicably, but she wasn't in such a mood now.

What passed between them on those infrequent occasions was not exactly romance but he was there to listen to her and she needed someone to speak to. Gormlaith suddenly received the vivid impression of herself and MacGauchie joined in marriage. Perhaps she had displaced her longing for Seward, for his return was an impossibility, onto John. Perhaps that MacGauchie wealth, modest as it was, helped to lubricate her mind to the thought. It was only upon reflection of this that she realized the buzzing in her ear was John speaking to her again.

"You are too beautiful, too desirable ..."

"What, what is that you say?" She asked.

John was slightly taken aback, for Gormlaith did not look pleased. A trace of mockery seemed to enter her eyes, though he stumbled forth in his soliloquy. "You are a sweet, pleasant thing of beauty. Like these roses."

"Very poetic," she replied. "You yourself have the figure of a God." He hated the look she gave. She laughed at him. She was cruel. She thought him a buffoon and wasn't bothering to hide it.

He looked defeated. "I accept your derision. I deserve it."

At last she thought of a way to be rescued from him. "Can you make a poem?" she asked.

"Of course my love," he replied. She had but jested earlier, and had recovered from her evil mood. The shock of her teasing was gone, it must be borne, he thought, for it was playful fun she had at his expense no harm meant by it.

She picked a rose, then scratched him with its thorns, "Make a poem of that," she said. She looked at him with hatred. "You go home now." As he walked away, she called out in a barking way. "You seductive bastard. Go and seduce some sheep."

He suffered a paralysis of will. 'Seductive bastard.' How could she call him, *that,* and do everything to him that she had this day. He arrived home and never remembered afterward how. She was cruel beyond bearing.

Not deterred, the next day and the day after that he went to her door with some trifle. A peculiar warmth grew ever more, until he seemed not so much a fool or a bald stout man, she saw the good in him and realized how much better he was than her, and how she must mend her ways and respect him, for he deserved that. She had been immature on the day of the rose. Although he might not pick up sarcasm and low jokes, he was not stupid. Somehow he was too pure to understand the low depravity of the jackals that each and all societies have amongst them, and whose traits, at times, were, her's. Her family did everything in their power to get him to take her. They liked him, they wanted her to wed and they knew better than she did what an appropriate match it was.

Gormlaith learned to curb the worst of her ways, she watched others and took notice of their actions and felt inspired to be pleasant, really wanted to change, but it was in her nature to be as she was. However, when she jibed him, his calmness of expression didn't stoke the fire of her spite or appear worthwhile cause; he brought her temper down, and it had to be thus for he couldn't understand nor adapt to her ways. John smiled at her tantrums, for it was the surest way to resolve them and make a smile appear on her face.

John MacGauchie offered to take her as wife, to which Gormlaith complied with fervor, she wasn't getting any younger. There existed no a long line of suitors, though often she said half the village men were in love with her. Didn't her looks compare with the loveliest maidens? She was pretty, but it was her uncouth mouth that turned heads away. Seward would be a good match. Gormlaith, looking across the heather imagined Seward and Morgund riding over the hills. They were a way off yet, but she felt they would return. But then she felt they would never return, neither of them had been heard from for many years.

COMING TO A sizeable town, the last before entering the highlands, provisions were obtained. Doubting if coins would prove useful to them where they were going, Morgund suggested a night on the ale. Paten and Seward thought it rash to enter a public house, but Morgund disagreed. He strove to convince the others arguing strongly that where last they encountered difficulties was far to the south, plausibly explaining that it would not have been told so as to travel. Moreover, it had been years since Morgund had been in Scotland, so it was unlikely that he be recognized. Seward had misgivings but agreed. Paten declined, he would care for the horses and the camp equipment. The ale house was a wattle hut, food and drink and smoke within. The darkness inside helped to hide Morgund's identity.

Morgund tasted much drink whilst Seward kept his head low in a corner of the ale house attempting to appear inconspicuous.

Morgund moved unsteadily to his companion to ask in a somewhat slurred voice why he was acting so aloof.

"Seeking to avoid notice Seward?"

Seward's curt reply, followed by an impatient glance even the gloom failed to disguise.

"Of course," Morgund replied, "Man, do you know what you look like? You're near seven feet tall, built like a ox and have snow white hair. And you think you won't draw notice? You draw more attention by trying to hide yourself under the table. If I brought a pig into the bar and it ordered a drink and *it* had an argument with the taverner on the price of the ale, I think it be commented on less." Morgund swaying, drawing an audience, acted up to them. "And if that pig played the pipes at the bar it would be less of note."

"Yes Morgund, thank you. You've drawn even more notice to us by going on so."

"Seward, hide under that table. If nothing else, it will shield my eyes from your wickedly ugly head." Morgund was greatly amused at his own wit.

Seward's reply in similar vein. "Oh, Morgund, you jolly soul, shovel some pie into your mouth. Watching you talk and eat it is like watching a boar at swill, but not quite for that is by far a more pleasant sight."

"It is well you've chosen to liken me to a boar, for I am that." Morgund alluded to his blood containing the ancient royalty. It was the ancient Scottish symbol of kingship.

But Seward prevented him from adopting a serious melancholy at the misfortunes of his clan. He interrupted him, "My wits addle me. Is not furtiveness our goal?"

"It might be yours. I am royal and hide from no man."

"Boar's innards for sense, you mean." Seward said and regretted it instantly for Morgund was loud again and more people were looking their way. Seward thought to break this flow of conversation with a jest, "Morgund the darkness provides a good cloak to hide your evil head."

"The lack of an appealing visage you accuse me of. Look at you. Probably better not, if you've a weak stomach that is." This was applauded by his listeners.

"Morgund you are too clever for me." Seward said, hoping to quieten him.

"Aye, that I am Seward and twice the swordsman."

Seward had reached the limit of his tolerance at Morgund's drunken nonsense. "Think yourself a future king of Scots! Morgund, you're not fit to be! Without me to guide you you'd be some poor slave trapped in Southern England. It took me to rescue you. If not for me you'd be sitting somewhere in England book reading." Seward looked disgusted. "You're incapable of governing yourself let alone anyone else."

Morgund sat down. "You low-down wretch!" After a while he looked at Seward and said, "Dog."

"Dog." Seward repeated. "It took a while to take it in, then replied, "You are the dog. Be careful, or I'll turn you into a dog. It is no empty boast. The witch queen herself initiated me into the magic arts."

"That evil bitch I suffered greatly at her hand, do not remind me of her, I take the harm she has done me to the grave," Morgund said.

"It was a fog on my mind, to speak thus," Seward said.

Morgund misheard him, thought himself called a dog again. "Be careful I will cut your head off and feed it to dogs. Do you think I will not?" Morgund said.

"Probably not," Seward said, meaning that Morgund wouldn't have the heart to.

"Probably not," Morgund replied, "But then again ... I might."

Seward was angry. "Well, I'll say it again then." Thinking to repeat the dog insult but then changed his mind. "No, I will not call you a dog, you're a worm and not a dog, a dog is loyal at least, you're overly arrogant, with nothing to recommend you."

"Nothing?" Morgund asked.

"Nothing!" Seward replied angrily.

"There must be something ..." Morgund asked.

"Perhaps but do not ask me of it now," Seward said.

"You yourself have many qualities that I aspire to. Honour friendship and great manliness," Morgund said.

"Thank you."

Smiling at Seward Morgund said. "Friends." When Seward didn't respond, Morgund smiled and then said again, "Friend, may I buy you a drink?" Morgund asked. He was sick of fighting with Seward.

"It would serve well, Morgund."

"Then honour is satisfied. In haste I depart to favor your whimsy." Morgund made a show of hurrying. He was in a fit, humorous state.

But he did not return. After much looking Seward spotted him. Morgund had his arms around two men and was singing. If anyone had had a doubt as to his identity, they didn't when Morgund shouted. "You have seen me, verified my existence in Scotland. Fellows, put your hand in the hand of Morgund MacAedh, descendant of kings and like to join that company."

Next, he abused Alexander. "Alexander is unsparing in his deception that is what I say. Would it not serve better that I unmake the tyrant and betrayer? Remove him to dust and take his crown? He soils it with his touch." Morgund pointed to all those about. "And he destroys Scotland by pandering to and advancing the Normans at the expense of the old blooded folk."

As if under a spell everyone responded to Morgund's call, sought his favor and wished destruction upon Alexander. Drink and the magic of Morgund's words spoken with true ardor had effect. Everyone waited for him to go on, expecting a discourse on national events and of what steps he would take to win the throne, but he told instead of his life and of sights and adventures. Enjoying being well loved, he sought to grasp all the enjoyment he could from them with inventive tales of heroic deeds, some his own and some never performed by a human being but all were displayed under the banner Morgund MacAedh. He seemed a legend, and in the tavern that night, he was.

"Back to Alexander. Personally, I disagree with his pedigree, it is of a second rate kind compared with mine. He is bred from English daughters - I have that taint diluted and am almost as pure as a drop of rain untouched. Scottish to the core. I do not want to live as an Englishman for I am not one, but he does, being almost one himself. Were he a true man he'd settle this issue on open field." Morgund banged the table. His audience loudly agreed.

Seward heard someone's comment. "This lad's certainly got spirit."

Seward's mind travelled back to a timid cringing boy. He smiled at the thought for Morgund's pledge to reinvent himself had been made good. That he'd certainly done, and though stretching the truth tonight he was in fact a brave man and a worthy soldier. Looking around him Seward could not believe how outrageously good-natured everyone was. It seemed like none had a worry in the world. He longed for this scene to go on. Now Morgund was on to mythical beasts, a debate was raging.

"In truth, they exist, inhabiting inaccessible parts," Morgund proclaimed.

Seward and Morgund, the most travelled men present, were listened to as if learned scholars. Morgund proclaimed himself an authority on the subject.

Remembering texts dealing with these beasts Morgund brought up interesting insights concerning their habits, filling in gaps with the most outrageous lies he could conceive of. Thoroughly entertaining was it, tears of mirth stained every cheek. This night he could make any comment, bend words his way, within dark corridors devoid of humor find a narrow beam of light, a merriment, thereupon pierce it squarely, these shafts were incisive, displaying truths familiar to every soul.

His cup was constantly replenished and spilling forth with mirth. It was as if he was surrounded by a band of storytellers who were taking turns trying to surpass one another with their inventive tales and from Morgund the audience learned them. Ever more stomach tugging, becoming a raging fire feeding off itself, this humor.

Men sought to empty bellies which could not hold after such attacks, and mouths ached, smiles were torture, and ever Morgund could think of a humorous twist, which amazed. Being possessed of boundless energy Morgund wished to stay up all night, but the time to go, had come, it was very late. Sleep must be gained for tomorrow the magic would be gone. They would be a lot less exuberant and had to travel far for he had caused them some danger by his behavior. Seward and Morgund whistled as they walked. That they had been able to share this was an added pleasure.

"How do you explain a night like we had, Seward?"

"I don't know. I think everyone partook of a portion of goodness, and someone convinced them that you would be the most fascinating person they would meet in a lifetime, and God tonight made you thus. It is a sign things will turn out well."

They travelled slowly stopping frequently to relieve Seward and Morgund's suffering. Paten was humored by it. Having no pity for them he taunted them. Some good was salvaged from the night at the inn, for word travelled ahead of them and all were aware of the famous personage amongst them, Morgund MacAedh. With his antics at the tavern, he was popular and fed well hereabouts. This wasn't the only reason for the marked good will. Alexander was someone to be watched and never trusted, many Scots had bitter experience of him, they had learned the measure of Alexander. The further Morgund, Seward and Paten travelled north, the number of people and settlements became fewer, and they passed beyond the last of the simple farmers struggling amongst the hills and entered the highlands proper. The three subsisted on deer killed in the glens.

Home was not far now and Morgund and Seward shared odd combination of emotion; that particular urgency of a long homecoming, mixed with the anxiety proceeding into the lands of the old enemy, MacCainstacairt. Unknown to Seward and Morgund, the tenants of Ross loyal to the MacAedhs were dispossessed having been driven far to the north They clung to wind swept cliffs on waters verge where they were beyond Alexander's reach, or prayed they were, for they had suffered through his rule.

One morning they came across an old man herding sheep. He was a man who told them of the remnant of clan MacAedh. He asked who Morgund was, thinking to have seen his face before.

"I am Morgund MacAedh," Morgund said. "The Earl of Ross."

"MacCainstacairt is that." The man eyed Morgund with disdain, and continued. "There are many mountain passes here, a few men placed at each. We knew there were only three of you, and we'd heard that you was less than a man."

Seward's retort was sharp. "Say no more or I will kill you."

"Kill a man who gave thee warning, being the saving of thee."

"Then, speak with more respect to Morgund the Earl," Seward said.

The man replied quickly, "He has changed. He is sturdy."

"What of my clan?" Morgund said.

"Your people are gone. MacCainstacairt governs here now. This is not your homeland. MacCainstacairt is Earl of Ross and has been made so by the king. All is his."

Morgund stiffened. "What of my mother. What happened to her? Where are they, my people?"

"Away north. The king sickening of their disloyalty, swept them far."

Morgund attempting to deal with this startling information knew only this, all was not lost for whilst he could still draw a breath he would find them. He turned to MacCainstacairt's retainer. "You told me in good faith. Go."

They set off again on horseback, continuing northward, in a country now alien and harsh, a land they once called home. They wished to leave the general locality of MacCainstacairt quickly, for not all they met along the way might be as peaceable.

After half a day and the horses faltering, they decided at the next settlement to seek rest and direction. But people were rare. Many miles they travelled before they saw a man who hid, so from him they learned nothing. Further on they sighted a small group of dwellings clustered on the shore of a mighty loch, surrounded on the remaining three sides by sheer mountain cliffs. Either they must back track, or leave the horses and cross by boat.

None here could enlighten them. They had little experience of the outside world, for they shunned it, as those of the surrounding countryside shunned them. Centuries earlier, as best as their ancient and half-senile story tellers could recall from their demented predecessors, Norse raiders had attacked.

The survivors forced to cling to this almost inaccessible place. The Viking customary depredations had approximated the last semblance of trade and had evidenced the last infusion of new blood. Now most were hunched, stunted and malformed. Some bore curious abnormalities of feature beyond even that, bulbous eyes staring glassily out of narrow heads. The worst of their kind, the elders had said, dwelt in the caves in the cliffs where they lit strange-colored fires at night and made strange carvings in the rock.

Morgund, Seward and Paten spent a very uncomfortable two nights with these strange, isolated people, eager to leave the horses in exchange for provisions and to be away. The mountainous countryside was not suitable for horses, though these folk seemed not to mind. Indeed, the beasts were almost utterly intractable around the strangers, though they regarded the horses with keen, eagerness. Disturbed and unsettled by the place and its dwellers, they left before the moon grew full.

## TO SUCCUMB TO LOVE WHEN LOVE IT ISN'T

MORGUND THOUGHT OFTEN of Mirium, about her welfare and that of the child that might have been born. He knew she would be safe at least, with Cristo. All was not well with Mirium, however. She suffered no ill a physician could cure, for although in full health, she descended into depression. Morgund had left her. Dumped her with a strange family deep in the woods. In his wake, a girl abandoned and expectant, the space he used to occupy in her mind was now a void that was alternatively filled with confusion and anxiety.

Morgund was far away, and after all this time, she remembered his features only dimly. She was confused and fragile. Morgund's destiny was to be in Scotland and that she had acknowledged before he left, yet she couldn't help feeling that if Morgund truly loved her he would not have left her before the child was born. Did he want to see this baby? What could be more important than the birth of his first child? Such thoughts brought creases to her brow. Unfortunately for her the desolation she felt was compounded by deep loneliness.

The loneliness of the forest drew Mirium and Simon, Cristo's son together. Whenever her was near, Mirium could feel the beat of her heart race as the rhythm made by an anxious drummer before a battle. Simon himself had never thought he would find someone to share his forest home with, until now.

The season's shifted and golden leaves fell in the cooling breezes. During the ensuing weeks and months Simon and Mirium spent many hours together. Simon craved not only the joy this distraction brought, but knew how she felt about Morgund's continued absence. Guilt plagued him when he thought of Mirium so, and he took care to shield his eyes from her's whenever they took in the curve of her breast or hips, or the swelling of her belly, with more than familial amicability. One sun setting afternoon they walked to the river. Water lapped around their ankles. It surged over their legs as they walked deeper. Mirium and Simon found rocks to sit on. They watched the eddies in the water and the occasional silvery flash of darting fish. Past them swirling in the currents, fleeting offerings of plants trapped and speeding away and gone.

Good vantage was theirs, perched here in the river's path. Mirium found it mesmerizing, and it went some way to precluding any musings on things that didn't concern the beauty of the river. She massaged her feet into the small, rounded pebbles on the riverbed.

Charity of spirit can only exist in a charitable vessel, Simon was no such thing, his only concern before he met Mirium was himself. Now, constantly he thought of her and had done so since their first meeting. She had a maddening effect on him for years of bachelorhood vanquished a balanced disposition. His eyes met hers, and held them. She looked away, but looming was the moment when she would not. Then he would have her, of that he was certain. By passing sly comments on Morgund's absence he made her head spin. He pushed on, despite the upset it caused, relentlessly mentioning him, exploring reasons for his absence. It wore her down. They walked downstream and sat on soft river sand.

Laying there, with his head on her shoulder, Mirium said contemplatively. "I should not be doing this." She moved away. "Yet I am lonely Simon." A single tear trickled down Miriam's cheek as she spoke. "I am so very, very lonely and with my baby coming it does cause me much anguish."

"Do not worry. I am here," he responded. "You are not alone. You should not be without him, it is wrong. He should be here."

"I know. Do not remind me of it, Simon."

He held her close, an embrace she returned. "She returned the closeness." He spoke this thought within his mind.

And, as if in a dream she heard Morgund's voice. "Forsake me not, for I will return." His smiling face was many miles away and he seemed a stranger now. Nonetheless, it served to make her loosen her grasp on Simon.

"Why is he not here now, Mirium?" Simon demanded through clenched teeth.

"I don't know." Her voice was slight and small.

He held her again. Feebly resisting, she could not herself now, release his hold. One tear squeezed out, then another and another. So, so many tears, a wrenching cutting pain, a sudden rush of anguish. The baby inside her deserved better than she betray its father. Mirium looked into Simon's eyes and saw only icy orbs surrounded by a dispassionate and equally cold countenance. A plan of action tormented Simon's mind, that would have distressed her if she had known it. When she had loosened her hold him the last time he hadn't. Enraged, that she did not share his desire those eyes of his narrowed.

Both his fists tightened behind her back. He had had enough of waiting, and would take her by force if that was required. Her rigid posture collapsed. She knew she was powerless, and resistance would endanger her child, a truly tragic thing.

Simon held both her small hands in one of his. He could feel her hands trembling, and the sensation gave him a queer thrill and sense of confidence and power. Mirium, on the other hand, was fearful and felt utterly powerless. When she hesitated he would drag her, and she being only slight and heavy with child was in no condition to resist. She knew why Simon was leading her into the deeper wood, knew what he wanted. Yet part of her, the part that hated Morgund for abandoning her, wanted this. The part of her that still loved and longed for Morgund wanted to fight against it. Trapped somewhere between the two opposing forces of will, she realized ashamedly that she no longer cared what befell her, and warm tears erupted, spilling down her cheeks like a torrent. As if a symphony, the wind whistled discordantly through the trees and lightning flashed to the north. The first heavy drops of rain began to fall, cold and unwelcome.

They came to the shelter provided by an ancient oak tree. Simon pushed her in front of him, pressing her face first into the uneven bark. She felt it scratch her face and the palms of her hands, now that Simon had released them. There was a long time when he did not hold her, and the only noise was that of the pattering rain and Mirium's suppressed sobs. Then she felt him lift her skirts from behind and grab her roughly, one hand on her hip, the other by the throat. Mirium felt him thrusting away, disgusted when he tried to speak words into her ear, words of love. His breath stank of sour milk.

Simon grunted like a pig. He shared none of the tenderness Morgund had given her, and exhibited no care for the burden of her unborn child. More than once did she have to protect her belly from being slammed against the tree with her hands and when she released her grip on the hand at her throat she felt him grasp tighter. With a final shudder Simon finished, pulled away and left her slumped weakly against the oak. Her garments remained unceremoniously tugged up around her waist, and she could feel his seed spilling down the inside of her thighs. Eventually she turned and collapsed onto hands and knees, tasting bile and feeling used, shameful and abandoned. She hated Simon for doing this to her, and Morgund for leaving her with Cristo's family. She hated herself for letting all go this far. Simon had left her to the falling leaves and rain.

She shivered. "Rain?" Wondering how long it had been raining. Worrying about her babe, she fervently hoped it was unaffected. She had asked him to be gentle. He wasn't. The pelting moisture had been softened by him taking most of it upon his back but a drop here and there got through and was enough to wet her. Now, she was getting drenched.

Wishing she had a cloth to get away these clawing droplets that clung there reeking on her legs. The leaves were gliding down driven by the wind she felt they had a message for her, that an end had come, for the leaves were as lost and as far from their home as she herself was. They were crumpled and all their life gone, just like her. To be nothing, to feel nothing. Life was a nightmare, full of pain. Where was Morgund? Gone. Why had he abandoned her? Previously unaware she was being rained upon, now, she felt cold and soaked.

What had changed? Morgund had gone, leaving her alone. As had Simon. Leaving her alone and abandoned he had left her, to. Was their no one who would stand by her side, none who loved her. Did she not deserve love? After this, probably not.

What did this mean? In just one small moment her whole world had changed and her life's journey was now upon a very different course. It could be no other way. What she did, was inexcusable. Mirium would regret these events many times in the future, wondering, how different, things could have been. Betraying, Morgund, herself, and their baby! Whilst feeling lost, in her utmost misery, needing someone and Simon was there. Drowning in self pity she had grabbed at whatever she could. Her mother had a turn of phrase that she was reminded of, "When sinking, some will take hold of a snake to prevent from going down." So it was with her. Just as constant hunger eventually cannot be denied, love pressures some in different ways, it will drive action upon all beset by that condition, and sometimes that which is unwise. She returned to the croft, in silence.

Only Edith made it possible for her to continue living. Cristo tried to help, but like many men whose days of strength have passed them by, he was often morose. He would suddenly become angry, adding to her woes. She wondered what she had done to deserve her current predicament, and concluded much too much. Why had she not fought or held him off, or at least tried to? That she didn't know only added to her discomfort. She had led Simon on, blaming herself more than she blamed him. Wanting a solution so desperately caused panic and tremors.

If an answer came it might arrest this. But there was no answer. Morgund had told her he was coming back, so why hadn't she waited. Asking herself continuously why she committed this sin eventually she came to an answer of sorts. She had wanted Morgund so much, she told herself, that in her depression and confusion she had made Simon his proxy.

It didn't make sense to a stable mind but she was far from that. Death, she thought, might be the answer, and by her own hand. Such an ultimate sanction would suffice but the same debilitating depression that gave her that thought precluded any action.

Preoccupied with her suffering, the days stretched on timelessly. Would she ever have this baby? The waiting seemed eternal. Mirium held her belly. It was Morgund's firstborn child, and because of it she loved it greatly, often patting where she thought the babies head would be within her stomach. Mirium's was overtaken by a deep lasting sorrow, for she realized the enormity of her mistake and knew now there was no way of correcting it, or ending her life. For the baby, she must live for the baby's sake.

"What shall we call him?" Edith had asked.

"I want him to be proud of his Scots heritage, and to have a suitable Scots name, but not a name Morgund might choose for his heir. Never shall the boy be that. Morgund will have other children. He must have other children, and must find happiness with a truer soul than mine."

"William?" Edith asked holding Mirium's hand. "Is that not a royal Scot's name?"

"That is what we shall call him," Mirium said. "It is a name that will not mark him, from his fellows, for the name William is common in England."

"Be strong then. For William's sake," Edith urged.

"As much as I can."

Mirium, exhausted by guilt, slumped back on her cot. After some time her panicked voice filled the room. "What if Morgund bears another son, and also calls him William?"

Edith calmed her, and cooled the fatigued girl's head with a dampened cloth. "Fear not, dear Mirium. William it shall be. Should there be more sons we must trust to fate he shall be named other. Or, indeed, a daughter you might have."

Mirium smiled, imagining hugging little William to her breast. When she did, a glimmer of light entered her heart. Cheerfulness existed, she realized with wonder. Saying then. "He will be such a dear little man and so perfect. William will be mine to love, and be loved by."

Simon entered and he held her hand. She didn't blame him for coercing her. Whilst not holding any deep affection for him, she realized that without a man her baby and herself would most likely die. Simon would cast her out and Cristo wasn't strong enough to prevent it. She wouldn't be able face Morgund now, the pain of betraying him was too severe. Morgund was her past. The future was her concern, William. Therefore, Simon must be a part of her future, to.

———————————

THE SUMMER HAVING passed in fruitless searching for the MacAedh. Unremarkable adventures. Occasionally evading the allies of Alexander. As northern Scotland became colder, Seward, Morgund and Paten built a shelter on a riverbank underneath tall trees, finding protection there from the wind and rain. Wood was cut and stacked neatly.

Of meat, they had ample, a supply they had stacked in advance for winter. The forest was silent and empty now. At the end of the month driving snow piled in, forcing them to dig out. Days rolled on, the winter long and hard, showing no signs of slowing soon. In time, however, the freezing grip passed and days became longer. Rivers broke their banks. They waited for still further warmer weather to arrive. When the anticipated change came, having discussed much what to do, the decision was made that they would thread their way through a series of boggy and rock strewn valleys, unwelcoming country but where they were unlikely to be intercepted.

The refuge of clan MacAedh remained undiscovered. Despite continual setbacks and disappointments the partly kept searching, questioning whomever they could without arousing undue suspicion, and scouring the horizon for any sign of smoke which may betray an establishment. In early April they approached a pleasant wood, mountains rising above in the distance. Within an hour of entering the wood it had become dense nightmare and the going slow. The wood encompassed them on all sides save to the east, where an ice-cloaked mountain was visible. They set themselves to continue north, despite the near impenetrable forest.

Hour after sweating hour, cutting their way through the dense growth, the lead man hacking away with his blade whilst the other two followed in his narrow path. All alternating, in taking the lead. When possible they would crawl forward, threading through the woods, if only to avoid the laborious process of cutting through.

Eventually the trees thinned. After some continued journeying the trio encountered two men dressed in furs and rough homespun, who bore no surnames nor belonged to any clan. They were solitary men, and there were others alike them in these wild parts. They told of the remnants of the clan MacAedh, dispossessed and fugitive, half a day north.

Shortly after parting from the two, armed horsemen rode ahead of them, Normans, the banner, De Moravia, the Lord of Murray, aloft and resplendent waving in the crisp air. In times passed the Normans rarely if ever frequented so far north. The outcasts hid as best they could amongst the trees of a small grove, uncertain as to whether they were seen.

Fearful approaching a large loch with open spaces around it. In this severe aspect certainly they could be seen from afar. Horseman could ride them down. They needed to go quickly across this open country to escape detection, but had travelled many miles without sufficient rest, they stumbled like drunks.

"Now I am a deer chased, and it feels not good," Morgund said.

"This is the life you have chosen Morgund," Seward replied exhaustedly.

Far out into the open space, horsemen circled out in front of them.  Apparently they had been seen.  Carefully moving low to the ground, they sank down, covered by the grass, almost completely hidden.  Laying still, swords held tightly, they listened with racing hearts to the sounds of an approach. All was silent ... bar the sounds of nature, then alarmingly they identified the sounds of men.

The sounds of the men dimmed.  For hours they waited. To expose themselves on foot against a mounted foe was to forfeit their lives.  Upon the coming of long shadows, Morgund and his companions crept out.  None were near them.  They pressed on.  That night they spent on high ground.  The next day they crossed a river and  continued north, reasonably certain they had lost any pursuit.  Leisurely following the waterways towards the coast, they smelt salt air and heard the sound of breakers.

The sea suddenly appeared before their eyes.  White rippling tops, expanding, incoming, curling, ever growing, until; crashing, pounding, arcing downwards, rolling-white surging. Great waves rising and breaking far out on black spires of rock jutting out of the sea.  The crashing waves filled the air, and Morgund found himself entranced by the sound and spectacle. The greenery reached almost to the ocean itself, for only a thin line of grey-black sand and pebbles demarked the coast.  The place lured him to sacrifice himself to the sovereign sea.  He stood on the narrow beach for some time, gazing out upon the expanse.  He removed his boots and felt the stones and grit between his toes.  The occasional wave spilt over his feet, the icy coldness both thrilling and a balm to the blister and sores. He stood alone on the shore, all the anxiety and distress of friends lost tearing his heart asunder.  Tears rolled unbidden down his cheeks and he collapsed to his knees praying for a successful conclusion to his quest.

"No disrespect intended to you son, but are you staying here? I chose to make this my place for solitude."

"What?" Morgund, opened his eyes to a hermit with extremely long hair, his beard, matted and unkempt, which had obviously not been cleaned or trimmed lately.

Morgund tried to digest the meaning. "Where are you from?" Morgund asked.

"Not far, further along the coast."

"I think, I know you, before that?"

"Away south in Ross."

"Then I have found my home."

"Aye." The man eyed Morgund warily. "Have ye?"

A realization dawned upon the hermit that this might be Morgund MacAedh. He discounted it quickly, however for this one was not possessed of nervousness or timidity, but instead he bore the trappings of an accomplished warrior. Rumours had reached the clan, and even if told by enemies had an effect. They encouraged people to form a poor opinion of Morgund. Then there were the memories of Morgund MacAedh, of old, a quiet boy not seen as having any marked potential. As a boy small and inconsequential. Unlike so many of the MacAedh's who were large, soldierly and proud. However, in adulthood he was fated to be a greater man than those who carried his name before him, a prophet named Duibne who visited them had said He assured Morgund's mother the two would meet again.

The hermit remained unsure of the young man's identity, the rarement of his garment marked him as one of the privileged, and when given enough time looking at it his face it was strikingly similar to Morgund's as he'd known it – yet, so much time had passed.  When the young stranger spoke again the old man was certain.

"I have found my home.  I am Morgund MacAedh, Kenneth's son."

Tears trickled down the hermit's face as he placed a hand on Morgund's shoulder.  "I am your servant, boy, and you are right.  This is home."

"Adhering to the MacAedhs has brought you only misery and death, and the clan will blame me for causing it."

"Morgund fear not."  A look of total compassion was on the face of the old man.  Morgund, taken aback by the hermit's mercy and sincerity, began to stutter out a series of sounds that his emotion-choked throat failed to articulate into words.

The hermit smiled and interrupted.  "... They will be glad to see you son, they will not blame you"

"But why?"  Morgund begged.  The gravity of the persecution endured by his clan because of his own unwelcomed survival was personified in the derelict old man before him.  "After all you people have suffered, why?

"You are one of our own.  Our memories run deep, and in our hearts we must honor thee.  As a descendant of kings can we do less?"

"If the villagers were not connected to me, they'd still have homes in Ross. Those that are no more would be alive."

"Have no fear. Such will never extinguish our love for you. Alexander is to blame, as are the evil men who advise him, the likes of MacCainstacairt. Not you, who lost his father. Only friends await you here." Morgund looked doubtfully at the man. Not fully trusting the reassuring cast to his features. "You will see for yourself, son."

The hermit led the way to the village. A short walk brought them to it. The place was little more than a huddle of a dozen round houses, with wattle walls and thatched roofs. Racks of fish and strips of venison were smoking. The faces of village seemed blank, downcast and unimpressed by Morgund. This seemed hardly the welcomed home coming any of them expected. Morgund was disappointed to learn this was all of clan MacAedh, no other larger settlement existed.

"Morgund," Seward told his friend, "This reminds me of the day I arrived in your village." Seward winked at Morgund. "It is all yours."

Morgund felt a strangely dulled sense of relief, for few were the faces he recognized, and then only faintly. He, who should have been the leader of these people, was an outcast, an outcast and a stranger.

The bedraggled hermit called out giving himself the air of importance. "Does any amongst us know who this is?"

The people gathered around, summoned by the hermit. They looked at Morgund with more interest. Morgund was now a large man, well built, built for war, with a hardness of feature which was totally alien to him as they had know him. He was not like his father. He was a fighter.

"He has the MacAedh nose," Morgund heard a woman call out. "Aye, he most certainly has the MacAedh nose."

Another added, "He is a big lad. He must eat better than me. Where did you find him?"

Another had another thought and spoke. "He is related to Mary MacAedh beyond doubt. There is something so alike between him and Mary, in the eyes, not the color, the shape."

A woman stepped forward, her hair grey and face crossed with age. Despite this, Morgund detected a certain familiarity in her features. By the woman's expression, Morgund could see that she recognized him. "I know this boy," she said. "My, how you have grown, Morgund."

There was a general murmur of engagement from the assembled clansman. Sienna, Malcolm's wife embraced Morgund, her arms not long enough to encircle him, fully. "Morgund," she wailed, tears flowing freely. "Morgund MacAedh! I never thought to see you again. It is so very good to do so, my dear Morgund." She lifted her smiling, tear-stained face from his breast. "Who would have thought it?"

""MacAedh!" exclaimed another. "I thought the boy was dead!"

"Release me, woman," Morgund commanded, the tears welling in his own eyes. "Or I shall die of shame."

Others crowded around, the full import of a surviving MacAedh in their midst slowly dawning on people who had surrendered all hope a decade and more ago, that he lived. He felt women clasp their hands upon his arms in thanksgiving, and reassurance, on the shoulders, men nudged and slapped him with goodwill.

"Tell me Sienna," he begged. "What news is there of mother?"

"Worry not, son. She is well, but away. Come, we must feed you, and you must tell us your story."

The clansmen included Seward and Paten in the welcoming celebration. Sienna wept openly as she embraced Seward, kissing him many times upon brow and cheek in the manner of a mother.

"How did you find us, so dispossessed and abandoned as we are?" Malcom demand. Seward seeing Malcolm embraced him like a son.

Morgund, with Seward at his side, recalled his orating in the alehouse, with his ability to rouse a crowd. He recounted their tales, including only the most heroic and noble deeds. The narrative of Paten's escape he recounted in vivid detail before presenting Paten as living evidence of their exploits. "The pipes led us home." Morgund continued with passionate vigor. "They led us here, in our hearts we heard them. Ten armies could of stood in our way and not stopped us."

"Aye," Seward agreed. "It's true! We felt it in our breasts, and with that sound as our guide nothing could halt us from coming home."

As if on cue, the first discordant notes of the bagpipes began. The people parted to reveal the player, the unkempt hermit from the beach, who had hastily retrieved his instrument. His fingers played expertly over the pipes and his chest heaved to keep the bag inflated.

"Piper thou is more than I took thee for." The piper nodded in acknowledgement of the compliment. Tonight," Morgund proclaimed. "Tonight is for rejoicing. Piper, cheer us!"

"A wonderful instrument," Seward said. "So good to hear it once more."

"That is more than a fact, Seward. I am Morgund MacAedh who half of Scotland and England tried to kill and could not." Thereupon Morgund showed his perfect teeth.

The fact that this was Morgund MacAedh amazed them. He'd been gone so long and had changed so much. No MacAedh held a title for many years yet these people thought him still noble. His breeding made for respect. He looked a worthy successor to the ancient kings.

"To you all and to Scotland," Morgund shouted out.

As they listened to the piper, they understood how it gave the determination to overcome obstacles, to conquer perils. The piper, igniting spontaneous gaiety and dancing. Girls enticed partners. The younger ones demonstrating skilful steps in teams and as individuals. A woman possessing a singular vocal talent began to sing.

Morgund found the tune somewhat mournful, despite the uplifting words. The entire village stopped to listen, and the anthem of love and the pipes chorused into the surrounding countryside.

When the initial energy of the celebration began to wane, men talked. First, tales of bravery and heroism. But as the fires burned low into the night, and the alcohol began to take its effect, Morgund detected a shift in attitude. The tales of bravado were replaced by lamentations of hardship and loss, of abandonment and alienation. Morgund observed the furtive, confidential looks some of the men exchanged, an indication of caution and fear. He understood that the people were torn between two opposing forces, joy at the discovery of a successor to the MacAedh line but apprehension that because Morgund survived they could once more be subject to oppression.

Many believed that if they stood with Morgund against Alexander they would suffer again. Although they called him my Lord, he wasn't fooled by such a title. He was however, very determined to lead them.

Morgund spoke. "Alexander has caused, so much of ill, but he can and must be stopped. The disfunctioning state of the realm is to our benefit. Alexander's unpopularity is the key. Strike hard and many will join in."

It appeared to Morgund he may well have been suggesting to them jumping from a cliff onto rocks for all the eagerness they showed.

The next day Morgund organized a party to travel southwest to meet his mother. Accompanied by those versed in the stealthy ways to their destination, avoiding clans that supported the crown, and others who were noted attackers of any interlopers. An uneventful journey through the hills finally complete, at a large castle situated in a loch with a narrow causeway leading to it. One of Morgund's escort called out and was acknowledged by a hearty reply. The outer drawbridge was hastily lowered onto the stone platform that jutted out into the loch. The drawbridge once lowered, linked to the gatehouse, and on into the castle bailey. The iron-bared portcullis was raised and after Morgund's party drew forth inside, the portcullis slid into place behind them.

An old gatekeeper asked of Morgund. "Be thou Lady Mary's long lost son?"

"Has thou heard?"

"The word is out. Art thou, the MacAedh?"

"I am Morgund MacAedh, son of the murdered Kenneth MacAedh, Earl of Ross," he stated matter-of-factly, pride and sadness combining to swell in his breast.

The old man and guards bowed their heads submissively. "Come forth." The gatekeeper outstretched a hand taking Morgund's hand in his.

Morgund, entered and waited in the central hall. The sun shone in through high apertures. A single lit brazier cast its warm glow upon tapestry and stone. The place was very quiet and Morgund was reluctant to create any noise. It felt empty, and still. There came the sound of walking from behind a door. Steps seemed to have a sense of urgency about them. The door opened, and Morgund gasped aloud in thanksgiving and wonder.

"Mother." He muttered, through the sound was barely audible, as if lodged in his chest. Again he spoke, this time with the eagerness of a child. "Mother!"

It was indeed Mary who rushed towards Morgund her finery and trappings of nobility all but forgotten. She came with her arms outstretched, embracing the son she had long thought dead. "Morgund, oh Morgund," Mary repeated time and again, hugging him kissing him and hugging him. She wept and laughed in equal measure.

After a long time she held her boy at arm's length. "Let me look at you." Her mouth caught in the flux between a smile and sorrow. The child, who she had last set eyes upon in his thirteenth year, was now a man. A very handsome man.

Where he had once been a small, timid child, his shoulders and arms now bore the girth of one familiar with the sword. He had grown in height so much. Morgund was no longer her sweet boy. His jaw had certainly lost that fineness and delicacy of youth, yet his brow was uncreased with worry. The silken face of her child had been cast away, to be replaced by the current likeness that looked to be roughly hewn from the granite that made the mountains of the earth.

Morgund, too, used the opportunity to gaze upon her. She had certainly aged, though he thought time had been gentle on her. The wrinkles at the corners of her eyes emphasizing her smile, and the graying of her hair akin to spun silver. She was still an attractive woman, even in her greater age and with her childbearing years now behind her. There was, however seriousness and gravity about her that had embedded itself into her features. Morgund, now looking upon her, saw it for what it was, the burden and sustained grief at having lost both a husband and son. At least his presence could alleviate some of her sorrow.

"We have no oil for lamps, I must take myself to get some," Mary said.

"No stay mother. The fire will be enough."

It became darker and the fire seemed to glow brighter and the light tantalizingly caught her auburn hair, which was strikingly harsh now, her hair blazed along like a displaced ember flickering as deep as any particle inside it, her hair entwined with the living heat, until she moved away.

'You have your father's eyes, my son," Then braking her gaze by falling into Morgund's arms again.

"I love you, mother," Morgund stammered, his voice becoming thick again.

"And I you, Morgund," she replied her voice muffled by his chest. He held her in silence for a long time, until eventually she added, "I have the handsomest son in the world."

She smiled and felt more genuinely happy, than she had for so long, perhaps ever. It came to mind that Kenneth stole her heart, with his eyes, as Morgund would of any girl who looked into his. She looked at him with a look of love, and said. "I am never letting you go, again, ever."

Together, they walked to a large aperture overlooking the loch. The breeze from the north blew Mary's hair. She clutched Morgund's arm as they gazed at the majestic scene of the countryside before them.

Putting her hand down on his, she said, "We are a clan of two."

With that they returned their eyes to the horizon, to the setting sun, and to the promise of history yet unwritten. The two became twenty, two hundred, three hundred, a thousand, a million. Alexander was defeated in that Morgund survived and founded a great family, the Mackays.

Fearchar MacTaggart prostrated himself on the dusty floor of the church, yet unfinished, the walls almost fully erect but the firmament above serving as the building's roof. The floor was cobbled in neatly hewn stone, the space before him recently upset. He had lost his second son to illness and his body had been laid to rest beneath the dressed stones this very day. MacTaggart wept openly, his fingers clawing impotently with grief upon stone. The injustice tore at his heart; would not the Lord protect his family for building of a church? Had he not put his wrongs behind him? He refused to accept this could be a judgment upon him for his part in the deposure of Kenneth MacAedh,

Though he had assumed control of MacAedh lands, he lamented that the land may be cursed by the blood of the unjustly spilled. Yet in time his eldest son would fall to the blade of Morgund MacAedh himself. The bloody feud would continue, with MacTaggart's third and youngest son William growing into a hardy warrior, who would himself war against Morgund's progeny. The first MacTaggart Earl of Ross, was Fearcher, his grandson would die at Bannockburn, beside the descendants of the Morgund, fighting for Scotland's hero king, Robert the Bruce.

Fearcher felt the hand of the priest upon his back. "The rain," he quoted, "falls upon the just and the unjust alike. As does the sun."

As the sun that cast long shadows over MacTaggart's prone form it filled the narrow windows of William Comyn's apartments as he argued bitterly with Alan Durward, the Earl of Athol. Both these men had encountered Morgund during his time in Edinburgh. Now that news of the MacAedh's survival reached them, and from no other than Alexander himself, William plagued the Earl of Athol's ears with profanity and ill oaths.

William Comyn's descendants would stumble, and be transformed from one of the pre-eminent Norman families during Alexander's reign to being a scattered remnant struggling for survival after contesting Robert the Bruce for the Scottish crown.

Durward sat, grinning. A Celt was not so easily put down as Alexander and Buchan had found out. He was sick of Buchan and hastened his departure. His concern was cementing of his family's position, by the marriage of his daughter to MacDuff, the Earl of Fife. It would fall to the MacDuff line to crown the kings of Scotland, yet Alan Durward's own grandson would refuse to crown Robert the Bruce and forfeit the titular role. He would serve as the last MacDuff Earl.

Edith, the wayward daughter of Cristo, brought another pail of water into the house. The last rays of the setting sun were filtering through the forest trees before the gloom of night shrouded all. She set the water down and sponged Mirium's sweat-soaked brow with a cloth. Mirium screamed, the childbirth entering it's third hour. After a great deal more exertion and the fall of night, the child was born, and Mirium held the struggling, purple babe exhaustedly.

"It is a boy, healthy and strong, dear Mirium," Edith told the almost, child-mother.

Mirium nodded, fatigued. "And what shall you call him?"

"As we spoke of, William."

Mirium smiled, pondering the child and his future. In time the names MacAedh and MacWilliam would be used in close connection, sometimes even interchangeably, especially during the uprisings that would transpire only short years ahead. Although the exact nature of the relationship would become forever lost to history, the boy child bore an uncanny resemblance to his father, a trait that would continue to bless and curse the line for centuries.

Seward watched the same sun near the horizon and a girl as she spoke to her companions. Occasionally she would glance his way, and the dimming light failed to disguise her blushing. He admired her physical beauty long before he realized fully why he did; the hair so light brown to be almost blonde, her eyes clear and blue and a constellation of freckles across the cheeks and bridge of the nose reminded him heartily of his lost homeland, Scandinavia. Seward could not help but feel a natural attraction towards her.

He asked one of the villagers still fussing over him who the girl was, to be informed she was visiting from one of the nearby hamlets. As he paced towards her, he noticed she blushed again. "My name is Seward," he introduced himself.

"As mine is Colcha," she replied sweetly.

Seward would marry this girl. Unfortunately, in horrific circumstances she would die and the child she bore Seward would lay dead, slain along with her. Seward would have a descendant who he never met. The Gunns established a long and prestigious history. It is believed that a member of clan Gunn was with Henry Sinclair, Earl of Orkney, whom some believe travelled to the New World in 1398 traveling to Greenland, Nova Scotia and New England.

In northern Scotland, the sun cast its rays upon the loch, upon two figures on castle battlements. Morgund's mother retired indoors, leaving her son to reflect alone. Morgund's eyes wandered the darkened sky, illuminated by the crescent moon and the myriad stars. He pondered his years of adversity and what the future held in store for him. Seward, Mirium, Edith, Cristo, his parents, MacCainstacairt and Alexander. They all played significant parts in his life, as actors upon a stage, for better or worse. Morgund would never face Alexander in battle, despite his wrath and desire for revenge.

Morgund's revenge would take at once a more subtle and more profound form; the establishment of a great family that would out survive the reign of any one man. In the decades and centuries to come, the name MacAedh would become MacKay, and those bearing it almost beyond counting. Whether Morgund himself considered such potentialities, he fought hard for his name displaying pride in being a MacAedh.

This night, he contemplated instead upon the hills, rivers and mountains that made up his land. He recalled the friends he loved and foes he hated. He considered all he had lost, and all he had gained. And knew he had been above all, very lucky to survive.

And lastly if you are a MacKay you have a small sample of Morgund's blood in yours, noble blood it is, and it is ... **Celtic Blood ...**

**THE END**

# ABOUT THE AUTHOR

The Author has held a life long interest in Scottish history, and history in general. After reading the novels of he Scottish author Nigel Tranter he was inspired to attempt his hand at a Scottish historical novel. He has co-written a feature film. He lives in Brisbane, Queensland, Australia and is married with two children.

Made in the USA
Charleston, SC
25 January 2012